THE PERFECT LIFE

VALERIE KEOGH

ALSO BY VALERIE KEOGH

Psychological thrillers

The Three Women

The Dublin Murder Mysteries

No Simple Death

No Obvious Cause

No Past Forgiven

No Memory Lost

For my sister, Joyce Doyle. With thanks for so many happy memories over the years and for sharing your wonderful family with me.

The Perfect Life – it's an illusion, a fantasy, a lie we happily live in until someone switches a bright light on outside our make-believe world and we see the cracks, holes and huge gaps. In panicked disbelief, we try to fix it by smoothing over the gaps, patching the holes, filling in the cracks, and when the light goes out and it all looks perfect again, we think we've done it.

Anon.

1

Molly Chatwell woke and slid her hand across the bed to where Jack usually lay flat on his belly with his arms stretched out over his head. Her hand moved across the space without meeting resistance; he was already gone. She wasn't surprised or concerned. Jack regularly woke at six. He'd slip from the bed without disturbing her, use the main bathroom to shower and shave, and dress in the spare bedroom. As soon as he was ready, he'd leave, buying a takeaway coffee from a café near his office on his way and having it at his desk.

In their early days together, before they were married and for a couple of years afterwards, he'd come in and kiss her goodbye before he left. Sometimes, when the children were younger, they'd wake when they heard him moving about and would come running, jump into their bed and snuggle against her. Jack would come in, wrap his arms around all three of them and kiss them goodbye. Molly's heart swelled at the memory, a piercing regret for times long gone.

Nowadays, with Freya and Remi off at university, Molly preferred the extra rest and usually slept until her alarm went off at seven. It hadn't gone off yet. She shut her eyes, hoping for a few more minutes and had almost dozed off when the loud beep beep of a reversing vehicle made her eyes open in surprise. It wasn't a sound she usually heard so early... unless, of course, it wasn't... rolling over, she grabbed her phone and looked at the blank screen with dismay. She never forgot to charge her phone... never... and she had to start today?

Two weeks before, and after one too many cocktails, she'd told her friends how wonderful it had been to see her two children embarking on the first step of their exciting future, Remi off to the Massachusetts Institute of Technology, Freya to the Sorbonne. 'They're living their dream, their future perfectly mapped out,' she'd said, slurring her words slightly. 'For the first time in twenty years, it's only me and Jack.' It was easy to be enthusiastic after a few drinks; she didn't mention that she found the house too quiet, and she wondered what she and Jack were going to talk about now that their children had left. *Flown the nest.* It was an expression she hated. It implied they wouldn't come back, but of course they would. It was into that moment of doubt that one of her friends had dropped what had seemed like a wonderful suggestion.

'All this extra time on your hands now, you should have a party.'

A party! 'That's a brilliant idea,' Molly had said, lifting her glass. 'And you're all invited.'

The next morning, her head thumping with the first hangover she'd had in too many years to remember, she mentioned the plan to Jack.

'Great,' he'd said. 'But have it on a Friday night. It will suit my work colleagues better; a lot don't like to come back into the city on a Saturday.'

Molly had been thinking of friends rather than work colleagues, but she shrugged. A few more people wouldn't make a huge difference and it would be nice to have some of her work colleagues over too. What, after all was the point in having the perfect house to entertain, if they never did? 'Fine, fine,' she'd said. 'We'll have it on a Friday night.'

And tonight, was that night.

With no idea what time it was, she leapt from the bed and dashed out to the landing where an ornate clock stood on the windowsill. It had been given to them as a wedding present, twenty-two years before. Jack loved it, she detested it, but she had to give it credit, it kept perfect time, and it told her clearly, she was very late.

Back in the bedroom, she plugged her phone in to charge and dressed quickly in her standard workday clothes of tailored black trousers, white shirt and black jacket. As a single woman, she'd been an adventurous dresser, and would think nothing of spending an hour or more putting her look together in the morning. Marriage hadn't altered her routine much, but the arrival of the children had. Returning to work after maternity leave, she discovered the convenience of wearing a smart trouser suit. Initially, she'd matched it with a variety of coloured shirts, but one day she bought a white Armani shirt and from then on she wore one every single day.

The only variation was the jewellery she added. Today, she picked up a string of dark blue Murano beads they'd bought in Venice on their first wedding anniversary and hung them around her neck. They were heavy, went almost to her waist, and made any outfit look good.

Make-up applied with practised ease, a brush flicked through her straight auburn hair and she was ready to go. She grabbed her bag and the barely-charged phone and rushed down the stairs with one final thing to do — grab the list she'd stuck to the front of the fridge freezer. Her eyes ran down it and she swore softly.

What a stupid, stupid idea this had been!

Up till a few weeks ago, they'd had a housekeeper. Ten years before, following a succession of unsatisfactory au pairs and unreliable childcare, they'd been alerted by a friend of a friend to a woman looking for part-time work. Rebecca, an English teacher who'd taken early retirement to look after her terminally ill husband and now widowed, wanted something less onerous than teaching. Freya and Remi had taken an instant liking to the kind woman who appeared to have an endless supply of patience and good humour. She'd come on a temporary basis and stayed, running the house in her calm, unhurried way; there every day when the children came home from school, always waiting with a pot of tea ready when Molly arrived home after a stressful day at work. Rebecca had become part of the family; celebrating when Remi and Freya got the university places they'd wanted, sobbing along with Molly when first Remi, then Freya had left.

A week later, Jack insisted there was no longer a reason to have a housekeeper. 'It's hard to justify the expense for the two of us,' he'd said.

Molly had looked at him, horrified. Get rid of Rebecca... he couldn't be serious. Molly was going to argue that they both had busy, high-pressure jobs and it was a relief to come home to an organised house, the words on the tip of her tongue slipping away when she saw his troubled expression.

There had been grumbles recently about work; she'd thought nothing of it – the world of finance tended to be volatile – but maybe this was something else, something worse? He had been working late more than usual, coming home with heavy eyes, refusing to discuss it, brushing off her concerns. He was drinking more too. Recently she'd noticed a smell of alcohol on his breath when he came home from work. She'd commented on it once; he'd said he'd bumped into an old friend and had joined him for a quick one on the way home. The next time she'd noticed, a day or two later, there was a look in his eyes that said *don't ask.*

'Is everything okay in the office?' she'd ventured, giving him the opening to tell her if there were a problem. She didn't expect an answer; Jack was notoriously reticent about his job, preferring to keep his work separate from his home life. She'd tried to convince him more than once that it was healthier to talk about things, more cathartic and better for his mental well-being, but each time he'd laugh and accuse her of spouting psychobabble.

'Everything is fine,' he'd said, giving her a peck on the cheek along with the answer she'd expected. 'But that doesn't mean we can throw away money, Mol. The kids are going to cost us a fortune over the next three to four years.'

'But we've paid for their tuition, Jack.' She hadn't wanted to pay it all upfront, it had made a deep dent in their savings, but he'd insisted, and as usual, she'd given in.

'Accommodation, living expenses and so forth,' he'd said with a shake of his head, 'we haven't paid for that. It's all going to mount up.'

Molly knew only too well. The Sorbonne wasn't that expensive but living in Paris certainly was. And as for MIT, it was astronomically expensive to study there and cost almost as much to live in Boston as in Paris. Molly remembered blinking when she'd seen the invoice for three years' tuition and the first year's compulsory on-campus accommodation. For a moment, she'd thought they'd put an extra zero in by mistake but no, the six-figure invoice was correct. She'd not told Jack, but her eyes had watered when she'd done rough calculations as to how much both children were going to cost them over the next three years.

Perhaps it wouldn't do any harm to tighten their belts a little. 'I suppose you're right,' she'd said reluctantly, 'we don't really need Rebecca anymore.' Molly felt like a traitor. 'I'll speak to her tomorrow and give her a month's notice.'

Rebecca, as it turned out, wasn't too surprised. 'I was beginning to feel a bit of a fraud rattling around here on my own. But I'll miss you.'

Molly had started to cry, so had Rebecca, the two of them, arms wrapped around each other, consoling themselves for change's inevitable loss.

She wasn't gone a day, when the cold hard light of reality dawned on Molly. Despite it being Jack's idea to get rid of the housekeeper, he wasn't interested in doing any of the shopping, the laundry or the mountain of ironing Rebecca had done and he still came through the door in the evening expecting a dinner to be ready. When Molly had complained, he cited exhaustion and wiped a hand across his eyes.

Molly wanted to argue that her job was equally as exhausting, but he'd looked unusually pale so she'd said nothing. She looked around the living room. She was aware that many women juggled child-rearing, running a house and working full-time without outside help; had she not had a housekeeper and cleaner over the years, no doubt she'd have learned to cope too. But she had been able to afford help and wasn't interested in learning to juggle things at this stage.

She set an account up with a local supermarket and ordered everything they needed from there; it meant some compromise, but it was worth it. For convenience, she set it up as a repeat order; every Saturday morning the same items would be delivered.

Molly had never entertained the idea of getting rid of Terry, their cleaning lady. To Molly's relief she was willing to come for an extra couple of hours a week to do the laundry and ironing. 'But you will make sure the house is cleaned properly, won't you?' she said to her, watching as Terry nodded with more vigour than she'd ever seen her use while she cleaned.

'Of course, Mrs Chatwell.'

'Fine,' Molly said, relieved, 'we'll give it a trial.'

Unfortunately, it seemed that Terry's idea of taking on extra work was to leave everything half-done. Now, only two weeks after Rebecca's departure, the house was looking uncared for, some of Molly's white Armani shirts had a pink tinge, and their clothes never looked better than half-ironed.

Molly tucked the to-do list in her pocket and looked around. The L-shaped living room was the ideal space for entertaining and one of the reasons they'd bought the house. A long, narrow, marble-topped unit separated the glossy high-end kitchen in the short arm from the rest. To the front of the long arm, a circular table sat in the deep bay window where floor-to-ceiling windows overlooked the garden and allowed light to flood the room. French windows opened from here onto a wide veranda. The other end was furnished for comfort; two huge sofas facing each other across a wide, low table. On the wall, a large ornate picture frame disguised the TV. It was a perfect space for entertaining but now, thanks to Terry's half-hearted efforts, it looked decidedly unkempt.

Pulling open a drawer, Molly tore a page from a notebook and scrawled a message: *make sure you do a good job today, we're having friends around.* She propped it against the kettle where Terry, who drank copious amounts of coffee in the few hours she was there, was sure to see it.

Molly speed-walked to South Kensington station, squeezed on with the mass of blank-faced morning commuters and stood sardine-like for the short journey to Hyde Park Corner. Her head was spinning with all she had to do and here she was, the day of the damn party and already running late.

2

The headquarters of Dawson Marketing, the prestigious company Molly had worked for since qualifying with a degree in marketing, was only a ten-minute walk from the station. Thanks to her senior position, she was paid extremely well, earned ridiculously large bonuses and, best of all, worked hours that suited her. Normally eight till four thirty, she had planned to leave at three today to organise the party but here she was, over an hour late.

The ten-minute walk she'd travelled every day for so long required no concentration, every corner and crossing taken automatically while her phone was glued to her ear, her focus on her plans rather than the journey. Conscious of her low battery, with a minimum of words, she confirmed the caterers and the delivery of six cases of their usual wine and arrived at the front door of her office building, already stressed.

Chatter floated around her as she took a packed lift to the fourth floor. Why had she agreed to a party? She could have proposed they go out to dinner, take over a club, something, anything that didn't involve all this time and energy.

There were too many people in the lift, standing too close to her. A wave of heat rushed through her, colour flooding her cheeks, claustrophobia sending her heart pounding. She had to get out of the lift. *Now*. When it stopped at the first floor, she pushed through and out into the airier corridor. Luckily everyone was too concerned with the start of their own day to give her more than a surprised glance.

There was a stairway. It was cooler, quieter, she took the steps slowly, calming down, trying to relax. She knew damn well why she'd agreed to the party. A desperate desire to fill the house with noise and life, a determination to pack the void left by Freya and Remi's departure with excitement and fun. Muttering to herself that she seemed to have missed out the fun part, she checked the time, swore softly and increased her pace.

By skipping a lunch break, she managed to catch up with what she needed to do and as her desk clock clicked slowly from 1459 to 1500 she switched off her computer, grabbed her bag and threw *bye, have a nice weekend, see you Monday* to her PA, the last couple of words trailing behind her as she hurried from the office.

She rolled tense shoulders as she sat on the tube ride home. A stop later, a man got on and sat opposite and stared intently at her for the remainder of her journey. She ignored him without difficulty; years of commuting had inured her to the weird cross-section of humanity who used the tube. Anyway, she was far too busy ticking off the list in her head. A quick phone call to remind Jack to be home early... in case he conveniently forgot... and she was back on track and in a more relaxed mood as she walked the short distance to her home.

Their house was on the quieter tree-lined end of Elystan Street in Chelsea, a two-storey Victorian house squashed between a five-storey apartment block on one side and a three-storey apartment block on the other. There was only a tiny pocket of a front garden between the pavement and the front door but behind the house there was a long walled garden, lushly planted, and so well designed as to make it appear endless. When the nearby apartments had been built, many years before, a condition of planning had ensured they were built in such a way as to ensure the privacy of their garden was maintained.

Before the children had arrived, Molly and Jack used to take advantage of this, sunbathing naked in the summer, staying outside until the only light was the tiny solar fairy lights she'd had festooned around the walls. The carefully-tended lawn was like velvet under their skin as they made love to the background symphony of London. And when they'd decided it was time to think of babies, she had a fairly good idea that Freya had been conceived there.

A smile lingered as she pushed open her front door, feeling more relaxed about the upcoming party. The smile froze as loud, angry voices coming from the living room brought her to a halt, her eyes widening in sudden fear. Burglars? A home invasion? She'd heard and read so many awful stories. Heart pounding, she'd taken one step backwards, preparing to run into the street and scream for help, when the loud voices changed to raucous laughter. Puzzled rather than terrified, she approached the living-room door and held her ear close to it. All she could hear now were low voices. With an indrawn breath, she grabbed hold of the doorknob, turned it and slowly opened the door.

Terry, oblivious to Molly's entrance, was slouched down on the sofa with her feet in a pair of tatty trainers resting, ankles crossed, on the coffee table. A movie blared from the TV, filling the room with noise. Terry, a mug of tea in one hand and a cigarette in the other, was engrossed in it and cackled open-mouthed as a character blew another away with a blast of a shotgun.

Molly's jaw had dropped open; she snapped it shut and yelled, 'What the hell is going on?' It was a rhetorical question; she could see from looking around that not much was going on at all. There was a pile of clothes on a chair waiting to be ironed. The vacuum cleaner was sitting to one side but by the look of the floor, it had yet to be used.

'I was having a break,' Terry said, looking up at her without a trace of guilt. She dropped her cigarette end into her coffee cup and stood.

'You were smoking.' And from the smell, Molly guessed it hadn't been her first.

'You never said I couldn't.'

No, Molly hadn't. She didn't think she needed to. 'This isn't working,' she said, holding a hand to her head. 'I'm sorry. I'll pay you for today but that's it. I need someone more reliable.'

'Suits me,' Terry said, and with a shrug of unconcern, put the mug down on the coffee table. 'I'll get my coat.'

Molly looked at the pile of ironing with a feeling of dread. Maybe she'd been too hasty; who was going to do it? Then she looked at the mug with its disgusting contents, there were some compromises she wasn't going to make.

The echo of the front door banging behind Terry hadn't faded when Molly realised how much extra she had to do before the party that night.

With a jolt of panic, she wondered if it were too late to cancel the whole damn thing, plead illness or temporary insanity. She couldn't, of course, standards to maintain and all that. Her friends teased her about having the perfect family, the perfect life. While she'd always denied it with a smile of forced humility, until recently she had thought her life was pretty much perfect. *Until recently.*

Something had changed and she couldn't put her finger on what that was. She and Jack had had little time for each other over the last few months between their busy jobs and the preparations for Freya and Remi's departure but she'd thought that was understandable, that when it was only the two of them once more, they'd get back some of the intimacy they'd always enjoyed. Instead Jack had become more distant, more wrapped up in his work, working later in the evenings and working some weekends which he'd never done before.

And now, with Rebecca gone, Molly came home every day to a house empty of life, the rooms quiet, echoes of the laughter and voices of her two children almost haunting her.

With a grunt of frustration, she changed into leggings and a T-shirt and got on with the work that Terry had abandoned. There was only so much Molly was going to have time to do. Ironing would have to wait. She shoved the overflowing wicker basket into the utility room. There were such things as laundry services; she'd have to investigate.

With the vacuuming done, she ran a duster around, plumped up cushions, reorganised chairs.

An hour later, she stood and looked around with satisfaction. The stage was set.

3

'You mean you fired her?' Jack said later that evening, as Molly raced around doing the last-minute titivating while he busied himself putting the food, that had been delivered an hour earlier, onto fine china platters. It wasn't complicated and despite his eating far more of them than he should, she left him to it.

'She was smoking,' Molly said, 'anyway, she was never very good and a million times worse since she took over the laundry. We'll get someone better.' She didn't tell him how difficult that might be, how getting someone, even someone as unreliable as Terry, might be impossible. If it came to it, they'd have to do some work themselves. She was using the royal *we*, but she knew Jack wouldn't lift a finger, he never had and was unlikely to start now. At the back of her head was the thought of ringing Terry and begging her to return, then the clear memory of the cigarette floating in the coffee dregs came back to make Molly shudder. No, she'd not ask her to come back. Something else would come up. Maybe one of her friends would have someone they could recommend.

With a last look around the room, she turned back to Jack who was carefully arranging prawn hors d'oeuvre around the edges of a square dish. 'They'll need to go in the fridge for the moment,' she warned him. She took one, popped it into her mouth and smiled to see his irritation at the upset to the pattern he'd painstakingly made.

He rearranged the display and put the dish into the fridge. When he'd shut the door carefully and turned around, there was a bottle of beer in one hand. 'A reward for all my hard work,' he said, reaching into a drawer for an opener and immediately slurping the foamy beer from the neck of the bottle.

Molly swallowed the criticism she wanted to make – that it was early to start drinking – and there was a time she wouldn't have hesitated in saying something, but his temper seemed so much more volatile recently and he took umbrage at little things that would once have rolled off his back or made him laugh.

Over half of the forty people they'd invited were his work colleagues, only a few of whom she had met before. The turnover of staff in the financial consultancy company where he worked was high; at every party there were new people and she depended on him to do the introductions and for his support to make the party a success.

'Take it easy,' she settled for saying before heading up to shower and change.

An hour later, she was back in a low-cut cherry-red silk dress she'd bought a few weeks before but never worn. She wasn't sure about it, wondering if she looked a bit mutton-dressed-as-lamb, wondering too if she could carry the cherry-red colour with her auburn hair. Freya would have told her; she would have stood with her head tilted to one side and assessed her outfit carefully before breaking into a smile that was so sweet that whatever she said – good or bad – was always acceptable. Molly missed her every day.

'What do you think?' she asked Jack when she came back to the living room. He was standing by the window, the bottle of beer in one hand.

Turning, he raised the bottle to his mouth and took a gulp before answering. 'Isn't it a bit...' He waved a hand at his chest.

She glanced down, adjusted the neckline slightly and frowned. 'Am I showing too much cleavage?'

He waggled the bottle from side to side. 'No, I suppose it's fine.'

She'd hoped for *you look amazing;* she'd even have settled for *you look nice* but this damning with faint praise was upsetting. Looking down at her dress again, she hesitated. There was time to change into something else.

'No, I'm sorry,' Jack said, coming over and putting an arm around her waist. 'You look lovely, don't mind me.'

'You sure?' she said, putting a hand on his shoulder.

'Positive, you look amazing.'

Molly smiled. It was what she'd hoped he would say, a little later than she'd have liked but she'd take it.

Turning from him, she checked the room, straightening cushions Jack had knocked askew.

'Relax and stop fussing,' he said, opening the fridge and taking out another beer.

'I want it to be perfect.' Molly adjusted the flowers yet again, wondering if she should have chosen a different colour scheme. She took a step back and tilted her head. 'Do you think these are a bit blah?' When he didn't answer, she turned, frowning to see him drinking the beer from the bottle. 'They'll be arriving soon, Jack, use a glass.'

'It tastes better from the bottle,' he said, holding it to his mouth and gulping a quarter down. 'And the flowers look fine. It's all fucking perfect so stop obsessing.'

Molly blinked. Jack rarely swore. 'There's nothing wrong with wanting everything to be–'

'Perfect,' he interrupted before holding the bottle to his mouth again and draining it. 'Yeah, yeah, I know but lighten up a bit.'

Lighten up a bit? There was nothing wrong with wanting everything to go well, was there? He was the one always keen to impress work colleagues. Molly turned away, hurt feelings forming a lump in her throat.

Luckily for the success of the party, Jack reached for her, pulling her back into a hug. 'I'm sorry, Mol,' he whispered, his lips buried in her hair. 'It's my night for apologies. I've a lot on my mind, it's making me grumpy.'

Don't take it out on me! The words were on the tip of her tongue and she'd have used them if the doorbell hadn't chimed, silencing her. She pulled away from his embrace. 'I suppose I'd better let them in.'

Forty people had been invited and almost everyone turned up. By eight-thirty, the room was buzzing with the sound of laughter and conversation. Molly moved from group to group with a wine bottle in her hand, topping up glasses, adding comments into conversations, introducing newer friends to older ones, work colleagues of hers to work colleagues of his.

'Have something to eat,' she urged everyone, waving towards where the hors d'oeuvres were laid out. 'And don't worry, we didn't make them,' she added to a chuckle of amusement from those friends who knew her well. She was, as she'd rush to admit, not a good cook.

Nods of appreciation came from those who did partake of the food, and Molly was pleased to see Jack doing his bit. He was standing chatting to Amelia, one of her oldest friends. He didn't like many of her female friends, found them too domineering, too, as he always phrased it, *in your face.*

Too intelligent. That's what she thought. Her friends were vocal, clever, bright women who took no prisoners. She never told him, because he'd have been horrified, but in the intelligence stakes, he lagged far behind most of them. It hadn't been his brain she'd fallen for. She'd been swayed by the humour in his blue eyes, his cheeky grin and the way his dark-blond hair curled back from his forehead like a Roman emperor. From the first time they'd met she knew he was the one, and twenty-one years later although he frequently drove her crazy she loved him just as much.

She watched as Amelia threw her head back and laughed at something he was saying and smiled. The party was a success. Molly allowed herself to relax.

She turned to chat to a group of Jack's work colleagues, the new ones, the stalwart few long-timers like Charlie Forster and a couple of others who'd been with them for several years. She greeted Charlie with a smile and a kiss on both cheeks. 'It's been a while,' she said, looking around for his wife. 'Zara not here?'

Charlie shook his head. 'Didn't Jack tell you? We split up. About six months ago.'

Colour flared in Molly's cheeks. 'I'm so sorry, I didn't know, Jack never said.' Suddenly claustrophobic, she pointed towards the garden. 'It's very warm in here, I'll go and open the back door.'

Molly pushed the French doors open and stepped into the chilly night, feeling immediate relief. Why hadn't Jack told her about Charlie and Zara? He should have warned her. How damn embarrassing. She'd return and apologise, but it was a couple of minutes before her body temperature returned to normal.

Bloody hormones. She flicked her hair, pinned a smile in place and headed back into the party.

She looked around for Charlie and saw him in the far corner of the room deep in conversation with Jack, their heads together, both looking serious. Talking shop, Molly guessed. She'd give them a few minutes, then go and drag them apart before more of their colleagues joined in and it ended up being a work meeting. She wondered what happened between Charlie and Zara. Maybe Jack was giving him a pep talk. She hoped so. She liked Charlie, he was one of those people who brightened a room when he walked in and unlike some financial types, didn't take himself too seriously.

Not like another of the long-timers, Stuart Mercer, who was making a beeline for her, a crooked smile on his lips that she guessed he thought made him look interesting. It didn't; he was handsome in a bland, forgettable way, the twisted smile made him look as if he'd swallowed something unpleasant. She hoped her social smile didn't look too false as she greeted him. 'Hi Stuart, I thought you were still in Hong Kong.'

'No, thank goodness,' Mercer said. 'I've been London-based now for a few months. Hong Kong lost its magic after the first year, to be honest. I've had a promotion; it'll keep me here for the foreseeable.'

'A promotion? Congrats, Jack never said.' Seriously, she'd have to have a word with her husband. It would be nice to know these things so that she didn't look a complete twat when she spoke to his colleagues. 'I wish Jack didn't have to travel so much. He's already been to Vegas several times this year and has to go back next month.' She laughed. 'He keeps asking me to come with him, but it holds no allure for me, I'm afraid. Now, Hong Kong,' she added, 'I'd have gone there all right.'

'Vegas,' Stuart said, a puzzled line appearing between his eyes. 'I didn't realise we had business there.' He shook his head.

'We work in the same building, but we might as well work in separate cities. Since my return, I've been so busy between the promotion and moving to a new house that I've had no time to catch up with what's happening with everyone. Travelling as much as I did was quite isolating, it'll be good to be settled.'

Molly felt a twinge of pity for the man as she recognised the hint of longing in his eyes; he was lonely. Perhaps she could fix him up with one of her friends. She rested a hand on his arm and leaned closer. 'You know what you need, Stuart,' she said, and was about to suggest introducing him to one of her single girlfriends when a commotion on the far side of the room claimed her attention. 'Oh dear, I'd better go and see what's up,' she said, smiling at him. 'I'll catch up with you later, okay?'

The commotion was nothing more than a dropped glass and spilt wine, but there'd been enough alcohol consumed at this stage to turn a minor incident into a tragedy. Brenda, one of her work colleagues, flushed with embarrassment and alcohol, muttered, 'I'm so sorry,' and dabbed uselessly at the small puddle of wine with a scrap of tissue.

'It's fine, don't worry about it,' Molly insisted, manoeuvring her out of the way, trying to stop another guest, whose name she couldn't remember, from picking up the pieces of shattered glass with his fingers. 'It's okay,' she said, putting a hand on his shoulder. 'Please, if everyone would move back, it'll be sorted in a jiffy.

Her words, cajoling but firm, did the job. Guests moved and were soon engrossed in conversation.

Left to clean up the mess, Molly fetched a paper towel, dustpan and brush. The glass had flown across a corner of the room. She had to stretch under a low coffee table to brush some out, banging her head as she did so, swearing softly under her breath.

'I heard that.'

Molly straightened with a dustpan filled with glass in one hand, rubbing her head with the other. 'You were lucky that was all you heard,' she said, turning to smile at Amelia. 'I've barely spoken to you. Let me get rid of this and we can have a natter.'

A few seconds later, with a quick look around to make sure everyone had their glass full, Molly gripped her friend's elbow and led her from the room. 'Come into the study,' Molly said, pushing the door open, and waving her in. 'I need five minutes to recoup my strength.'

'It's getting a bit rambunctious.' Amelia pulled a chair from under a desk, sat into it and looked around. 'What are you going to do with this room now that the kids have left?'

Molly frowned. 'They'll be back.' She ignored the raised eyebrow that was her friend's only comment. 'Anyway, tell me what you've been up to?' She tilted her head. 'Love your dress, by the way.'

'This old thing?' Amelia ran her fingers over the fabric before laughing. 'I bought it last week. It's pretty fab, isn't it?'

'Fab,' Molly agreed. She and Amelia had met in university and they'd maintained an erratic friendship over the years. Amelia had married her older hotel manager boyfriend, Tristan, shortly after graduating and spent the next several years following him from one far-flung city to the other. Only a rare meeting when she was in the UK, the occasional long email and in recent years short WhatsApp messages had kept the friendship alive.

'How are the renovations going?' Molly asked. Six months ago, when Tristan had retired, they'd bought a two-storey apartment in Pembridge Square Gardens. Molly had had serious house envy when she'd seen it.

'Almost finished,' Amelia said with a toss of her expertly-highlighted blonde hair. 'Everything should be done by the end of next month; we'll have a party to celebrate.'

'Great,' Molly said. 'I think I prefer going to them rather than giving them.'

'You give good parties. Free-flowing alcohol always helps.' Amelia looked at her from under her lashes. 'I met Stuart Mercer recently at a party in the Hong Kong embassy. He's an attractive man.' She leaned forward and said in a conspiratorial whisper, 'He's been giving you some strange looks. Is there something you're not telling me?'

'Don't be silly! He struck me as being lonely, that's all, and I was about to suggest setting him up with one of my single friends when that idiot Brenda made such a drama out of dropping a glass.'

Amelia arched a plucked eyebrow. 'It looked to me like he was more interested in you, he was certainly staring at your ass when you bent down.'

'You always did have a vivid imagination,' Molly said, shaking her head.

'If you say so.' A shrug of one shoulder said as clear as words that Amelia wasn't convinced.

Molly smiled at her. 'I do say so. Jack is still enough for me.'

'Not surprising, he's still one of the sexiest men I've ever met.'

For a microsecond, Molly thought she saw a look of lust cross her friend's face and felt a pang of anxiety. It had been over twenty years since they were naïve university students who had bonded in a collective struggle to survive, but different life experiences had moulded them into women who had very little in common. Truth was, she wasn't sure she even liked Amelia much anymore. Recently, Molly had been taken aback to discover that her friend's idea of fidelity was to sleep with one man at a time.

'Fidelity,' Amelia had said after a couple of cocktails, 'is vastly overrated.'

Had Molly imagined the look of lust? After all, they were friends – she wouldn't, would she? Would Jack? They'd looked very friendly when she'd seen them laughing together earlier... too friendly?

She caught Amelia staring at her with a look of concern and managed to smile. 'We'd better go back; they might be running out of drink.'

'Before you go,' Amelia said, holding a hand up to stop her. 'Tristan and I are going away next Saturday for a few days. It's a bank holiday weekend. Why don't you and Jack join us? There's a golf course but the hotel is also a health spa with a pool and a top-of-the-range gym. It would be a lovely break.'

Nowadays, with no school schedule to adhere to, Molly hadn't even realised a bank holiday weekend was imminent. They used to organise to go away as a family, Freya and Remi excited no matter where they were going, as happy to go to Devon as France or Italy. She'd fully intended to book a nice weekend somewhere for herself and Jack, but she'd forgotten about it.

'Do come,' Amelia pushed. 'It would be so much fun.'

Maybe a weekend away with Amelia and Tristan *would* be fun. Jack was a good golfer; he'd enjoy winning a game or two. 'Do you think we'd get a room at this late stage?'

Amelia smiled, pulled a mobile phone from a tiny clutch bag and seconds later was making an enquiry. 'They have a room available,' she said, holding her hand over the phone. 'Say yes.'

Why not? Molly made a snap decision and nodded. 'Yes, why not.'

'You'll love it,' Amelia said, putting her phone away after making the reservation. 'It's a beautiful and incredibly peaceful place a little outside Semington, in Wiltshire. 'The hotel gardens sweep down to a canal that's perfect for walking or running alongside. You still run, don't you?'

'I do,' Molly said. The thought of running along a canal in the country rather than the footpaths of London was very appealing. 'It sounds amazing, thank you.'

All she had to do now was convince Jack it was a good idea. How hard could that be?

4

———

'A weekend with Amelia. Absolutely, no way!' Jack said next morning, when Molly told him what she'd committed them to.

Maybe, he'd have been more amenable if she'd waited until he'd recovered from his hangover. She rested a hand on his arm. 'It would be a nice break. The hotel is on a canal, we could go for long walks, enjoy the peace and quiet.'

His eyebrows rose. 'The peace and quiet? With Amelia rabbiting on and Tristan expounding his views on share prices?'

Jack had never quite come to terms with the fact that Tristan had made some clever and very lucrative choices, allowing him to retire in what they considered comfort, and most people including Jack considered extreme luxury. Molly lifted the cafetière and filled his mug. 'I wouldn't mind a break for a few days. It's been a manic six months, between the kids, work and having to deal with everything at home since Rebecca left.'

'I suppose that's my fault,' he said, his lips thinning in annoyance. 'If you remember, you agreed we didn't need her.'

Yes, stupidly, she had. Not one of her better ideas. Nor was letting Terry go. She should just have given her a warning, after all she had been correct, Molly had never told her she couldn't smoke in the house. The agency she'd contacted promised they'd *try* to find a replacement. They'd also promised to send someone around to help with the clean-up operation that day. She checked her watch; if they'd not arrived by now, she guessed she was on her own. 'I really would like to go,' she said. 'I think it would do us good to get some fresh air. We can go for a run along the canal.'

Jack ran fingers through his hair and groaned. 'I drank way too much last night.' He reached for the coffee and topped up his cup. 'I don't want to, Mol. Why not go alone? You and Amelia can sit and gossip while Tristan plays golf. And you can go for a run along the canal on your own, you know you prefer to, you complain that I slow you down.'

Molly screwed up her nose. 'I can't go without you, Jack.'

'Why not?'

'Why not?' She glared at him. 'Because it would look odd. Amelia would wonder if we were having problems.'

'Don't be ridiculous,' he said bluntly. 'You've gone on spa breaks without me before, why is this any different?'

'Because Tristan is going, for one. Anyway' – she reached out a hand to rest it on his shoulder – 'it's you I want to go away with. We don't seem to have had much time together recently.'

'I tell you what, go this time on your own, and we'll go away for a weekend, just the two of us, in a few weeks.'

Despite hints during the week, Jack didn't change his mind. Resigned to going alone, the following Saturday Molly packed her bags and took them down to the hallway.

Jack raised an eyebrow when he saw all she was carrying. 'How long are you going for?'

'Funny man,' she said, putting the bags down. 'I'll be back on Monday. Why don't you book a table for a late lunch in that new

Lebanese restaurant, maybe for two o'clock? I'll definitely be back by then.'

'Sounds like a good idea, I'll do that,' Jack said, putting an arm around her shoulder and pulling her close.

Her hands slid around his neck and she breathed in deeply. He smelled of the citrus shower gel he used, fresh and tangy. Some of her friends relished time away from their husbands, but she never had. When he had to go to Vegas for work, she felt like part of her was missing until he returned. Maybe next time she'd go with him. She wished he were going with her now. 'It's not too late to change your mind,' she said softly, nibbling his earlobe.

He kissed her quickly and pushed away. 'It is,' he said, 'even if I wanted to, which I don't, I have plans made.'

'Plans?' Her eyebrows went up.

He grinned. 'Don't worry, nothing more sinister than meeting Charlie and a couple of others for drinks and dinner tonight.'

'Fine, enjoy yourself, but not too much.' She ran her hand over his cheek. 'Maybe I will come with you when you go to Vegas next month.'

He grabbed her around the waist and looked into her eyes. 'You mean it?'

She kissed him gently. 'Yes, I know, I said *never* but now that the kids are gone, I'd be here alone, and I'd much prefer to be with you.'

'Great, I won't let you change your mind.' He picked up her bags. 'You've remembered your running kit?'

Nodding, she opened the front door.

'It's supposed to get quite warm,' he said, as they walked towards the car. 'Will you be able to get out early?'

Molly always preferred to run first thing in the morning, especially in the summer when the heat in combination with exhaust fumes made running in London unpleasant. She didn't think there'd be a problem with fumes along the canal, but she'd still prefer to be out early. 'There should be no reason I can't go whenever I want. You know me, I'm always awake by seven thirty.'

'Okay, be careful,' he said, as they reached their car a few yards down the road from the house. He threw her case and holdall into the boot. 'Have a lovely time, Mol. I'll see you on Monday.' He turned, cupped her face in his hands and kissed her deeply.

Surprised at this unusual public display of affection, Molly gave an uncertain laugh. 'Gosh, maybe I should go away more often.' She got in the car, shut the door and opened the window. 'Go,' she said, 'you know how long it takes me to input a postcode into the satnav.'

He bent down, gave her another lingering kiss, tapped the car door with the flat of his hand and with a wave, headed back home.

She watched him go with regret. But maybe it would be good to get away for a couple of days and put her worry about him into perspective. She watched in the rear-view mirror as he walked back to the house, admiring his long, ambling stride, his slim-hipped athletic frame that had barely changed since she'd met him. But then she noticed something odd, something that made her eyes narrow in concern. His arms weren't swinging, relaxed; instead they were held tightly to his side, each fist tightly clenched.

Her heart went out to him, but if he wouldn't talk about whatever was worrying him, there wasn't much she could do. She watched until he vanished before concentrating on putting the hotel postcode in her satnav. As usual, she fluffed it first time and had to start again. Finally, it was done. She checked the arrival time; if she were lucky, she'd be there in under two and a half hours. Indicating to pull into traffic, she stopped when her mobile buzzed to say she had a new message and reached for it with an expectant smile. Jack missing her already?

But it wasn't him. She didn't recognise the number and was taken aback to see the message. *Is there a chance we could meet up this weekend? Stuart.*

She looked at it, frowning. At the party she remembered feeling sorry for him. It had crossed her mind he might be lonely, and she'd thought about setting him up with one of her single girlfriends. What was it she'd said to him? Ah yes. *You know what you need...* Oh damn, she'd been about to elaborate when she was interrupted by something... that silly broken glass. She'd left him with a smile and a promise she'd find him again later. Had he seen those simple meaningless words and smile as something more than she meant? Surely, he didn't take them as an invitation. Amelia said he'd been watching her. She thought her friend was being silly, maybe now she'd been proven right. How dare he? She'd a good mind to tell Jack. He'd swing for him.

Molly looked at the message again. Stuart had gone to the trouble of getting her number. She vaguely wondered who from, then shrugged. It was on her business card; there were some on the hall table, he might have picked one up at the party. With a shiver, she deleted the message and blocked the number. She didn't think he was in any way stupid; he'd get the message.

'Honestly,' she muttered, indicating and pulling into traffic. Did he really think she was interested in cheating on Jack with someone in his office?

She wasn't interested in cheating on her husband, full stop.

And with that thought clear in her mind, she headed off to Wiltshire for the long weekend.

5

Thanks to horrendously heavy traffic on the M4, it was almost three hours later before Molly turned into the quiet village of Semington. Minutes later, hearing *you have arrived at your destination on the right,* she indicated and pulled over. She'd known from what Amelia had said that it would be lovely, but this was more than she'd expected.

Set back from the road, the buttery-coloured stone façade of the elegant house glowed in the early afternoon sun. Three tall sash windows sat to either side of the open front door and above were two further floors, seven windows on each stretching the width of the house with pleasing symmetry. An elaborate wrought-iron gate was set into an old stone wall that surrounded the garden; it opened onto a gravel pathway that led to the entrance, neat flowerbeds on either side holding a profusion of creamy blooms swaying in the slight breeze.

Lost in admiration, it was a few seconds before Molly saw the ornate arrow with *car park* in neat letters along its length. It directed her further along the road. She started the engine again, and drove slowly, turning between two stone pillars into the large car park.

She sent Jack a text, *it's lovely, you should have come,* before getting out, taking her bags and heading to the hotel. The gravel pathway to the front door crunched underfoot and the creamy blooms on either side danced as she passed. It was all rather perfect.

Inside, a grand entrance lobby held the reception desk and a cantilevered stairway that curved upward, dividing right and left on the first floor and vanishing from sight. Double doors at the back of the entrance lobby lay open and gave a view to a huge glass and brick extension. It was a combination of old and modern that worked well.

'Molly Chatwell,' she said to the smiling receptionist. 'I have a reservation.' With the formalities completed and declining assistance with her bags, she took the key that was held out, looking at it with pleasure. A proper key, not a key card. 'Have the Lovells arrived yet?' she asked, before leaving the desk.

'Yes, I checked them in myself an hour ago,' the receptionist said and proceeded to give Molly directions to her room.

Rather than taking the lift as indicated, she took the stairs, admiring the paintings that adorned the walls, a mix of old and contemporary art that shouldn't have worked but did. It took her a few wrong turns before she finally found her way and stopped outside number twelve. She slipped the key into the lock, turned it and pushed the door open into a large airy room.

It was a corner room, tall sash windows on two sides flooding the room with light. They were partially open, and a slight breeze caused long voile curtains to flutter gently. The décor – pastel shades, floral patterns and frills – was the right side of twee. Molly looked around the room and smiled. It was very nice indeed.

She dropped her bags and wandered over to the window. The room was in a modern extension to the back of the hotel and her breath caught when she saw the beautiful gardens. Immediately below, steps led down from a patio to a pathway that meandered through wide borders to end in front of a fountain. A plume of water, easily seven or eight feet in height, sparkled in the sunshine and danced in the breeze. On each side, a lawn so velvety green she wondered if it were fake, with topiarised boxes at each corner. It was all, she decided, an absolute delight.

At the end, barely visible through the thick shrubbery that surrounded the garden, she could see the glint of sun on water. The canal. She was looking forward to running along it in the morning.

Molly quickly unpacked her clothes, hanging the dresses in a cavernous wardrobe whose door creaked ominously when she opened it, and placing the rest into the top drawer of a bureau. In a neat folder on a small table, she found information about the hotel and spa and a list of salon treatments available. Amelia had told her she should book some in advance, but she hadn't bothered. If she couldn't get an appointment, she was happy enough to relax in the steam room or sauna after a few laps of the pool.

A glance at her watch told her it was three o'clock. She should have asked which room Amelia and Tristan were in, but if she knew her friend she wouldn't be hanging about and was probably already lying on a massage table. And Tristan, no doubt would be on his way to the golf course.

A quiver of annoyance and resentment shot through her that Jack had refused to come, followed by a shiver of hurt feelings that he hadn't wanted to spend time with her. Wasn't that what it came down to? She pressed trembling lips together, her good mood of only seconds before extinguished. Unable to find any enthusiasm for the spa, she picked up her handbag and went down to the lobby. She was almost there when she heard her name called and turned to see Amelia coming down the stairs behind her.

'Molly! Perfect timing, I was thinking about having a G and T, now you can join me.'

'I thought you'd be in the spa,' Molly said, smiling at her friend as she came alongside.

'I've a facial booked for five, darling, so plenty of time for a drink and a catch-up first. Where's Jack?'

'Unfortunately, he's got too much on so couldn't make it,' Molly said, having decided on the journey down that this was the best lie to tell. She saw expressions of disappointment and annoyance vie for a place on Amelia's face and wondered why. Maybe disappointed that Jack wasn't going to be there for her to flirt with and annoyed with having to entertain Molly. Whatever the reason, she was suddenly sorry she'd agreed to come.

As soon as they were seated in the lounge, a tall, exceedingly handsome young waiter bustled over to take their order. Amelia's eyes widened and she put on her best flirtatious manner as she asked for a G and T for them both. 'Plenty of ice, darling,' she said to him, her voice pitched low and husky. 'I'm feeling rather hot.'

'You're old enough to be his mother,' Molly said bluntly when the waiter had gone.

'You're too fixated on age, Mol,' Amelia said, unoffended, her eyes following the young man across the room before turning back to her. 'If he's interested where's the harm?'

Molly was about to laugh but seeing her friend's expression she raised an eyebrow in disbelief. 'You're serious? What about Tristan?'

'Tristan will be playing golf until the light fades, he always does. Anyway' – Amelia waved a hand dismissively – 'enough about my sexual exploits, what's going on with you and Jack? There isn't someone else, is there?'

'Don't be silly.' Molly ignored Amelia's sharp eyes and pointed towards the outdoor seating on the other side of the window. 'Why don't we have our drinks outside? It's a lovely day, seems a shame not to make the most of it.'

'As long as we can sit in the shade,' Amelia said, lifting a hand to attract the waiter's attention. When he looked her way, she smiled, pointed outside and gave him a wave when he nodded understanding.

The drinks arrived a few minutes later, the waiter putting the large balloon glasses down carefully in front of each of them. Amelia made a big performance over tasting her G and T. 'It might be the best I've ever had,' she said, smiling up at him.

'Thank you. Would you like to charge it to your room?'

'Absolutely.' Amelia swirled the cocktail stick around her glass. 'I'm in room seven.' When he brought her a docket to sign, she did so with dramatic flair before circling the room number heavily. 'There you are.' She handed it to him with a flirtatious smile.

'Could you make it any more obvious?' Molly said with a shake of her head when the waiter had left. 'You don't really think he's going to call, do you?'

Amelia shrugged and picked up her drink. 'My darling, I'd almost bet money on it but that would be stealing. Of course, he'll come, and hopefully well before Tristan gets back.'

Molly laughed thinking that this time, surely, she had to be joking. The laugh died quickly when she realised, once again, she'd miscalculated. 'But what if Tristan comes back and you're... you know?'

'If he walks in on us, he'll turn around and walk out again. The proverbial blind eye, the same one I turn on his peccadillos. We have what I suppose you'd call an open marriage, Mol.' Amelia sipped her drink and smiled. 'Don't look so shocked, it works for us. I love Tristan but he can be a bit of a bore in the bedroom department, so I get my excitement elsewhere.'

Molly looked at her with startled eyes, unsure whether she was shocked or slightly envious. Was fidelity an outdated notion? She picked up her G and T and frowned as a horrible thought crossed her mind. Amelia had come back to London about six months ago; around the same time she'd noticed a change in Jack. *There isn't someone else, is there?* Amelia's words echoed in her head. Had she been a fool? Was her friend dropping a not very subtle hint? Was Molly the classic last to know?

Amelia was swirling ice cubes around in her glass, looking relaxed. There was no point in asking her, she'd deny it. Anyway, it would mean nothing to her, just another in her long list of conquests. If she had a bedpost, it would be riddled with notches.

But Jack was a different type. Molly knew him so well, if he were indeed cheating on her, the guilt would take its toll. Maybe she'd have been better staying in London and having it out with him. She shut her eyes and swallowed the lump in her throat. Have it out with him? What would she say – are you having an affair? And if he said no – would she believe him? And if he said yes – what then?

'Right,' Amelia said, draining her glass. 'I'm off for my facial.' She stood and looked down at Molly. 'See you for pre-dinner drinks? Around seven thirty?'

'Sounds good,' she said, conjuring up a smile, even as she wondered if she could think of a reason to leave, to head home to London and... what? She watched as Amelia sauntered across the lounge; she was a very striking-looking woman. The young waiter wasn't the only man whose eyes followed her.

Molly sipped her G and T and checked her phone, pleased to see messages from both Remi and Freya. She read them with a smile. They were such good kids. An exciting future lay ahead for both, a world of promise waiting to be explored. A dart of what she recognised as glossy-green envy startled her. She remembered being there, it seemed only a blink ago. Where had those years of promise gone? When had she become a dull middle-aged woman with a worried, increasingly distant husband? *Increasingly distant*. She shook the self-pity away. They had two gorgeous children. *Who'd flown the nest, and would probably never live at home again, might never even live in the UK again.*

And she would be proud of any and every choice they made. She *would* be proud. It was part of being a parent, wasn't it? You reared them, gave them all you could, and you let them go. A heavy sigh escaped her at the thought.

The evening ahead was unlikely to be a bundle of laughs. Listening to Tristan drone on – Jack had been right there, he did tend to fixate on the most boring of subjects. Her cheeks would ache from the plastered-on smile she'd wear that would probably look as false as it felt.

It might have been a good idea to go to the gym or do a few lengths in the pool, but she couldn't rustle up enthusiasm for either. Instead, she returned to her room and lay on her bed reading until it was time to get ready.

At seven thirty, wearing a pale-blue, knee-length silk shift dress that was an old favourite and more importantly, loose and cool, she headed back to the lounge.

Although Amelia had said seven thirty, it was obvious she'd been there a while, ice-cubes from a finished G and T melting in the bottom of a glass, the second in her hand, half drunk.

'Molly!' Amelia's voice was raucous, a good indication that the drink in her hand wasn't the second.

'Hi,' Molly said, taking a seat opposite.

'What'll you have?' Tristan asked, getting to his feet.

'A mineral water, please.'

Amelia snorted. 'Water! You're going to be a bundle of laughs.'

Tempted to say that it looked as if her friend was drinking enough for the two of them, Molly took a breath and let it out. There was never any point in crossing swords with someone inebriated. Instead, she gave her a friendly smile. 'I'll catch up later, I'm a bit thirsty.'

When Tristan returned with her drink, he suggested they move into the restaurant. 'I'm starving,' he admitted, patting an abdomen that strained against his shirt buttons.

'Fine with me.' Molly picked up her handbag and stood, waiting for Amelia before heading from the lounge.

The restaurant was a breathtakingly beautiful room. The clever use of mirrors on the rather low ceiling gave the illusion of space and reflected light from the numerous candles and carefully-positioned lamps. The walls were dark with a profusion of paintings set into ornate silver picture frames. Overall, the look was a gothic fantasy. It was, Molly decided, fabulous.

It was also very flattering. In the soft light, every woman there looked ten years younger.

'This is lovely,' she said as they sat around a circular table set for three.

With food ordered and wine poured, they relaxed into social chit-chat. It wasn't until they were on coffee that Tristan, more verbose after several glasses of wine, looked at Molly intently and asked, 'Have you never been tempted to change jobs... in all these years?'

Molly had worked for the same company since graduating. Working her way up, certainly, but for the same company. The thought suddenly appalled her. How incredibly dull it sounded. What had happened to the exciting ambitious woman she'd been in university? It would have been easy to blame marriage and children, but unfair; Jack had supported her through every promotional opportunity. And, between au pairs, childminders and the wonderful much-missed Rebecca in the last ten years, she'd had plenty of help with the children. Intelligent and experienced, she could have gone anywhere. But she'd stayed put.

'They've been very good to me,' she said. 'Plus, it's secure, lucrative, well-regarded. There is a certain cachet about working for Dawson Marketing that I wouldn't have had elsewhere.'

'But the same company, all these years?' He raised his hands, palms out. 'I'm sorry, that was rude.'

'No, it wasn't. You're right. It sounds appalling,' Molly said, with an attempt at a smile that failed.

Amelia, obviously bored with the conversation, told them a long, rambling, barely coherent story about a mutual acquaintance that was amusing enough to lighten a mood that had turned a little oppressive.

When Tristan suggested retiring to the lounge for after-dinner drinks, Molly pleaded tiredness and made her escape. Amelia, she noticed, made no attempt to persuade her to stay.

Back in her bedroom, Molly flopped on her bed and groaned. What a night! She lay for a few minutes before she gave a chuckle and sat up to reach for her handbag. Opening it, she pulled out her mobile phone and pressed a speed dial button.

When it went to answer machine after a few rings, she grunted, hung up and dialled again. It wasn't until the third attempt that the call was answered. 'Hi,' she said, adding a fake breeziness to her voice, wondering where Jack was, who he was with. She could hear voices and the faint sound of laughter too light and high-pitched to be anything but female. They'd probably gone to a pub after dinner, she reasoned, there was nothing to be concerned about.

'Hi, darlin', you havin' a good time?'

'Wonderful,' she said. It wasn't a complete lie; the food had been good. 'You in O'Dea's?'

'Yeah, me an' Charlie, we're havin' a few pints.'

It sounded like he'd had more than a few. 'Tell Charlie I said hello,' she said. 'I wish you'd come here, Jack, the hotel is really lovely and there are beautiful gardens that run down to the canal. The towpath is along the other side, I'm going to go for a run along it in the morning.'

'At cockcrow, I s'ppose.'

She smiled. 'If the cocks are crowing at seven thirty, then you'll be right. Okay, go back to your pint, I'm heading to bed. Chat tomorrow. Love you.' She waited until he echoed her words before hanging up.

6

Molly expected to sleep well; the room was almost eerily quiet, the bed extremely comfortable, the pillows perfect, everything designed for a peaceful, relaxing night apart from churning thoughts in her head that kept her tossing and turning. Wide awake before the first light of dawn chased the shadows from the room, she lay still, concentrating on her breathing, hoping to get another hour's sleep. It didn't come, but she lay there anyway, uneasy about wandering around the hotel so early. The distant but distinct sound of a cockerel's cock-a-doodle-doo followed by the sound of footsteps on the gravel outside her open window made her throw back the duvet and swing her feet to the floor.

Checking her phone, she was surprised and pleased to see a message from Jack. It had been sent at four, she guessed the long drinking session with his friends had had its inevitable consequences and he'd used the toilet break wakefulness to text her before going back to sleep. *Be careful running on the canal, I worry about you.* His concern made her smile. Whatever was wrong, they'd get through it. She sent a quick reply. *Heading off soon, wish you were here.*

Padding over to the window, she peered around drapes she hadn't bothered to pull shut and looked out. It was a beautiful day with that just awake fresh greenness that made her open the window wide and take a deep breath. There was no one to be seen, but the murmur of voices drifting from somewhere below indicated the hotel staff, at least, were up and about. She took her running gear from the drawer and pulled it on, tied her hair back with a scrunchie and a minute later, was quietly opening her bedroom door. She stood a moment, listening, then stepped out into the corridor and shut the door behind her.

Downstairs, she was surprised to see quite a few guests were up and about and she had to wait until the one receptionist on duty was free before she could ask her about access to the canal.

'There's a path that cuts through the hedge on the right,' Molly was told, the receptionist pointing towards the hotel gardens. 'Follow it to the bridge, cross it, and you'll be on the towpath. You can run for miles in either direction. Keep your eyes open for herons, and if you're really lucky you might see a kingfisher.'

Molly's eyes widened. 'I've never seen either.'

'You should see a heron, they're fairly common; a kingfisher is harder.' The receptionist smiled as she admitted, 'I've never seen one, to be honest.'

'I'll keep my eyes open,' Molly said. 'What time does breakfast finish?'

'It's served seven thirty to ten thirty, you've plenty of time.'

With a nod of thanks, Molly headed across the reception to a door leading out onto the patio. It was a perfect morning for running, cool but with the hint of a warmer day ahead. Following the directions, she easily found the path through the high hedge, stepping carefully over slimy, slippery leaves in its deep shade.

A short while later, she was walking over an old, stone humpbacked bridge. On the other side, the towpath stretched each way. Both directions looked tempting, each having enticing bends to lure her on. She'd go one way today, the other tomorrow. And with that easy decision made, she ran, slowly at first, getting a feel for the rough path underneath, then increasing her speed until she was moving at a steady pace. She ran in London, despite the fumes, but this was sheer pleasure.

The path was separated from the farmland beyond by lush hedgerows filled with life; birds twittered, butterflies fluttered, bees buzzed. Molly wanted to laugh aloud at how perfect it was. She would have missed the heron, if her eyes hadn't been scanning the canal on the lookout. It was standing on the edge of the path ahead, staring into the water, waiting for a sign of prey. She stopped and stood watching it, mesmerised at how still it was before edging closer to get a better look. The heron moved its head slowly, beady eyes focusing on her, then with a slight bend of its long legs, it launched into the air, wide wings flapping gracefully as it skimmed over the water. It didn't go far, coming to a halt on the other side several feet ahead.

It ignored her as she ran past a moment later. She guessed a kingfisher would be harder to see, especially as she needed to keep her eye on the towpath as she ran; it was far more uneven than she'd expected, with potholes and raised stones underfoot and the odd arching bramble extending from the hedgerow.

Almost thirty minutes after leaving the humpbacked bridge, she saw a wooden bench ahead in the shade of a large tree. Maybe she'd sit a moment and see if she could spot a kingfisher before starting back, but when she got closer she saw she'd been deceived by a shadow... the bench was already occupied.

She slowed to a walk, her eyes scanning the canal, peering into the branches of the trees on the far side, searching for a splash of colour. There was nothing and it was time to turn back. She'd seen a heron; she'd have to settle for that.

'Hi.'

One husky word. It brought her attention to the man sitting on the seat. He'd turned to look at her, his arms lying casually along the back of the bench, legs stretched out in front, ankles crossed. There was a curious stillness about him as he waited for her response.

It would have been rude to ignore him. In London, she'd have done so, would probably have turned back as soon as she'd seen him, but in the country, it was more appropriate to acknowledge him before moving away. She never understood why, there were surely as many criminal types in the country as in the city. Nevertheless, she nodded, said, 'Hi,' and trying to be casual, stopped and stared at the water for a moment.

'Do you have the time?' the man asked, bringing her focus back to him. She was close enough to see that the eyes fixed on her were an unusual shade of blue, almost turquoise. A striking shade in a handsome face.

She glanced at her watch. 'It's five past eight.'

'Early to be jogging,' he commented casually, holding her attention.

'Early to be sitting there too.' Despite a natural distrust of strangers, she took a step toward him. 'Are you hoping to see a kingfisher?'

The man's smile was slow, beguiling. Molly was drawn by it.

'I saw one,' he said, lifting his hand and pointing toward the far side of the canal. 'A minute before you arrived. Wait, and you might see it.' He took one arm from the back of the seat and patted the space beside him. 'You can sit, I don't bite.'

She laughed, the sound a nervous titter she didn't recognise. With a shake of her head, she walked over and sat. The wooden seat was small, there was room for two, but there was the merest whisper between them. Molly caught the scent of his aftershave and a slight hint of... body odour... no, she corrected herself, it wasn't the right word... it was the groin-tingling smell of virile masculinity. And it sent a shiver down her spine.

She should have got up and left then and she would have done, she wasn't Amelia, wasn't given to fancying or flirting with strange men. Molly would have stood and carried on back to the hotel if she hadn't felt his eyes on her... those amazing turquoise eyes.

He spoke about seeing the kingfisher, how beautiful it had been, his voice low and melodic, almost hypnotic. And all the time, his eyes stayed on her. She could have turned and met them, but she was afraid to – afraid of the sudden dart of lust that swept through her. She felt the man beside her move closer and turned slightly to see the perfectly-sculpted cheekbones, the delicious curve of his lips – didn't she deserve such excitement?

She jumped to her feet, the movement startling him as much as it did her. 'Have to go,' she said, and without another look in his direction, she ran as fast as she could, to put as much space as possible between her and the utterly gorgeous, fabulously-tempting young man. She resisted the temptation to look back to see if he were watching her or, God forbid, following.

A minute later, a frisson of anxiety made her stop and glance behind, but she'd come around a bend and all there was to be seen were fields and trees. No heron, sadly no kingfisher or young man.

She ran on. *Young man.* Maybe only a few years older than Remi. He was younger than she by twenty years, maybe more. Movie star good looks, a lean athletic body. And those eyes! Amelia, she knew, wouldn't have hesitated to have taken advantage of the situation. She'd probably have dragged the poor man into the fields and had her wicked way with him.

Molly laughed, feeling lighter than she had in days. The

brief encounter was beginning to take on a dreamlike quality. They hadn't even really touched, only a brushing of arms and yet it had been the most erotic experience she'd had in a long time.

Crossing back over the bridge, she slowed to a walk as she approached the hotel. She'd been gone over an hour and in that time, it had completely woken up. Already, with the day warming, there were people sitting on the patio. Gardeners were tidying flower beds, waiting staff were darting about with trays held high. Conscious of her dirty running shoes, she slipped them off and walked barefooted across to the stairway. The silence of early morning had been filled with sound. Voices drifted from the restaurant; she imagined she heard Amelia's amongst them.

Back in her room, Molly quickly undressed and stepped into the shower, a smile playing over her lips. She remembered the stranger's intense stare – and felt a shiver of desire. Would it have been so wrong to have given in to that moment's madness? Who was it that had said that the only thing they'd regretted were things they'd not done? She couldn't remember but they were wise words – or words of justification. She couldn't decide. The shiver of desire was replaced by a pang of regret for what might have been.

It had only been Jack since their marriage. And before that, a few college fumbles, and quick sex with forgettable men. She pushed a hand through her hair in frustration. What was she trying to prove? That she was still attractive? No, she was glad she'd not stayed. But that innocent meeting, that feeling that she was still desirable, still fanciable, had made her feel good about herself. That she should need such validation from a stranger worried her, then she brushed that aside. Sometimes she was guilty of overthinking. It had been a moment; no harm had been done and it had made her feel good. And that was all that mattered.

Molly stood at the restaurant door and looked around. Tristan was sitting alone. He didn't look too pleased. Feeling sorry for the man, she crossed the room to his table.

'Good morning, do you mind if I join you?'

Tristan half stood before flopping back into his chair. 'I'd like nothing better.'

'What happened to your golfing buddies?'

'Early birds,' he said with a shrug. 'They had breakfast at seven thirty and headed straight out.' He smiled. 'I'm a keen golfer but not that keen. I thought I'd have a leisurely breakfast with Amelia and head out later.' He jerked his head to the ceiling. 'She decided to have breakfast in bed.'

Molly picked up the menu and glanced at the choices, but her appetite appeared to have deserted her. 'Coffee and toast, please,' she said when the waiter came to take her order.

'You should have more,' Tristan said, cutting through a fat sausage. 'You're not on a diet, are you?'

'No, but I don't feel too hungry this morning.' She looked across the table to where his belly stretched his polo T-shirt, unable to take her eyes off it as her mind slipped unconsciously to the young man by the canal. His leather jacket had hung open, his T-shirt taut across a muscled torso.

A flush of heat rose to colour her cheeks, she fanned herself with the menu, eyes darting to the doorway. She'd ask the waiter to open it when he came.

Luckily, Tristan didn't appear to notice. He sat back with his three chins resting on his chest and made no effort to engage her in conversation. 'You don't regret leaving the hotel business?' she asked, knowing it was something he liked to talk about.

It was the perfect topic and gave Tristan the opportunity to expound on what he had done since he'd resigned, and all Molly had to do was nod and smile. Meanwhile, her thoughts were elsewhere, a smile lurking in her eyes as Tristan was going over some financial dealings he had with someone or other.

They'd almost finished breakfast when Amelia came in and joined them.

'I suppose you were out for a run this morning,' she said by way of greeting, taking the chair between her husband and friend.

'Yes, and very nice it was too.' Had she been alone with her, Molly might have told her about the man she'd met. They would have laughed over it and wondered what if...

'You coming to the spa? I have a massage booked for midday. We could go beforehand.'

Agreeing to meet her there, Molly went back to her room. Jack was sure to be awake; she took out her mobile to ring, feeling an urgent need to hear his voice. She had to settle for his voicemail when it rang unanswered. He was unlikely to still be asleep. He'd probably taken the Sunday papers to a nearby pub to read over brunch. She left him a voice message. 'Having a lovely time but wish you were here,' and hung up.

A few minutes later, her robe tightly belted over her swimsuit, she made her way down to the spa. The pool was large and inviting. Molly hung her robe up and slipped in, shivering for a second before immersing herself completely and starting to swim lengths. She had done several before Amelia turned up, and she swam to the side to meet her. 'It's a lovely pool,' she said, wiping water from her eyes.

'It looks nice, but I don't feel like swimming. I'm going to the sauna. Coming?' Amelia didn't wait for an answer, sauntering across, hanging her robe on a hook and going inside.

Molly swam to the steps. She'd all day to spend and although she preferred the steam-room to the sauna it would be nice to spend some time with Amelia. Molly could get back into the pool when Amelia had gone for her massage.

They had the sauna to themselves. Molly sat on the cooler lower wooden bench, leaving the hotter top one to Amelia. It was the perfect opportunity to tell her friend about her unusual encounter by the canal. Whether she was confessing or boasting, she wasn't sure. With the benefit of a few hours' distance, the episode had taken on an almost otherworldly quality, a black-and-white scene from a vintage Hollywood movie. She cast herself as the mature elegant leading lady and him as the younger glamorous leading man in an old-style romance of thwarted love.

Amelia's reaction put a damper on her imagination. 'He sounds amazing... if slightly unbelievable... seriously, does anyone really have turquoise eyes? It sounds like you were carried away by the romance of it all, when what you should have done was drag him into a nearby field for a quick fuck.' She raked Molly with hard eyes. 'It would have done you good, you know. Honestly, one of these days you'll realise that you're way too uptight.'

The bubble of romance burst, and Molly regretted having said a word. She was relieved when Amelia changed the conversation.

'How are the kids enjoying Paris and Boston?'

'Great. They love it.'

'You must miss them terribly.'

'I was never a stay-at-home mother, so although we're very close, I'm happy they're following their dreams.' Words she'd said to herself so often she almost believed them. Who was she trying to fool? Sadness pushed the corners of her mouth down. 'That's the official story, the one I trot out when anyone comments. Nobody has ever challenged it, but the truth is I miss them like hell. The house is like a mausoleum without them clattering around.' She gave a short laugh and turned to look up at Amelia. 'I bet you're sorry you asked now?'

'No, I'm not. You looked a little sad, sometimes it's good to talk. It sounds to me as if you're suffering empty nest syndrome. It's very common.'

A frisson of irritation flashed through Molly. She didn't want to be defined by some pseudo-psychological bullshit. 'Perhaps,' she said, her voice a shade cool.

'I bet you're menopausal too.' Oblivious to the effect her words were having, Amelia leaned down and used the ladle to throw water over the hot rocks, sending a burst of steam into the room, raising the temperature.

Molly wanted to stand up, storm out of the sauna and from the hotel, but she didn't. She wasn't a stupid woman and despite her suspicions about Amelia and Jack, there was something in what her annoying friend was saying. Maybe Molly had been overthinking everything, all her worries and concerns the result of hormones and a bloody empty nest. It might be that Amelia had hit the damn nail squarely on its tiny little head.

'No, I'm not menopausal,' Molly lied automatically. Denial, it wasn't a bad place to linger. 'That joy still awaits me.'

'Then perhaps you're in a rut. You should try something new, do something different.' A trace of boredom crept into Amelia's voice and a few minutes later, she stood and stretched. 'I'd better go. I'll see you later.'

Molly followed her out and headed into the steam room. There were other people there, a couple of younger women with their heads together discussing something important in murmured undertones and an overweight man who appeared to have fallen asleep, a gentle snore coming from his direction.

There was an outdoor jacuzzi but Molly's earlier prediction that the day would turn warmer had been wrong. Dark clouds had swept in through the early afternoon and light rain had increased to a deluge that blurred the boundaries of the garden and shimmied over the patio. The hotel wasn't taking any risks – a sign went up to say the jacuzzi had been closed for safety reasons. So, for the rest of the afternoon, Molly drifted between the pool, sauna and steam room.

Amelia didn't return after her massage. Molly wondered if she had an assignation with the waiter; he'd never been mentioned again. She hadn't wanted to ask, and Amelia hadn't volunteered information. Perhaps she hadn't wanted Molly spoiling her fun.

Rain, driven by the wind, played a noisy staccato rhythm on the floor-to-ceiling windows that surrounded the pool and in the background, much further away, there was a low rumbling of thunder. Molly pulled her robe on over her swimsuit and stood looking out over the deluged garden. After such a promising start, the day had taken on grim shades of grey that suited her mood. She wished she'd not told Amelia about the man she'd met. It had been a harmless fantasy, now it was spoiled. Molly shivered and wrapped her arms across her chest.

Turning away from the window, she looked at the clock that hung over the entrance. It was four thirty. She'd go back to her room and ring Jack. Maybe later, she'd come back and do a few more lengths before calling it a day. It wasn't as much fun on her own.

Back in her bedroom, she picked up her mobile and pressed the speed dial key for Jack, breathing a huff of pleasure when it was answered. 'Hi,' she said.

'Hello, hang on.' Sounds in the background told her he was in a pub, the noise fading as a door opened and closed. Wherever he'd moved to, it was quiet enough to hear him clearly. She thought he sounded a little tense. Had she interrupted something?

'Hi,' he said, 'still having a good time?'

'Really good,' she lied, wondering as she did, why she felt the need to pretend.

'Did you get out for your run this morning?'

It was the last thing she wanted to talk about. 'Yes, it's very pretty around here. How's your weekend going?' What she really wanted to know was who he was out with. Charlie again... or someone else. At least she could be sure, it wasn't Amelia.

'Fine, quiet,' he said. 'I'm with the lads watching the match in Masterson's. Will you go for a run again in the morning?'

The lads. That all-encompassing term. She resisted the temptation to ask who was there. 'Yes,' she said, answering his question, although she wasn't sure she would go for another run. 'I'm heading back down to the pool now. Have a good evening, if it's not too late and I'm not too tired I'll give you a ring after dinner, okay?'

'Okay, I love you.'

She rubbed a hand over her forehead. Was there a hint of

overemphasis in those three words, as if he were trying to convince himself? Or was she stupidly overthinking again. 'Love you too.' Hanging up, she swung her legs up onto the bed and lay back against the pillows. Feelings of regret, worry and guilt were scrambled in her head. She closed her eyes, trying to shut the thoughts away and despite everything found herself drifting to sleep.

When she woke, eyes snapping open in confusion, it was almost dark. She brushed away the brief disorientation and sat up, her hand searching for the phone. Seven thirty. She swore softly. There had been no mention of meeting for drinks prior to dinner but she guessed that was the plan.

She'd not made it back to the pool. Her hair was a tangled mess, and she saw with a grimace that her swimsuit had soaked through her robe to dampen the bedcover beneath. It would dry without leaving a mark, she hoped, smoothing the cover out.

Ten minutes later after a quick shower, she tied her hair in a French knot and slipped on a silver-grey dress. She looked at her reflection in the mirror as she did her make-up and pulled back the creases around her eyes, wondering, not for the first time, if she should have a bit of work done. Dropping her hands, she turned away. *Empty nest syndrome*. There had been so much stress over Freya and Remi's exams, then the excitement of the results and their move overseas. She'd gone with each of them in turn to help them settle in. Paris and Massachusetts had both been so exciting... then it was all over for her, she'd left them to it and come home to the same old, same old.

Old.

Was that what it all came down to? *Menopause. Empty nest.* All symptoms of what she should be seeing as the natural order of things; hormones were supposed to change, children were supposed to go out into the world and make their own lives.

Maybe she needed to take a page from Amelia's book and grasp this different life with both hands, break out of the rut she was in and try something new.

It was worth thinking about.

8

When Molly went down, Amelia and Tristan were still in the lounge, an almost-empty glass in each of their hands. Amelia's discontented expression brightened when she saw Molly hurry across the room. 'Where have you been?'

'I'm so sorry,' she said, 'I think I must have overdone it between the run and the pool, when I went to my room I lay down for a moment and fell asleep.'

'You should learn to relax more.' Amelia waved towards the restaurant. 'We'd better go in before they give our table away.'

Since the hotel was quiet, unusually so for a bank holiday Sunday, Molly didn't think there was much chance of that, but she said nothing and followed them from the room.

The food was once again excellent but there was little atmosphere in the half-empty restaurant. Conversation between the three was in brief bursts followed by long periods of silence. Tristan complained about the weather ruining his golf; Amelia gave an in-depth account of her massage, and Molly added a word here and there as required and wished Jack was with her. If he had been, he'd have told some funny anecdotes that would have livened the mood. She missed him.

After coffee, Amelia suggested drinks in the lounge, but Molly had had enough. 'I'm tired,' she said, pushing back from the table. 'I'm going to head to bed. I'll see you at breakfast.'

Back in her room, she took out her mobile and checked for messages. There was one from Jack. *Hope you're still having a good time. Charlie and I are going to a movie. Chat tomorrow.*

A movie! She'd hoped to be able to speak to him and felt a lick of disappointment bring tears to her eyes. Perhaps if she'd told him the truth earlier, he might had advised her to come home, and she'd be there now, with him, laughing about the weekend, putting the young man and his ridiculous eyes behind her. But she hadn't told him the truth, and now it was too late. She tapped out a suitably vague and ambiguous message. *Wonderful, but it'll be better when I'm home tomorrow.*

She wasn't sure she'd sleep following her long afternoon nap and was surprised to find herself drifting off as soon as her head snuggled into the pillow. But it didn't last; every creak and whisper of noise woke her to send her tossing and turning in a hunt for oblivion. When the first streaks of light slipped under the curtains, she stopped trying. Her hand stretched out and fumbled to find the lamp switch, eyes shutting tightly when the room was flooded with light. She blinked and looked at her watch. Seven.

She'd half thought about skipping the run, but the one the day before had been so lovely, wasn't she being a bit silly to deprive herself. It was highly unlikely that the stranger would be there today. Anyway, she'd go the other direction and enjoy the fresh country air before returning to London.

The morning was dry but the heavy rain of the day before had left its mark. The ground squelched underfoot, wet leaves on mud making it slippery in places. Once she crossed the humpbacked bridge, it was safe to start her run. She glanced the way she'd gone the day before, gave a slight smile and headed in the other direction.

There were a couple of narrowboats moored. Molly ran past, picking up speed, careful to avoid the worst of the puddles. There were locks along this stretch of the canal; she looked up as she rounded a bend and the first came into view. Painted white, they stood out against the predominately green surroundings, but it wasn't their colour that made Molly stumble and slow to a halt.

There was a man standing beside the lock, leaning on one of the lock paddles. His back was to her, but she could tell from his slim-hipped broad-shouldered physique that it was the man she'd met the day before. Perhaps he lived on one of the narrowboats she had passed? Or perhaps he was a figment of her overactive imagination? An illusion conjured up by her paranoid, confused brain.

She stood staring, shifting her weight from foot to foot. What had Amelia said? *You should try something new, do something different.* There would be no harm in going over and saying hello, would there? Then Molly was beside him, a tentative smile on her lips. 'Hi.'

It was a second before he turned as if he were lost in his own thoughts, a second that gave Molly time to admire the classic line of his jaw, and acknowledge the lust that had set her groin tingling and her heart pounding.

When he turned, stunning turquoise eyes boring into hers, her first thought was that Amelia had been wrong, that colour eye did exist and the second that she had been equally wrong, she should never have stopped.

'Hello,' he said. 'Aren't canal locks fascinating?' He moved around the paddle and stood at the edge of the lock chamber staring down.

She stood uncertainly, watching as he leaned forward, then

she took a few steps to stand beside him. The walls of the deep chamber were green with moss and slime, the water at the bottom dark and eerie. It wasn't pleasant. She turned to him instead.

'Some lock chambers have ladders in case people accidently fall in. This one,' he said, 'doesn't.'

Molly had no interest in the lock; she was mesmerised by the man, by his chiselled cheekbones and sculpted lips, his low husky voice as he spoke about the workings of the lock. She remembered an expression Freya had used about some movie star – sex on legs – it was a description that suited him perfectly. When his hand reached for her, sliding around her waist, she decided Amelia was right, she was going to grab the moment and to hell with the consequences.

She felt the heat of his hand through the thin material of her T-shirt and leaned towards him, chin raised, her lips parting in invitation... waiting for his response... and in that second of waiting, she knew she'd got it wrong... he reared back, mouth thinning in distaste, eyes narrowing in disgust. She'd got it all wrong... he'd not been reaching for her, he'd been putting a hand out to prevent her falling in... to prevent a woman old enough to be his mother from making a stupid step and falling into the damn chamber.

Unfortunately, he hadn't managed to stop the pathetic stupid woman from making an absolute fool of herself.

With a cry of anguish, she pulled away. His hand had tightened on her T-shirt, she could feel the material stretch as he tried to stop her and she wrenched it away, then ran as she didn't think she'd ever run before, her feet barely touching the ground as she flew on the heat of mortification. She heard him call out, then the heavy sound of his feet crunching on the path as he chased after her, but he was no match for her speed and within a minute, she had left him behind.

. . .

Back in the hotel, she went straight to her room, grabbed her clothes from the wardrobe and bureau, changed quickly and jammed everything into her bags. Humiliation stung with almost unbearable pain and all she wanted to do was leave, to go home, hide away to lick her wounds.

At reception, she left a note for Amelia, explaining that something had come up that required her to leave early. Her brain was too fraught to come up with a reasonable explanation, she'd think of one before speaking to her next. She settled her bill and headed out to the car park.

Pines from an overhanging spruce tree decorated her windscreen. She brushed them off, wiping her hand carelessly on the leg of her trousers and sat into the car, throwing her bags into the footwell of the passenger seat. There had been no early morning text from Jack, he was probably still fast asleep. She took out her mobile to tell him that she was on her way, then changed her mind, she'd be home before he woke.

She turned the radio on, scrolling through stations to find music then increasing the volume so that the sound filled the car and her head, leaving no room for recriminations, for scalding guilt and searing gut-wrenching humiliation.

Despite bank holiday Monday traffic, she made good time. The music helped to drown the demons and, by the time she pulled up near her house, she was calmer and suitably embarrassed at her behaviour. It would have made a good story to share at parties if it had only happened to someone else. Now all she wanted was to forget about it.

The downside to their beautiful London home, the only one, was that there was no parking. Today the gods were smiling down on her, perhaps in sympathy, and she found a space a minute's walk away. She picked up her bags and headed for home. *Home*, she thought, pushing open the door and feeling instantly relaxed.

A sudden piercing *beep beep beep* told her the alarm was set. She dropped her bags and hurried to key in the code to switch it off. Maybe her plan to surprise Jack hadn't been such a good idea after all. He'd probably woken early, gone out for the newspaper and taken it somewhere to read over breakfast.

Heading upstairs, she pushed open the door to their bedroom, planning to drop her bags and ring him, her eyes widening when she saw the bed. Jack was being unusually tidy. Normally, if he did anything, it would be to pull the duvet up but today the pillows were plumped, the bedspread in place and tucked under them, the way she liked it.

Leaving the bags on the floor, she walked over and ran a hand over the bed, her forehead creasing in a frown. So neat; just the way she'd left it before she went away on Saturday. If she didn't know better, she'd have sworn he hadn't slept in it at all.

But that was ridiculous.

Wasn't it?

9

Molly had unpacked, thrown a wash on, and was sitting with a mug of tea before she heard the front door open and Jack's irritating off-tune whistle.

Her eyes were glued to the kitchen door. She hadn't bothered to ring him, so he wasn't expecting to see her. He wouldn't notice that the alarm was already off, he'd assume he'd forgotten to set it, as he often did. She was shocked when the door opened and he stood staring at her with his mouth slightly open... he looked terrible. She'd not noticed before but absence, no matter how short, highlights change; she'd thought he'd lost weight recently but now she could see it, his face was full of angles and planes that were new. There was a greyish tinge to his skin, and dark circles rimmed his eyes

'Molly,' he said, faltering in the doorway.

She attempted a laugh that fell flat. 'Don't sound so surprised, I'm only a couple of hours early.'

'It's great... great... just unexpected, you should have phoned to let me know,' he said, stumbling over his words. 'That's great,' he said again, his smile looking as false as the heartiness in his voice. He dropped the holdall he carried and closed the distance in two swift steps, dragging her into a hug, burying his nose in her hair.

She could feel his breath damp on her neck and the slight tremble that ran through him. Pulling back abruptly, she looked at him. She saw confusion sweep across his face and... was that a trace of fear?

'What's wrong, Jack?' she asked, reaching a hand up to his cheek and holding it there.

He shook his head. 'Not a thing,' he said, putting his hand over hers, 'although I might have overdone it at the gym.' He patted his stomach. 'I've lost a bit of weight recently and thought I'd better tone up. Haven't been in ages.'

'Oh, I see,' she said, wishing she believed him.

'Yes' – he patted his stomach again – 'I swear I feel more toned already. A good workout, you can't beat it.'

She sat and picked up her tea. 'It's still hot if you want some.'

Nodding, he reached into a cupboard for a mug. 'Are you okay?' he asked, lifting the teapot. 'You look pale.'

'I'm fine,' she said, with a reassuring smile. 'Amelia wasn't as much fun to go away for a weekend with as I'd expected, so I made an excuse to leave early.'

'Really? I thought you said you were having a great time.'

'It was okay.' It would have been nice to share her humiliation, to have him laugh over it. But of course, she couldn't – couldn't tell him about her moment of weakness where she had lusted after a young man so much that she would have followed him into the fields and revelled in him like an escapee from a Thomas Hardy novel. 'But I'm glad to be home and looking forward to having lunch with you.' She caught Jack's puzzled look. 'You did remember to book a table for lunch, didn't you? Remember, we discussed trying that new Lebanese restaurant.'

Jack shook his head as he poured tea and added milk. 'It

went out of my head. I'll give them a buzz, I'm sure it won't be a problem.' The tea was too hot, he slurped it noisily. 'You've already unpacked?' Putting his mug down, he went to the cupboard for biscuits, rummaging through a selection of packets before deciding on one. He took it out and struggled to open it. 'Damn things,' he muttered and tore the top with his teeth.

Taking his seat, he shook out a handful of biscuits and slid the rest over to her.

Shifty. It was the only word Molly could use to describe the way he was looking at her. 'Yes,' she said finally. 'I've been home about an hour.'

'Did you see?' he said, taking a sip of his tea.

She blinked in confusion. 'See what?'

His mug went down with a clatter and he threw his hands up in the air. 'What? The bed I made so perfectly. Weren't you surprised?'

He'd made the damn bed. He hadn't put on the laundry or emptied the dishwasher. But she knew the easiest course was to give him the praise he was seeking. 'I was pleasantly surprised.' She didn't mention that it looked as if it hadn't been slept in. She still wasn't convinced it had.

'I knew you were unhappy about losing Rebecca, I thought I'd show you that I could help out more.'

'Great,' she said, trying to sound enthusiastic, knowing by the tightening of his mouth that she hadn't succeeded.

He drained his mug, left it on the table and went into the study to check emails before they headed out to lunch. With a sigh, Molly picked the mug up and put it into the dishwasher with her own. There was a beep as the washing machine finished the cycle. She went into the small utility room, opened it and transferred the clothes to the tumble dryer.

With the idea of putting Jack's gym clothes in for a wash, she went back to the kitchen. But he'd taken the bag with him. So much for being helpful. She scowled; she wasn't going to go looking for it.

Despite Jack's assurances, the Lebanese restaurant didn't have a table free for lunch. Instead, they went to an Italian that, although excellent, was too traditional, conservative even, for the Instagram-obsessed customers who frequented the restaurants in their area. No flowers, no fantasies, just food.

'So, tell me about the weekend,' Jack asked her. 'Amelia wasn't much fun, you said.'

'I was mostly on my own, Amelia vanished somewhere. I think she was having a fling with one of the waiters.'

One of Jack's eyebrows disappeared into his hair. 'Seriously?'

Gossip, it was never kind. She laughed. 'Of course not, I was kidding. Amelia likes her own space, that's all. She wasn't expecting to have to babysit me, she thought you were coming, remember?'

Jack, in the middle of lifting his pasta-laden fork, stopped and stared at her. 'So, you're blaming me for the weekend not being up to your standards?'

'No,' she said, 'I'm trying to explain why it was a bit of a washout.' She put her fork down, her appetite suddenly gone as she thought about the weekend.

'You and Amelia have been friends forever, but you've hardly spent any time with her in the last ten years. People change, Mol.'

What about in a year? She wanted to ask him what had changed between them, because something had. It was easy to blame work or to imagine he was cheating on her with Amelia or any number of women. Too easy perhaps. The dim light of the restaurant emphasised the shadows and shades on his face.

Was the distance that had grown between them her fault? She'd been so caught up in Remi and Freya's departure, the organising and arrangements, invoices that needed to be paid. All of it had fallen on her shoulders. She hadn't minded but maybe he had. Maybe, not only did he miss the children but also resented her total immersion in them and felt left out.

The grip on her fork tightened. So maybe he had looked elsewhere for attention. Maybe he'd been tempted to cheat on her, the same way she'd been tempted to cheat on him – only with more success. Was that why he'd looked so shifty and spun her that crazy story about making the bed? She was convinced it hadn't been slept in, so where had he spent the nights? She dropped her fork and pushed the plate away.

'You've hardly touched it,' he said in surprise, reaching over with his fork and jabbing it into a piece of her chicken.

'I ate a lot over the weekend,' she said, pushing the plate closer to him. 'The food in the hotel was excellent.'

After lunch, they walked the short distance to St Luke's Gardens. This late, the flower borders held little interest, but it was still a pleasant, quiet place for a stroll. Molly was conscious of the silent man at her side, of the need to make conversation that before would have flowed. Since when had they struggled for words to fill the gaps... since when had there been gaps?

A sideways glance told her he was lost in thought, a set look to his profile. She slid her hand into his and saw his quick look of surprise – she'd never been the hand-holding type. But she could change; now that the children were settled, she could concentrate on him. If there was one lesson she'd learned from the calamitous weekend, it was how easy it was to be led astray. If Jack were having an affair, she'd fight for him.

'Let's go away for a weekend,' she said, squeezing his hand tightly. 'Maybe to Venice for a few days. What do you think?'

He pulled his hand away and bent to retie his shoelaces.

They didn't look to Molly as if they needed to be retied and when he stood, and they'd resumed their walk, she noticed he didn't reach out to take her hand. On the contrary, he moved slightly further away as if to prevent her doing so.

She felt a weight in her chest. They were in more trouble than she'd thought.

He hadn't answered her question.

'Well?' she said, trying to keep her voice light.

She saw him turn toward her, a puzzled lift to his eyebrows. 'Well, what?'

'About my idea of a weekend away,' she said, unable to prevent the trace of exasperation.

'Oh, that? Maybe in a few months, I'm way too busy to take time off work now.'

There it was, work again. Maybe it *was* at the root of it all. There was no point in asking him; if there was a problem at work, he'd not talk about it. He became stupidly macho about things like that. To her, it was simple, if there was a problem, he needed to sort it out... sort it out or leave. He was an experienced finance investment manager; he'd easily find something else. And if he didn't, they'd cleared the mortgage on the house a few years ago, they'd easily manage for a while on her salary. But she knew his stubborn pride wouldn't accept that situation.

She needed to find out what was going on. Her friend, Petra, knew someone who worked in a different department in the same company. She'd get her to do a bit of digging.

After a leisurely walk around St Luke's, Jack wanted to go for a drink. She'd have preferred to go home, chill in front of the TV and have a glass of wine. Instead, she forced her lips into a smile and nodded enthusiastically. 'Good idea,' she said, wondering at how easily lies came these days.

O'Dea's was a popular pub, and always busy. If she'd hoped Jack might open up over a pint or two, her hopes were dashed when they were greeted by an acquaintance of his, a man she'd met a few times and found amusing when sober and a bore when drunk.

Luckily, this time he was sober. 'Jack, Molly,' he greeted them, drawing them into the group he was with, making introductions, names fired around, forgotten as soon as heard.

Molly smiled at everyone, accepted the drink bought for her and perched on a stool. She'd stay for one, then make her excuses. She saw the signs; these men were there for the long haul.

Apart from the occasional nod and smile, she wasn't called to contribute to the conversation and was able to concentrate on her own thoughts. When she got home, she'd ring Petra.

It was time to take the first step and find out what was going on.

10

Molly made her excuses after one drink, noticing that Jack, on his second pint, looked settled for the evening.

'Don't be too late,' she said into his ear before she left.

'I won't be, I'll have one more and follow you.'

It seemed she wasn't the only one to whom lies came easily these days. With a casual wave to the rest, she headed out onto the street, the light already fading, the darkening clouds promising rain before long. It made her quicken her pace and she was home as thunder rolled and the first crack of lightning shot across the sky.

Inside, she hung her coat over the banisters, kicked off her shoes and walked barefoot to the living room as she scrolled through her list of contacts for Petra's number. Molly flopped onto the sofa as she waited for the phone to ring, hoping her friend would be at home.

She was in luck; it was answered almost immediately. They chatted regularly so it wasn't unusual for her to ring, and her friend greeted her with her customary cheerful, 'Hiya Molly.'

Relaxing, Molly spent the first several minutes telling her friend about the weekend. 'I should never have gone without

Jack.' She was tempted to tell her about the stranger she'd met but she didn't. Not because she was afraid her friend would be surprised or shocked, she'd long come to realise that Petra was virtually unshockable, but because the episode had taken on an unreal dreamlike quality. If she didn't talk about it, the whole thing, along with the guilt and humiliation, would fade away. It was better that way.

'I was surprised you did,' Petra said. 'Actually, I thought you were crazy. Amelia is a lovely dash of psychedelic colour in our conservative grey world, but I've found a little of her goes a long way.'

'She's probably saying the same about me,' Molly laughed. 'I've been a bit preoccupied recently and possibly wasn't the best of company.'

'You're missing the kids. A touch of empty nest, I'd guess.'

Molly swallowed a groan. Why was everyone so quick to practice their armchair psychology on her. At least, Petra hadn't asked if she were menopausal too. Before she was tempted to do so, Molly brought the conversation around to the real reason she had phoned.

'How's Simon?' she asked as a first step and listened to Petra telling her how wonderful her darling husband was for several minutes. When there was a miniscule lull, she dived in. 'Good to hear,' she said. 'Jack has been a bit stressed recently and he's looking very pale. It seems to be a bit manic at work. I'd love to be able to empathise with him.' She thought that sounded suitably psychobabbly. 'But it's hard when I don't know what's going on, and he's like your Simon, way too macho to admit if there are problems.'

'Gosh, yes, they're two of a kind.'

Molly gave what she hoped would pass for an amused laugh. 'Peas in a pod. Men, we have to protect them from themselves, don't we?' She waited for her friend's laughter to die down. 'That pal of yours, Nicole, who works in Jack's firm, you wouldn't fish a little, see if you could find out something, would you?'

The indrawn breath told her that, for once, she'd surprised her friend. Molly shut her eyes and swore softly under her breath.

'You want me to ask her to spy on him?'

Molly had forgotten Petra's liking for drama and intrigue, and immediately regretted having asked. But it wasn't the kind of thing you could step back from. '*Spy* is a little OTT,' she said calmly. 'I see it more as looking out for my husband's welfare, the same as I'd look out for yours if the situation were reversed.'

'Gosh, yes,' Petra rushed to comment. 'I know you would, Mol. We women have to stick together after all.'

Putting her hand over the mouthpiece, Molly let out a whoosh of relief, not really listening as her friend rambled on about women's solidarity. 'Thanks,' she said, when there was a pause, 'yes, it's the only way, isn't it?'

'Absolutely. You leave it with me.' Petra's voice held the fervour of one on a mission. 'I'll give Nicole a shout tomorrow and ask to meet her for coffee, it will be easier to pump her for info face to face.'

Petra might be a bit of a drama queen, but she was also an astute woman. If there was anything to know, she'd find out.

A few minutes later, Molly said goodbye, dropped the phone on the sofa beside her and sat back, resting her head on the cushion behind. She wanted it to be trouble at work, however difficult that might be, because the alternative didn't bear thinking about.

She reached a hand up, her fingers lingering on the fine lines she knew had appeared around her eyes. An affair with Amelia, bad as that would be, wouldn't be a risk to her marriage. Amelia wasn't looking for something permanent after all, but if he'd found someone younger, prettier. Someone in Vegas perhaps?

With difficulty, Molly put the idea to the back of her mind and picked up her phone. Despite being asked to contact her every day, there were no messages from either Freya or Remi. They'd plead their case with excuses of being too busy, too exhausted, too *something* rather than the truth that they'd not thought about her. If they were in trouble, she'd hear about it fast enough. She'd no real worries, they were good kids, but she wished they'd at least send a message. The apron strings still tugged, she didn't let them hurt, but they did irritate at times.

As the evening crept on, she wondered about getting something to eat. Instead, she made a cup of tea and switched on the TV. Nothing held her attention, a documentary was too boring, a drama turned out to be less than gripping. The ten o'clock news came and went, and Jack still hadn't arrived home. The pub did food, he'd probably had something to eat and would fall in the door later, stinking of garlic and onions. She put her mug in the dishwasher and headed to bed. If he was very late, he'd sleep in the spare bedroom so as not to disturb her. He often did.

More often recently? She tried to think if this was the case and gave up.

Crawling between the sheets, she lay and listened to the gentle sounds of the house settling for the night, the soft gurgle of the ancient plumbing, pipes creaking as the heating switched off, soft ticking sounds that lulled her to sleep.

At home, she usually slept well, falling quickly, waking suddenly. Reaching for her phone, she checked the time just as the alarm sounded. Seven. Time to get up. She opened the bedroom door and looked across the landing to the spare room. The door was ajar and through the gap she could see Jack sprawled face first, arms bent, hands shoved under the pillow.

Moving closer, she saw the pile of discarded clothes lying on the floor. With a glance at Jack's gently snoring body, she picked up his trousers and slipped her hands inside the pockets. She found nothing; embarrassed with herself but unable to stop, she moved quietly to the jacket hung over the back of a chair. Here she found nothing more than a receipt for coffee and a few coins.

Jack's wallet sat on top of a puddle of coins on the bedside table. It was so tempting. She supposed she should feel guilty, but she wouldn't have to go to such extreme sneaky lengths if the stupid man would talk to her. The coins clinked as she lifted the wallet; she froze and kept her eyes on Jack. When he didn't stir, she flipped the wallet open. A row of cards on one side she ignored, her fingers sliding into the compartments on the other. There were a couple of business cards but nothing else. Closing the wallet, she put it gently back on top of the coins.

Unlike her, Jack found it hard to wake and she had to shake him several times, each time with more force, before he finally opened one eye.

'It can't be time to get up,' he pleaded groggily, his words slurred.

'Afraid so. It's after seven.' She saw his eyes close again and knew he'd be asleep before she left the room. 'Come on, Jack, stay awake.'

'All right, all right,' he said, pushing up and shaking his head. 'You should have stayed last night. I wouldn't have drunk so much if you had.'

'Yes, it's all my fault,' she said with a grin. 'Have a shower, you'll feel better.'

Thirty minutes later, she was drinking the first of the many cups of coffee she needed to get through a normal day when he came into the kitchen. He might not feel better, but he certainly looked it. She poured coffee, added milk and three sugars and pushed the mug towards him.

'Thanks,' he said, picking it up and taking a mouthful before checking his watch. 'Damn and blast,' he said, draining the coffee and putting the mug down with a clatter. 'I've got to fly. There's an early meeting this morning, if I don't rush, I'm going to be late.' A quick kiss on her cheek and he was gone.

A wave of relief washed over her. It was work. She'd seen the worried look. Work. It could be sorted.

With a quick look at the time, she put their mugs into the dishwasher, grabbed her bag and coat and headed out the door. Eight minutes steady walk got her to South Kensington Underground and fifteen minutes later, she was in work. Her job as account manager for Dawson Marketing used to be fun, but recently she'd started to find the work stultifyingly boring and the day dragged. Finally, when her clock ticked to four thirty, she picked up her bag and left.

The journey home was one she could do almost in her sleep; sometimes, running on autopilot, she'd arrive home and not remember anything about getting there.

Today, she turned into her street, her mind on Jack. She wondered whether Petra had contacted her friend yet. It would be better to wait until she rang, she didn't want to appear too eager to hear, too worried about what she might have discovered. She stood on the kerb, waiting for a gap in the traffic to cross the street, her eyes drifting automatically towards her house, blinking in disbelief when she saw the man standing on her doorstep.

Her gasp was loud, automatic, pushing her backward; she stumbled even as she searched frantically for somewhere to hide. Desperation forced her to try a gate. It opened, she slipped through, closed it quickly behind her and leaned against it, trembling. She hoped whoever lived in the house wouldn't come rushing out to chase her away because she was incapable of moving.

There were a few detached houses on this side of the street interspersed between the towering apartment blocks. Many, like this beautiful Victorian home whose garden she was hiding in, had shoulder-high brick walls and wooden gates. There was a small garden between the gate and the house where dead summer flowers lay at drunken angles around a small patch of grass. There was no light showing in any of the windows; she was probably safe for a while.

She took a steadying breath before turning to peer anxiously over the top of the gate, ducking down quickly when she saw him. With a loud gulp, she leaned against the gate and slid down, her coat snagging on the rough wood. She felt sick and took deep breaths to try to control the panic. What was she going to do?

Heart thumping and breath rasping, she waited a minute before turning and inching her way up to look again, dropping down when she saw he had moved from the front door. He was standing on the pavement, staring down the street.

If there'd been any doubt before, there wasn't any now. It was him, the man with the turquoise eyes. The stranger she'd tried to kiss on the canal. He was supposed to stay a stranger. How on earth had he found her?

And, more importantly, what did he want?

11

Every few minutes, Molly peered carefully over the gate, frustration growing as she saw him move back to the doorstep and lean against the door. Maybe she should go over and confront him, explain that what had happened had been simply a moment's madness.

He was obviously intent on waiting for her. Squeezing her eyes shut, hot tears pushed through to trickle down her cheek. Jack was usually home by six fifteen. If the man didn't leave, he'd meet him. Would he tell? What would he tell? *Your wife tried to kiss me, she seemed up for it.*

At six, she peered over the gate again. She couldn't put it off any longer, she'd have to speak to him. Damn it, she'd say anything, do anything, to prevent Jack finding out how incredibly stupid she had been. She could have told him yesterday; could have made a joking reference to a handsome guy she'd met, brushing it off somehow. Now, no matter which way it came out, it sounded worse than it was. Their relationship had been a little shaky recently, she didn't want to be the one who tipped it over into the realms of seriously rocky. Not over something so stupid... so meaningless as this. She gripped the edge of the gate, preparing to open it and step out. Then, to her relief, she watched the man push something through her letter box before taking a final look up and down the street and heading away.

She waited five minutes to make sure he'd gone, then opened the gate and hurried across the street, a taxi blaring its horn as it braked to avoid her. Her breath was coming in ragged gusts by the time she opened the front door. She slammed it shut, pulled all the post from the letter box cage, found a single folded sheet of paper and jammed it into the top of her open handbag.

She heard Jack's key in the lock and hastily pinned a smile in place. Seconds. That's all she'd had to spare. 'Hi,' she said, dropping her eyes to the post, hoping the slight tremble in her voice wasn't obvious to him.

'Hi yourself,' he said, dropping his briefcase on the floor and his coat on the banisters. 'You're late home.'

'Oh, someone was leaving and there was a bit of a do in the office after work. I felt obliged to pop in for a few minutes.' Yet another lie falling glibly from her tongue.

He took her explanation without comment. 'Mine?' he asked, nodding at the letters.

'Yes,' she said, handing them over. 'I was expecting an invoice from Freya's university,' she added. It might have been true; all the invoices for both Freya and Remi's universities were addressed to her for convenience.

He frowned. 'Didn't you pay recently?'

'It was for extras.' She shrugged without elaborating.

Throwing his post, unopened, onto the hall table, he shook his head. 'They're going to cost us a fortune.'

It was impossible to miss the underlying worry in his words.

Molly opened her mouth to ask him if everything was okay, giving him an opportunity to tell her what the problem was, but before she could get the words out he'd walked away and into the kitchen. Following him, she watched as he took a beer from the fridge, swigging from the bottle as if he couldn't wait to get the alcohol into his system.

Her handbag was in her hand, looking down she could see the top of the sheet of paper. She was desperate to read it, and yet afraid to. What could the man possibly want with her?

'Bad day?' she asked, standing by the door.

'Usual,' Jack said shortly. 'What's for dinner?'

The wonderful Rebecca had always left something ready for them. All they had to do was pop it into the microwave or oven, following whatever instructions she left. *We'll eat out more often*, Jack had said when she'd pointed this out to him, but during the week they were rarely in the mood to leave the house once they'd come in from work.

She'd planned to stock up with quick frozen ready meals but so far she'd not got around to buying them. 'There's pizza,' she said, opening the freezer door.

'Again?' he muttered.

Clutching the door, she pressed her lips together. There was no point in getting into a row about who was responsible for dinner. 'Or we could go out?'

He finished the beer and dropped the bottle on the counter. 'Yes, good idea, let's go back to O'Dea's, the food was good last night.'

She shut the freezer, her hand resting on it for a moment before turning with a bright smile. 'Fine, I'll change into something more comfortable.' He'd go as he was; he was as comfortable in his suit as in casual clothes. On the rare time they went out during the week, she preferred to change, to have that distinction between work and her social life. Tonight, it was more of an excuse for a few minutes' privacy.

She shut the kitchen door quietly after her and forced herself to take the stairs slowly, when what she wanted to do was take the steps two at a time, desperate to see what was written on the sheet of paper. Closing their bedroom door, she pulled it from her bag and took it into the en suite. With the catch on the door, she sat on the toilet seat and unfolded it. It was badly written... childish almost... a spelling error in the six words that were sprawled across the page in a single line, no punctuation, no capitalisation.

we need to meat ring me

And underneath a mobile number.

She crumpled the page in one hand and held the other over her mouth. 'Oh God,' she whispered before smoothing out the creases to read again. The six words didn't appear in any way threatening. But why on earth did he want to meet her?

He had looked so disgusted when she'd tried to kiss him... surely, he wasn't thinking of blackmail. Apart from humiliating herself, she'd done nothing wrong. But was it a story she'd want told to Jack? Of course, it wasn't.

She stood and flushed the toilet, in case Jack had come upstairs. But when she opened the door, the room was empty. Reaching for her handbag, she felt inside until her fingers closed over her phone. She took it out and returned to the bathroom.

A minute later, after a few attempts, she had composed a text she was happy with.

I'm sorry I misread the signals. I don't want to meet you. Please don't come to my house again. I've told my husband how stupid I was. Now I want to forget it happened.

She looked at it for a moment. It would do, wouldn't it? It

said she wasn't interested in meeting him and hinted that there was no point in trying to blackmail her as her husband already knew. A convenient lie that looked convincing. Holding the page out, she keyed in the phone number and taking a breath, pressed send.

12

Jack's voice came from the other side of the door, making Molly jump and drop the phone with a clatter. 'What's keeping you?'

She stood and flushed the toilet again, raising her voice to be heard over it. 'I'll be down in five,' she called. Back in their bedroom, she put her phone into her bag and held the page for a moment before crumpling it into a ball and shoving it into her underwear drawer. Tomorrow, she'd take it to work and put it into the office shredder.

It took only minutes to change from her work clothes into jeans and a jumper. She ran a brush through her hair and went downstairs, her expression carefully neutral. She needn't have worried. Jack gave her a cursory glance before grabbing his keys and heading for the front door, leaving her to trail behind.

O'Dea's was popular and busy, and that night was no exception, the overwhelming cacophony hitting Molly when they stepped inside. There'd be no chance to talk. Was that Jack's plan? Maybe it was just as well. Her mind was too wrapped up in her own problems to deal with whatever was going on in his life. Anyway, before she heard his side of the conversation it would be better to be in possession of whatever information Nicole had. It would help to be forewarned.

The food was good, as it usually was. And she'd been right, there was no chance to carry on a meaningful conversation, every second word swallowed by waves of shouting and laughter. They called out *hi* to a few acquaintances who passed by, but she was relieved when nobody joined them. They might not be able to have an in-depth conversation, but it was nice to spend time together. She sipped her mineral water; drinking during the week was something she tried to avoid, it made her too tired the next day. Usually, Jack would have a pint, no more but tonight he had two. Plus, he'd had a bottle before they left home.

Was that the problem? She tried to pinpoint exactly when he'd started to drink so much but she couldn't narrow it down. It wasn't particularly excessive but more than she was used to seeing him drink. Maybe she should stop worrying.

They were quiet as they walked home, the distance between them more than simply space. In the busy streets, she felt very alone but then she thought about *him* and her eyes darted from left to right as they approached their house. But there was nobody on their doorstep.

'I'm going straight up,' she said as they took off their coats in the hallway. 'You coming?' There wasn't an invitation in her words; although they hadn't made love in a long time, she certainly wasn't in the mood tonight, not with turquoise eyes boring through her head.

'I'm going to watch some TV,' he said, 'I'm not tired.'

If he were late, he'd take the spare room again. Something that used to be the odd occurrence was quickly becoming the norm. As soon as she'd closed her bedroom door, she took out her phone and checked for messages. There was no reply to her text and she felt a slight easing of the tension that had squeezed her gut since she'd seen him on the doorstep. Maybe, he'd understood there was no point in pursuing anything.

There were messages from Remi and Freya. Bright, happy messages that made Molly's heart smile despite the ridiculous situation she'd managed to get herself into. She sent cheery messages back, telling them, as she always did, that she loved them and was so proud of them.

As soon as she woke next morning, she checked her phone again, relief washing over her when there was nothing from him. Surely now, she could put that whole episode behind her.

It was certainly put to the back of her mind when Jack pushed open the door into the kitchen, forty minutes later. She was dressed and ready for work, a mug of coffee in her hand as she idly listened to an early morning news programme. She'd no idea what time he'd gone to bed. Late, she guessed, taking in his red-rimmed eyes and pasty skin. There was no point in saying anything, she knew by his set look that he wouldn't appreciate any comment. And she wasn't in the mood to start the day with a row.

She made a mental note to ring Petra later.

As it turned out, she didn't have a chance, the day turning into one of those nightmares without a minute to herself. It was four thirty before she had a chance to ring and, annoyingly, it went straight to voicemail. She hung up without leaving a message.

In the station, anxious about going home in case *he* was there waiting, she hopped on a tube going the opposite direction, getting out at the next stop with the vague idea of visiting a bookshop someone had recommended. Following directions she'd been given, she found it easily enough, frowning when she took in its shabby, unexciting exterior. She was leaving without going inside, then decided she'd nothing to lose; anything was better than heading home.

The interior of the shop wasn't a vast improvement on the outside, with uninspiring mushroom-coloured paintwork and a slightly musty smell. Tall floor-to-ceiling shelves were set closely together with barely space to walk between them. It meant she could browse unnoticed, and it didn't take her long to discover that what the shop lacked in beauty, it more than made up for in its vast selection of old and rare books. She lost herself in them, taking out one after the other, turning crackly old pages in fascination.

She chose some to purchase, taking them to the sales counter. The middle-aged man behind it didn't glance up as she approached, his eyes glued to his phone. Nor did he look up when Molly put the books on the counter.

'Ahem,' she tried politely.

Eyes briefly looked up. 'I'm busy with something,' he said, focusing again on his phone. 'Give me a minute.'

Glancing at the books, she shook her head. She didn't want them that desperately. Without a word, she left them on the counter and exited the shop. A glance through the window as she passed, showed her the man hadn't appeared to notice.

Suddenly the absolute ridiculousness of her situation made her smile and with another shake of her head, she headed back to the station to catch the tube home. If Mr Turquoise Eyes dared to turn up, she was ready to confront him. She'd plead if she had to.

It was almost six by the time she turned the corner onto Elystan Street, looking ahead to the front of her house, closing her eyes on a brief prayer of thanks when there was nobody standing there, waiting for her. It was over.

Unwilling to make more excuses as to why she was late, she rushed into the house and up the stairs. A quick shower refreshed her, and when she came downstairs twenty minutes later in a pair of soft cotton pyjamas she was in a good mood and ready for a relaxing evening.

She put the kettle on for a cup of tea and investigated what they could have for dinner because, once again, she'd forgotten to buy anything. Maybe a big note on the kitchen counter would work. She picked up the house phone and dialled a local Indian restaurant that also did takeaways. They hadn't had one for a while, it would be a nice change.

She sipped lemon and ginger tea, feeling the stress of the busy day ebb while she waited.

It arrived thirty minutes later. Paying, she took the bag straight to the kitchen, leaving it on the counter in the containers. It would be easy to throw it into the microwave when Jack got home. She checked the clock. He was unusually late.

It was tempting to put off ringing Petra until the following day, but Molly dialled her number. It went to voicemail again but this time she left a message. 'I wondered if you'd managed to speak to Nicole,' she said. 'I'll be here all evening if you want to give me a call.' Throwing the phone on the seat beside her, she switched on the TV and sat back to watch one of her favourite property shows.

The programme was almost over by the time she heard the front door open. She waited for Jack to come through, but to her surprise he went straight upstairs. It gave her the opportunity to watch the end of the programme, but her heart wasn't in it. He'd know she was there, waiting, she almost always was. He'd probably had a tough day. Or a tougher day. She should have made more of an effort to contact Petra.

Scrambling from the sofa, she went to organise dinner, taking the containers from the bag and arranging them in the microwave in one lot. It would take longer but there'd be less faffing. Setting the timer, she pressed start.

She knew she'd regret it in the morning, but she opened the fridge and took out a bottle of wine. A half a glass would help her relax. The half was gone, and she'd poured another before the door opened. She opened her mouth to ask if he were okay, shutting it again without saying a word when she saw how pale and drawn he looked.

'You're very late. Bad day?' She injected as much sympathy as she could into her voice, feeling her heart ache for him, for whatever was going on. 'I wish you'd tell me what's wrong.'

'There's nothing wrong,' he snapped, reaching for the wine bottle. He filled a glass and drank half, his eyes never meeting Molly's.

She wondered if her friend with the turquoise eyes had contacted Jack somehow. Perhaps his bad mood, pallor and inability to meet her eyes was merely disgust because he knew about her futile seduction of a stranger. Her stomach churning, she watched him for a moment as he sipped the rest of his wine.

But when he turned to her, when he looked at her at last, his expression was guarded but not condemning. He didn't look at her with disgust... maybe she was being oversensitive.

'What's for dinner?' he asked, his hand going up to cover a yawn. 'Sorry, I didn't sleep too well.'

'I got a takeaway,' she said, nodding towards the microwave that had pinged several minutes before. She rested a hand on his arm as she passed him, relieved when he didn't brush it off. Removing the containers, she carried them to the table, returning for plates and cutlery. As usual, when she bought a takeaway she'd ordered far too much. She put spoons beside the containers and sat.

Jack used the same spoon to take a little from each container. If he noticed she was drinking, an occurrence so rare as to be worthy of some comment, he didn't say anything. She decided not to have any more, taking a bottle of mineral water from the fridge instead. It was safer to have her wits about her. Conversation was stilted, laboured, any comments she made met with a monosyllabic response. Finally, she gave up trying, and concentrated on her food, pushing it around the plate with little pleasure. She'd chosen a bad combination; either that or she'd completely lost her appetite. After a few mouthfuls, she dropped her fork and pushed the plate away.

Looking across the table, she realised Jack hadn't eaten anything. He hadn't even picked up his fork, sitting with his eyes on the food as if he weren't seeing it. 'Jack,' she said gently. He didn't look up. She tried again, worried now, her voice taking on an edge. 'Jack?'

He looked up slowly, his eyes dull.

'I'm worried about you,' she said, reaching a hand towards him.

He managed to drag his lips into a semblance of a smile. 'Don't be,' he said, 'it's nothing. Just work problems.'

What kind of work problems? She wanted to ask but she knew that was as much as he was going to tell her. 'Why don't you leave?' she said, grasping and squeezing his forearm. 'Hand in your notice and get something else? We'd survive on my salary until you did, you could say you want to leave immediately.'

'Survive on your salary?' He met her eyes, his mouth twisting. 'I don't think so, there are bills, debts.'

She forced a laugh. 'We're okay. The mortgage is paid off. Short-term, we'd be fine.' She pressed his arm again. 'We could cut back a little. Luckily, the kids' university fees are paid. At least say you'll think about it.'

'I'll think about it.'

But she noticed, this time, his eyes didn't meet hers.

After dinner, he excused himself, saying he had some work to do. It wasn't unusual, his job far more demanding than hers. There were plenty of opportunities for someone as experienced as he was, he'd easily find something else. She wished he'd give leaving some serious consideration.

When she'd tidied up, she sat on the sofa and picked up her phone. She dialled Petra's number again. This time it was answered, her friend's cheerful voice shouting *hello*.

'Hi,' Molly said, 'I've been trying to get you.'

'Yes, sorry, I saw your missed call, but we were about to have dinner, so I thought I'd wait.'

Getting straight to the point, Molly asked, 'Well?'

Petra's laugh was genuinely amused. 'Not big on the old foreplay, eh, Mol?'

This wasn't the time for what her friend always described as her quirky sense of humour. Molly wanted to know if there was anything she could do, to take that look of desolation from her husband's face. 'Please, Petra,' she said, 'this is important.'

'Fine. Well, I did go to the trouble of meeting Nicole for lunch today,' she said, her voice a little cool and stressing *trouble* to make sure Molly was suitably grateful. 'And I did pump her for information which, I have to admit, didn't take much doing.' Her voice thawed. 'I hadn't realised what a gossip she was.'

Pots and kettles, Molly thought, biting back the temptation to ask her to get on with it.

There was a long indrawn breath down the line before Petra continued with her voice quieter, as if she were afraid she'd be overheard. 'There's a lot of high-powered meetings going on, Nicole said. A lot of closed doors and whispers in the corridors. She said there were a lot of glum strained expressions.'

Molly held her phone tightly to her ear, afraid she might miss something. When there was silence on the other end, she said, 'Is that it?'

'What did you expect?' Petra said, sounding slightly annoyed. 'It confirms what you suspected, there is trouble in Jack's office. Isn't that what you wanted to know?'

'It's all a bit vague,' Molly replied. 'I suppose I'd hoped there would be something more concrete, something I could advise him on. This is...' She wanted to say *nothing,* just vague unsubstantiated gossip, but her friend had done what she could, there was no point in being ungrateful. '... a bit of a help,' she finished on the lie.

Petra seemed mollified. 'She did hear one of Jack's colleagues saying it was all to do with money, if that's any help.'

'Yes, that's great,' Molly said, lying again. It was a financial services business; it was always about money.

They chatted for a few minutes about more pleasant things, the new restaurant that had opened up, the sale that was on in one of Petra's favourite clothes shops.

Molly only half listened and was grateful when her friend said she had to go, dropping the phone on the seat and staring into space. She was no wiser except it confirmed it was work causing Jack's pallor and grim expression. Not another woman.

And it was nothing to do with *him.*

She picked up her phone again and checked. No messages. She'd have preferred if he'd sent a message saying he was sorry, that he'd leave her alone.

But this silence – she found it unnerving.

13

When Jack came downstairs, Molly looked at his grey complexion and dull, staring eyes and decided it was not the time to bring up the subject of leaving his job again. She'd planted the seed; it might take time for it to germinate.

'I'm heading to bed,' she said, reaching to plant a soft kiss on his cheek. 'Are you going to be long?'

He went to fetch the wine bottle from the fridge. There was a glass left in it, maybe a little more; he took it and a glass to the sofa and sat before answering. 'I'm going to watch TV and chill for a bit,' he said, pouring the wine. He didn't look at her as he picked up the remote, the blare of some music station accompanying Molly as she left the room.

She was glad Freya and Remi weren't here. Both were intelligent, they'd have picked up on the strange vibes in the house in an instant. She'd have to be careful when she spoke to them on Skype, inject some positivity into her voice. Lie. She smiled grimly. She'd lie.

It was a while before, finally, she shut all her worries away and closed her eyes. Within minutes, she was asleep and despite her concerns, she slept solidly until a noise disturbed her. The doorbell? Opening her eyes, she grabbed her phone and groaned when she saw it was only six. She must have imagined it. Turning on her side, she tried to get back to sleep.

But the doorbell went again, longer this time, the sound pealing through the house. She threw back the duvet and got up, grabbing a robe from the back of the door and pulling it on. There was no sound from the spare bedroom and she felt a twinge of annoyance that it was left to her to open the door to who knew what at such an ungodly hour.

She ran barefooted down the stairs, switched off the alarm and checked the safety chain was in place before unlocking the door. The chain allowed a six-inch gap. She peered through it, blinking in surprise at the two men on the doorstep, both holding identification. Police. Her heart plummeted and she shut the door, her fingers fumbling with the safety chain in her haste to open it. *Dear Lord, please, not Freya or Remi.* The words going around and around in her head, until at last she pulled the door open.

She stood, one hand on the door, the other on the frame, her white silky robe with its batwing sleeves making her look like an avenging angel. 'Not my children,' she said, her voice husky with emotion.

The men were tall, maybe six foot, and broad so that they filled the space in front of the door. The older of the two, took a half-step forward. 'My name is Detective Inspector Fanshawe, and this is Detective Sergeant Carstairs. May we come in?'

Their faces gave nothing away. Molly dropped her hands and stood uncertainly before standing back and waving them inside.

She indicated the door to the study. 'Please go in. I'll go and get my husband.'

DI Fanshawe held a hand up to stop her. 'It might be best if we speak to you first, Mrs Chatwell.'

She looked at him, feeling the ground move unsteadily under her feet. 'If it's to do with Freya or Remi, shouldn't he be here?'

'They're your children?' Fanshawe asked, waiting until Molly whispered a strangled *yes* before continuing. 'We're not here about them.'

She clasped her hands to her chest in relief, then frowned. It had to be something serious to bring two policemen to her front door at such an early hour, but if it wasn't about the children, what was it about? 'Would you like some coffee?' she asked. 'I certainly need some to wake myself up.'

When the men nodded and gave their preferences, she went into the kitchen to fill the kettle, her mind spinning as she waited for it to boil. What would they want with her? Her. Not Jack.

She made coffee, added sugar to one, milk to all three and, gathering them awkwardly, headed back to the study where the two men were still standing.

'Please, sit down,' she said, putting the coffees on one of the two desks that were still scattered with the remnants of Freya and Remi's studies. She waited until the men sat before handing them their coffee and sitting onto the small bucket chair in the corner. The coffee was hot, but she drank it anyway, hoping the caffeine would race to her brain to make it start functioning, maybe even give her some clarity.

She looked at the two men as she sipped. They were fairly handsome despite their ill-fitting suits and cheap shirts. The detective inspector was, she guessed, about her age, the sergeant a few years younger. Each had hard eyes and grim mouths but there was a fan of wrinkles around the older man's eyes; when he wasn't working it looked as though he smiled a lot. The younger man's face was just grim.

'Why are you here?' she asked, cupping her hands around her mug and wishing she'd insisted Jack be called.

DI Fanshawe took a few sips before putting the mug down and taking a notebook from his pocket. 'Before we begin,' he said, tapping it with a well-chewed pen, 'I think it's best if we read you your rights. Keep it formal and correct, you understand.'

Molly's jaw dropped. Shutting it with an audible snap, she forced an uncertain laugh. 'There must be some mistake, what am I supposed to have done?' In the television dramas she watched, this was where she was supposed to ask if she should get a solicitor. She wanted to laugh, but none of this was remotely funny.

Ignoring her question, Fanshawe said words she'd only ever expected to hear in TV programmes. 'Do you understand your rights, as I have informed you?'

She looked at him. She'd done nothing wrong, yet fear shimmied down her spine. 'Yes,' she said, she understood her rights, but she'd no idea why they were being read. 'Do I need to have a solicitor present?'

DI Fanshawe tilted his head. 'That is certainly your prerogative, Mrs Chatwell. We are merely looking for information; reading you your rights allows us to use any information you may give us. If you prefer, you can come with us to the station and we can wait for your solicitor there.'

She shook her head. 'No, that's okay. I'm happy to cooperate. I have done nothing wrong.'

He gave a slight smile, as if of approval, and sat forward, hands dangling between his spread knees to look at her with cold grey eyes. 'Do you know a man named Oliver or Ollie Vine?'

Her brow furrowed as she thought of all the men in the office. She was almost sure none of them was called Oliver. 'I don't think so,' she said hesitantly. 'There are always people coming and going in work though, one of the newer ones that I haven't met might be–'

'This isn't someone in your office,' Fanshawe interrupted her.

'Socially,' she said with more conviction, 'I don't know anyone called Oliver Vine.' Her eyes flitted from one man to the other. Neither was giving anything away. What the hell was going on?

Fanshawe turned a page of his notebook, placed it on the coffee table and gave it a little nudge in her direction. 'Is that your phone number?'

She picked it up. Was it? She'd no idea. 'I'll have to go and get my mobile,' she said, 'it's not a number I've memorised.' When he nodded, as if to give her permission, she lifted her chin in annoyance. 'I want to know what this is all about,' she said, crossing her arms.

But if that attitude was effective with junior members of her staff in Dawson Marketing, it wasn't with the two policemen who sat unmoving opposite.

'If you'd go and get your phone, Mrs Chatwell.'

She stood, threw him a baleful glance and left the room. Upstairs, she stood for a moment at the door of the spare bedroom. Jack would know what to do, she'd call him, he'd get rid of them. But there was something in the detective inspector's eyes that made her hesitate. Maybe she'd better wait and see what on earth was going on.

She grabbed her phone from the bed table, unplugging the charging lead. Looking down at her robe, she swore softly. The soft fabric made her look feminine and weak. Quickly, she took it off, pulled on underwear and a white shirt and jeans from her wardrobe. Better.

She didn't bother with shoes and ran lightly down the stairs.

The two men hadn't moved. They sat with the mugs of coffee in one hand, their legs spread in that relaxed masculine way as if they were there on a social visit.

She sat in the same chair, waving her mobile. 'Okay,' she said, 'my number is...' She read it aloud, her eyes widening as she realised they matched the numbers written on the notebook. 'It seems it is my number,' she said unnecessarily.

Fanshawe took his notebook back with a satisfied nod. 'So, although you don't know Oliver Vine, you were sending him messages.'

Colour leeched from her face. The man on the canal. Oliver Vine. She gulped. 'I didn't know his name,' she muttered. 'A message. I sent him one message.'

'Ah yes. What was it you wrote again?' He turned pages in his notebook, stopping when he got to one, throwing her a look before reading, '*I'm sorry I misread the signals. I don't want to meet you. Please don't come to my house again. I've told my husband how stupid I was. Now I want to forget it happened.*'

DS Carstairs, who'd not yet opened his mouth, gave an unamused snort.

'Were you and Oliver Vine lovers, Mrs Chatwell?' Fanshawe asked calmly.

She ran a hand through her unbrushed hair. 'No,' she said emphatically, then dropped her hand into her lap. 'No, we weren't.' She looked from one to the other of the men but if she expected a lessening of their stern regard, she was disappointed. They stared at her as if she was an object of fascination and didn't say a word.

She'd watched enough police series in her day, she knew they were waiting for her to speak, to talk herself into something. What that was, she'd no idea. She blinked, taking stock. She had done nothing wrong. Humiliating herself wasn't a crime.

'I'm not sure what business it is of the police,' she said, drawing her shoulders back and looking the detective inspector directly in the eye.

Fanshawe looked at her coldly. 'Where were you between five and five-thirty yesterday afternoon?'

She shook her head, confused at the change in direction. 'Why?'

'Because in that short window, somebody murdered Oliver Vine.'

14

In the silence of the room, Molly's gasp was loud. Covering her mouth with a shaking hand, she looked at the inspector. 'He's dead?'

'You understand now why we need answers to our questions, Mrs Chatwell,' the inspector said evenly.

She was frozen for a moment, then dropping her hand, she nodded.

'So, I ask you again, were you and Oliver Vine lovers?'

A flashback of the canal encounter came to her; the handsome man, his smouldering sexuality, those vivid eyes. Now, he was dead. A twinge of regret for such a tragic loss made her clasp her arms across her chest. 'No,' she said, 'we weren't lovers, it was a moment's madness.' She gulped, feeling a wave of nausea sweep over her. 'I need a glass of water.' And before they could say anything, she left the room.

In the kitchen, she let the cold tap run, scooping water up with her two hands and bathing her face, the water dripping from her chin onto her shirt. After a moment, she turned the water off, grabbed a towel and hid her eyes in its comforting darkness.

She had to go back. Answer questions. *Oliver Vine.* She squeezed her eyes shut on the memory.

Returning to the lounge, she sat in the same chair. She didn't wait for them to ask. In a slow monotone, she described the two occasions she had met Oliver Vine and what had taken place on the towpath. 'It is completely out of character for me to do something like that,' she said. 'It was a moment's craziness. He was so handsome, so... sexy... his turquoise eyes so mesmerising.'

'Turquoise eyes?' Fanshawe said, with a raised eyebrow.

DS Carstairs was less interested in the description. 'You met this man a couple of times and tried to seduce him?'

Colour flooded her cheeks. Had she really? Hadn't she simply wanted a moment – a moment of feeling desirable. But if Oliver Vine had responded, if he had lowered those gorgeous lips to hers, would she have done what Amelia had suggested, dragged him into the fields and had her wicked way with him? It sounded so unlike anything she would have done, and yet... Her eyes met Carstairs' hard critical ones. How could she explain, when she didn't really understand it herself? That for a while she'd believed this incredibly handsome man had found her attractive and desirable and it had made her feel good. That she'd relished the feeling and when the opportunity arose she'd taken it... and oh yes, she would have taken it further, would have lost herself in one crazy act, only it didn't happen because she'd got it all wrong.

'It wasn't like that,' she said. When neither spoke, her voiced hitched, a pathetic sound in the quiet room. 'I thought it was a mutual attraction. I was wrong.'

'So, you ran away?' Fanshawe's tone of voice said he wasn't sure if he believed her.

'As fast as I could,' she said, lifting her chin. 'Humiliation, I discovered, makes me a faster runner. Maybe I should market it.'

She saw pity in his eyes, she wasn't sure if it was preferable to his disdain. 'So that's as far as my...' she hesitated over the word... 'seduction, went.'

Fanshawe jotted in his notebook before looking at her with a critical light in his eye and giving a slight shrug. 'And this was in Wiltshire?'

'Yes, I was away with friends for a weekend in Semington House Hotel.'

Fanshawe wrote the name down, then looked back to her. 'And their names?'

'Amelia and Tristan Lovell.'

A murder investigation. Every stone was going to be moved, the dirt dug out and raked over. Tristan wouldn't be impressed; Amelia would likely be amused.

'And you are absolutely sure you didn't tell Vine where you lived?' Fanshawe asked.

'No,' she said firmly, 'I definitely didn't.'

'When did he come here?'

'The day before yesterday, he was waiting when I came home from work.'

Fanshawe scribbled as he spoke, 'What did he say?'

'I didn't speak to him.' She saw by Fanshawe's expression that she needed to do better than that. 'I saw him when I turned the corner and recognised him immediately. I didn't want to speak to him. That moment by the canal was something and nothing, I'd been humiliated, I didn't want to speak to him.' She looked from one detective to the other. 'I hid,' she said.

Carstairs snorted his disbelief. Fanshawe, one eyebrow raised, said, 'You hid?'

'Yes,' she said and rushed on. 'You have to understand, I didn't want to see him, or speak to him. I thought, if I didn't turn up, he'd go away. The houses across the road, they have high walls, and gates. I went behind one and watched until he left.'

'So, you never spoke to him?'

'No.'

'So how did you get his phone number? And if you didn't tell him, how did he know where you lived?'

How? She'd met him hundreds of miles away. 'I don't know how he found out where I lived,' she said. 'But the day he came here, before he left, he put a note through the door asking me to ring him. That's how I was able to send a text.' She blinked. 'I still have it. I meant to take it to work to shred, but I forgot.'

Fanshawe nodded. 'Can you get it, please?'

'Of course.' She stood immediately, left the room and raced up the stairs. The door to the spare bedroom was shut. She breathed a thanks for Jack's ability to sleep through anything, and went into their room.

The note was where she'd left it, crumpled in the back of her drawer. She smoothed it out as she returned to the room where both men sat waiting.

'Here it is,' she said, handing it over.

Taking it by one corner, Fanshawe read it aloud. *'we need to meat ring me.'*

He slid the note into an envelope that Carstairs held out for him, then looked at her. 'He went to the trouble of finding out where you live, then hung around hoping to speak to you. And you've no idea why? Are you sure you're telling us everything, Mrs Chatwell?'

'Yes.' The word caught in her throat.

'Yes?' Fanshawe's eyes bored into her. 'You don't sound so sure. Was the temptation too much to resist, Mrs Chatwell? Did you have a sexual relationship with this man, thinking you'd never see him again, that your husband would never find out. You didn't tell him where you lived, you thought you were safe but then he turns up on your doorstep and you had to get rid of him.'

Molly looked at him, appalled. This couldn't be happening. This kind of thing didn't happen to women like her... but then again, exactly what kind of woman was she? She used to be so sure.

She ran a hand through her hair. 'No, I swear. Nothing happened. I admit, I thought he was attracted to me, that he was reaching for me.' She gave a short embarrassed laugh. 'He must have been afraid I'd fall in; we were standing very close to the edge and the lock chamber is very deep.'

'Looking out for you, was he?' Carstairs said with heavy sarcasm.

She ignored him and looked back to Fanshawe. 'He was being nice, I suppose, and as I said, we were standing very close to the edge. He seemed to know about canals and locks, he mentioned that there wasn't a ladder so if you fell in, there was no way out. Perhaps, that's why he was being careful.' Molly shrugged as if it hadn't mattered, as if she hadn't been cut to the bone. 'I misunderstood, that was all.'

If she'd hoped that Jack would stay asleep until they were gone, the creak of floorboards over their heads indicated she was out of luck. She closed her eyes tightly.

'Your husband?' Fanshawe asked. When she nodded, he looked down at his notebook again. 'You said in your text he knew about your liaison. Is that true?'

Wanting to scream with frustration, she waited a few seconds before answering. 'It wasn't a liaison and no, he doesn't know. I said that in case that man was going to try to blackmail me.'

'Blackmail,' the inspector said sharply. 'You insist nothing happened and yet you considered that this might be an attempt to blackmail you?'

'Nothing did happen but I suppose,' she admitted finally, 'I had wanted it to. I was afraid he'd tell my husband–'

'That you were up for it?' Carstairs said, leaning towards her, a sneer twisting his mouth.

It was exactly what she'd thought but hearing the words on this obnoxious man's lips made it sound so much more sordid. 'Yes,' she said. 'Anyway, what other possible reason would he have for contacting and wanting to meet me?'

'And yet he went to the trouble of doing so,' Fanshawe said. 'You didn't hear from him again?'

She handed him her phone. 'Have a look,' she said, 'you can see he never answered.'

He took the phone and skimmed through without comment. 'You might have deleted them,' he said. 'We'll take it with us, if we may, and have it checked.'

It was a strange feeling, not to be believed. 'Of course,' she said.

Fanshawe put it into his jacket pocket and picked up his notebook. Turning to a clean page, he clicked his pen and looked at her expectantly. 'What time did you leave work yesterday?'

'I finish at four thirty,' she said.

'And you left immediately?'

She nodded and felt the blood rush from her as the seriousness of her position dawned on her. 'You can't think I'm anyway involved in what happened to him?' She reached a hand toward Fanshawe, pulling back at his stern expression. 'Oh my God, you do?' Crossing her hands on her chest, she took a deep breath.

'We're gathering information for the moment,' Fanshawe said, his voice cool. 'We don't speculate. It would be in your best interest to answer our questions as clearly and honestly as you can.'

A chill crept over her, making her shiver.

'So,' Fanshawe said. 'You left work at four thirty. Did you come straight home?'

Reluctantly, she shook her head. 'I decided to go to a bookshop one of my colleagues had recommended.'

Fanshawe looked up from his notebook. 'And where is that?'

'It's called The Final Chapter. It's a second-hand bookshop. They have a lot of rare and unusual books...' Her voice tailed away.

'Where?'

'It's on White Horse Street, a few minutes' walk from the station.'

She saw his expression change, eyes growing harder, lips pressing into a thin line.

'That's Green Park station, isn't it?' he said, exchanging a glance with Carstairs. 'How long did you stay in this shop?'

She lifted her hands. 'An hour or so.' She saw the inspector's look of disbelief and added, 'If you like books, it's a fascinating shop.'

'And the staff will be able to vouch for you being there for that length of time?'

It would have been good to have been able to say yes, but it was unlikely that the assistant would remember her. 'I don't know,' she admitted.

Fanshawe looked at her. 'We'll check it out. They might have CCTV.'

Molly had her doubts; the exterior of the shop had been rundown and tatty, but what did she know? Less and less by the minute.

'And what time did you arrive home?'

'A little before six,' she said, confident in this if nothing else.

He tapped his notebook with the pen. 'Between four-thirty when you left work, and six when you arrived home, did you speak to anyone?'

'No, there was no need to. I had intended to buy books in the shop, but the only assistant was so engrossed in his phone that he didn't bother to look up, so I didn't speak to him.'

'What did you do with the books?'

Surprised, she glared at him. 'I didn't steal them, I dumped them on the counter and left.'

The door opened and Jack stood there, looking confused. 'I thought I was hearing the radio,' he said. 'What the hell is going on?' Panic appeared in his eyes. 'It's not the children?'

DI Fanshawe stood, putting his notebook and pen in his inside jacket pocket. 'No, it's not, Mr Chatwell. I'm sure your wife will explain everything. I think we've got all we need for the moment.' He turned to look down at Molly. 'If you would keep yourself available for further questions, we'd appreciate it. And,' he finished, and for the first time she saw a sympathetic look in his eyes, 'it might be in your best interest to hire a solicitor.'

'Hire a solicitor! What the hell is going on?' Jack repeated, as the two men passed him by.

Molly walked with them to the front door and shut it after they'd left, resting against it briefly before turning to Jack. He was looking at her as if he'd never seen her before, and he didn't even know what it was about yet.

'There's something I need to tell you,' she said, trying to keep her voice as calm as possible.

He took the same seat the inspector had, and she sat opposite. Crossing her arms, she told Jack, in much the same way she had told the police, keeping her eyes down, unwilling to see the expression on his face change from anxiousness to disbelief. When she stopped, she waited a moment for his reaction and when he said nothing, she risked looking up.

She couldn't read his expression, he seemed stunned into immobility.

'You tried to seduce a total stranger,' he managed at last, each word spat out.

'I misread the signals, I thought he was attracted to me. He was young, gorgeous and I was flattered. I wanted to kiss him. That was all.' And what did it matter that it was a total stranger – would Jack have found it easier to take had she tried to seduce someone he knew? She felt a quiver run through her as she thought back to those brief minutes over two mornings that would change her life. Forever. The man had been murdered.

Jack continued to look at her in silence, as if she were some strange bug he'd never seen before.

'It didn't mean anything.' She wanted to shriek that nothing had happened, she hadn't dragged the man into the long grass of the field beside the towpath to fornicate like wild animals. *Because he didn't want you*, a little voice sneered. How much worse to be vilified for her pathetic failed seduction.

'It must have meant something to him,' Jack said, unconvinced, 'after all, he turned up on our doorstep. You must have given him our address. Maybe you were hoping to continue your little dalliance in London?'

'No,' she cried. 'I didn't give him our address. I've no idea how he found out where I lived. I promise you. There wasn't a *dalliance*.' She rubbed both hands roughly over her face before admitting, 'He didn't want me, Jack. He was appalled when I tried to kiss him.'

Jack stood and walked to the window. Keeping his back to her, he twisted his wrist to look at his watch and grunted in disbelief. 'I need to leave for work. I can't be late, there's too much going on. Tell me quickly, why are the police interested in your sordid behaviour?'

Molly had hoped he'd stay with her, but she saw his rigid expression and knew that wasn't going to happen. He was consumed by whatever problems were going on in his life, her *sordid behaviour* didn't count.

She didn't answer until he turned around. When he did, she stood. 'The man has been murdered, Jack. I think they suspect I might be involved.'

15

Jack dismissed outright Molly's notion that she was a suspect in the murder. 'Don't be ridiculous.' His eyes raked her from head to toe. 'You might be an unfaithful cow, but you're a placid one, guilty of playing around with him, yes, but not murdering him.' With a final look of disgust, Jack stormed off, slamming the front door so hard the empty coffee mugs on the desks rattled.

Molly collapsed back on the chair, her hand over her eyes. There was no point in arguing that she hadn't been unfaithful, that she hadn't had the opportunity. Eventually, she'd make him understand. Jack was right about one thing; she wasn't a violent woman, but the police wouldn't know that. And that inspector had, after all, advised her to hire a solicitor. How did you go about doing such a thing? The internet, she supposed, like everything else these days.

Her head was throbbing. She struggled to her feet and went to the kitchen in search of paracetamol, finding a packet in one of the drawers and popping two tablets, swallowing them dry.

Murder.

Her eyes drifted to the clock on the wall. It was almost eight, she'd watch the news, see if it was mentioned. She sat on the sofa, switched on the TV and waited, her eyes glued to the screen, widening when she realised that indeed the murder of Oliver Vine had made the news. She watched as the reporter, her voice suitably solemn, told of the murder of a young man in Green Park. There were few details, but a witness described the man staggering onto the pathway clutching his belly, the handle of a knife clearly visible.

'Stabbed,' Molly muttered, then closed her eyes. Green Park! So that was why the inspector's expression had changed when she'd told them where the shop was. She had been within a few minutes' walk of where Oliver Vine was murdered.

It was a coincidence. Only a coincidence. But she guessed it explained their advice. They may or may not believe she was involved in the murder, but either way she was sure to be dragged through a lot of mud before the real murderer was found.

Desperate for coffee to try to sort the scrambled thoughts in her head, she made a pot, but the first two cups brought no clarity. How *had* the man found out where she lived?

Perhaps, after all, he had followed her. She hadn't seen him when she'd looked back, but that didn't mean he wasn't there lurking behind the hedgerow. He might have seen her cross the bridge. You could see the canal from the garden of the hotel, so the reverse also had to be true. Maybe, he'd seen her go across the garden. Her pink Lycra T-shirt would have made her very visible.

She frowned. It was possible. Semington House Hotel was also the only hotel within a few miles; he might have assumed she came from there. If he'd called around, would staff have told him who she was, and more importantly where she lived? If he'd spun a good enough tale, it was possible. She rubbed her forehead, smoothing the creases away. Anything was bloody possible.

Restless, her head spinning as she tried to figure it out, she paced the floor, stopping to stare out the window. She couldn't sit around doing nothing; finding out how Oliver got her address would be a start.

The invoice from the hotel was in her handbag. So were scraps of paper and receipts from what seemed like hundreds of things. In frustration, she upended the bag on the table to search among the detritus, finding the invoice and smoothing it out to read the phone number.

She picked up the house phone and rang, tapping the table nervously as she waited. 'Hello,' she said, 'My name is Molly Chatwell, I'd like to speak to a manager, please.' Go straight to the top, it often worked.

She was holding on for a few minutes before a softly spoken voice said, 'This is Sylvia Reekie. I'm the duty manager, how may I help?'

A blend of truth and lies was the best approach. 'I was staying in your hotel over the weekend and I met someone... someone new... just briefly. There was no exchange of names or addresses and yet this person subsequently turned up on my doorstep here in London. I was wondering if there was any possibility he might have obtained my address from one of your staff.'

The softly spoken voice held an air of righteousness when it replied. 'We would never give that information out, Ms Chatwell, it is against our policy. We take an extremely serious approach to customer safety and that includes personal details.'

'But if he'd asked one of the junior staff, a waiter or gardener, say?'

There was the sound of an indrawn breath before the manager replied. This time there was steel behind the softness. 'Every one of our staff receives the same training regarding client privacy. Is this a legal matter, Ms Chatwell?

Something we here at Semington House should be concerned about?'

How far were the police going to follow up what Molly had told them? 'I'm sorry,' she said, 'I'm afraid I don't really know the answer to that. Not yet anyway.' She hung up without another word and sat staring at the phone. She needed someone to talk to. Rebecca would have been her first choice, the way she often had been over the years. Molly had spoken to her a couple of times since she'd left but it wasn't quite the same. She still felt like a traitor for letting her go.

She checked the time. Almost nine. Petra would be on her way to work. Work! Molly dialled her office, put on a throaty voice and said she wouldn't be in, hanging up on the words of sympathy.

Amelia was her next choice for someone to talk to and Molly was in luck, her friend answered at the first ring. To forestall recriminations for having left the hotel without warning, she jumped straight in. 'Amelia, I'm in trouble. Something happened at the weekend. I need to talk to you.'

A long sigh came down the line accompanied by the sound of well-manicured nails impatiently tapping. 'You didn't mention anything while you were there.'

Molly gripped the phone, preparing for disappointment, relieved instead to hear a quiet *okay*.

'Do you want to come here?' Amelia asked.

'Yes, I'll be there in an hour.'

Having something to focus on made her mind more settled, clearer. Looking down at her jeans and shirt, she decided it was a perfect uniform for the day. She ran upstairs and slipped on some loafers, grabbed a jacket, then went back to the study. Freya and Remi were always mislaying their mobiles and had acquired a few pay-as-you go phones over the years. A quick search found one, its charger wound around it. Plugging it in, she checked that it worked and was pleased to see there was ten pounds credit on it. She quickly sent Jack a text telling him she'd be using it for a while without saying why. There was no point in adding a *sorry*, she guessed she'd be saying that a lot over the next few days and weeks.

Unplugging it again, she put the charger and phone into her pocket and headed off.

16

Molly caught the Circle Line to Notting Hill Gate and walked the five minutes from there to Pembridge Square Gardens. She loved her home but always suffered a little envy when she visited Amelia's beautiful apartment. No expense had been spared on renovations and interior design, the rooms were spacious and high-ceilinged, and the outlook over Pembroke Square was perfect.

Amelia opened the door in cream silk pyjamas, waving Molly in with a less-than-welcoming expression. 'This isn't really convenient, you know, darling.'

'The police called this morning,' Molly said without preliminaries. 'They think I might be involved in a murder.'

Amelia laughed uncertainly, then stopped and reached two hands to grab Molly's shoulders to hold her still. 'You are joking, aren't you?'

'Unfortunately not,' Molly said. 'I'd better tell you the whole story.'

Dropping her hands, Amelia shook her head. 'Wait, I need coffee first. Something tells me I'm going to need caffeine for this conversation.'

Once they were sitting with mugs in front of them, Molly told her story again. It wasn't getting any easier to tell and she stuttered over the words.

When she'd finished Amelia looked at her in silence, a puzzled frown trying vainly to furrow her botoxed forehead. 'You think this guy, this Oliver Vine, arrived on your doorstep with the intention of blackmailing you? Isn't that a bit of a stretch? After all, as you say, nothing really happened apart from you being a tit.'

Molly smiled. 'A tit? Thanks. It beats what I've been calling myself and you, at least, believe me. I'm afraid both the police and Jack think something more must have happened for him to turn up like that.' She played with the handle of the mug. 'I've no idea how he found out where I lived.'

'Maybe he found out at the hotel. It's the only one around, he may have guessed you were staying there.'

'It's what I thought too, but I rang them, they said it was absolutely against their policy to reveal information about guests to anyone.' She shrugged. 'Have to admit, I couldn't imagine him walking in and asking staff who the woman running on the canal is, could you?' Picking up the mug, she drained it, shaking her head when Amelia lifted the pot to offer more.

Molly stood restlessly, then sat again, pushing her hair behind her ears. 'I had thought it was so romantic,' she said, her voice calmer. 'That this divinely sexy man found me attractive. From the first morning, I couldn't get him out of my head. Remember I told you about him, and you said he was wasted on me, that I should have dragged him into the field. And later, you said I should try something new. I had been feeling old, you know, worn out and past it. Then suddenly there he was again, and I had a chance to prove I wasn't, to feel that magic and excitement, to roll around in the grass in total abandon and feel like a teenager again.'

Amelia grinned, then she giggled. Molly looked at her blankly for a moment. Nothing about this story was the slightest bit funny. She remembered the young man's shocked expression when she'd leaned in for a kiss. Okay, maybe it was a little funny. She chuckled and soon they were both laughing like a pair of hyenas.

'Oh God,' Molly said, wiping her eyes, 'I suppose it does sound so ridiculous now.' Her worried expression returning, she stood and paced the room again. 'Not so ridiculous though when you think the poor guy was murdered. And, I'd still like to know how a stranger managed to get my address.'

'It's odd all right.'

Molly's eyes narrowed. 'I wondered if he could have followed me?'

'You'd have noticed, wouldn't you?'

'I looked back once and didn't see any sign of him. But I was thinking, you can see the canal from the hotel where they've cleared a bit of the shrubbery, maybe it worked the other way too, and he saw me crossing the garden to the hotel. I was wearing a bright pink T-shirt; it would have stood out.'

Amelia screwed up her nose. 'He'd have to have been staring at that gap when you passed by. Anyway, you haven't thought it through, if he knew the gap was there, then he already knew where you were staying, didn't he?'

Molly shut her eyes. Of course, how stupid. Amelia was right. Molly's shoulders slumped. It was a puzzle she wasn't going to be able to solve. 'It's a mess,' she said finally. 'I don't know how he found out my address, or why he was on my doorstep unless it was to blackmail me, and I certainly have no idea why he was murdered.'

Amelia looked at her, her expression troubled. 'You aren't serious about being a suspect, are you?'

'I don't know,' she said wearily. 'Jack says it's nonsense to think so, but the man was murdered in Green Park and I happened to be nearby at the same time.'

'You were always a little bit of an idiot, Molly, but you haven't a cruel bone in your body. Anyway, you were hardly going to murder the poor fool for rejecting your advances, were you?'

She'd been called a tit and a cow this morning, ignoring the *bit of an idiot* tag was easy. 'I told you, the police think we did more than kiss. Stupidly, I didn't help my case, I told them that he must have come to blackmail me because why else would he have come? And, yes, I probably would have paid him to go away if he'd threatened to tell Jack what happened.' She pushed a hand through her hair. 'Jack and I are shaky at the moment, Amelia, I wouldn't have wanted him to know that I'd made a play for someone else.'

Amelia reached across, took her hand and squeezed it. 'The police will look into it all but you're only a *little bit* of an idiot, Molly, you'd have known they'd find his phone and trace the text from you. If you'd murdered him, you'd have taken it with you, wouldn't you?'

'I've watched enough crime series, I guess I wouldn't have been *that* stupid.'

'The police will come to the same conclusion when they've done some investigating. And hopefully, when they dig around in this poor man's life, they'll find someone else with a much stronger motive.' Amelia filled her mug and picked it up. 'Did he really have turquoise eyes?'

A slight smile appeared on Molly's lips and her eyes softened. 'I know you said people don't really have turquoise eyes, but I swear he did, plus high cheekbones, perfectly sculpted lips and an amazing chiselled jaw. He wore a leather jacket over a white T-shirt and jeans – very young Marlon Brando. In short,' Molly said, 'he was sex on legs. And his voice was hypnotic. The second time we met, he was going on and on about the workings of the canal, leaning down to look into that gloomy lock chamber. But he could have been talking about anything, it didn't matter. I would have listened to him forever.'

Her smile dimmed. 'He was young, only a couple of years older than Remi and now he's dead and somewhere, some mother and father, maybe siblings, are mourning.' She felt a deep sense of sadness for the loss of this man she'd admired and lusted after but never known.

Amelia squeezed her hand again. 'He was probably involved with some shady characters, wait, you'll see; just because he looked good, doesn't mean he was.'

Molly was about to agree when her phone rang, her heart beating faster when she saw who it was. 'It's Jack,' she said, reaching to answer it.

'Where the fuck are you?' Jack said, before she'd a chance to say hello.

'I'm with Amelia.'

There was a moment's silence. 'Are you completely out of your mind? The police called around to the house. When they didn't find you there, they went to your office and when you weren't there, they came here. Here! I suppose I should be grateful they weren't in uniform and driving a damn squad car!'

Molly didn't have a chance to speak, she let him rant on until his ire ran out. 'I needed to speak to Amelia about what happened,' she said into the first moment of silence.

'Seems pretty clear to me.' His voice arctic cold, each word filled with anger.

Molly gulped back the tears. 'I was trying to find out how he knew where to find me.'

'And did you, detective?'

Ignoring his sarcasm, she fought to keep her voice calm. 'No, I didn't, I've still no idea.'

'Well, you'd better get your ass back home. They want to ask you more questions.' And without waiting for a reply, he hung up.

Hurt, Molly dropped the phone on the table. 'Jack's pissed.'

When it rang again, seconds later, she gave Amelia a weak smile and felt a shiver of relief. He'd be ringing to apologise, to say he forgave her and that he'd stand by her through the mess she'd got herself embroiled in. Her relief was short-lived. It wasn't Jack; the number displayed on her phone wasn't familiar. She hesitated, her heart thumping, before picking it up to answer. 'Hello?'

'Mrs Chatwell, it's DI Fanshawe. We did ask you to keep yourself available for further questions, but it seems nobody, including your husband, knows where you are.'

They could only have got the phone number from Jack; he'd neglected to tell her he'd given it to them. She bit back the feeling of abandonment and instilled some strength in her voice. 'I'm in Pembridge Square Gardens with a friend.' She didn't think there was any point in adding she'd come to discuss her situation.

But Fanshawe wasn't a fool. 'Your friend? The one you went to Semington House with when you ran into Oliver Vine?'

She was tempted to point out that she had more than one friend, but she didn't think the detective would appreciate the sarcasm. 'Yes,' she said without elaborating. Let him think what he wanted. He would anyway. Would he think there was some kind of conspiracy? That she and Amelia had plotted together to kill Oliver Vine? Molly looked across at her friend, who was regarding her with concern, and managed a smile. 'She is offering me some support. Jack said you had more questions for me. I'm happy to answer any you might have.'

There were muffled voices in the background. She guessed he was speaking to someone else, his large hand covering the phone. 'Okay,' he said, his voice suddenly loud and clear. 'Here at West End Central Station at two, if you please.'

In the police station, not at home. She swallowed the lump in her throat. 'Perfect,' she said, her voice cool, and hung up.

She put the phone gently down on the table with a shaking hand. 'It was the police, they want to see me today, at the station.'

17

Amelia stood, moved around the table and enveloped Molly in a hug. 'You haven't done anything wrong, remember?'

'I don't think Jack would agree with you,' Molly said, giving a loud sniff. 'And the police... I know they don't believe me.'

'They have to dot all the i's and cross all the t's. It's the way it works. You'll go, answer questions you've already answered, and come away wondering why you were worried.'

'Sounds like you're speaking from experience.'

'I read all those crime novels and watch every crime drama,' Amelia said, sitting back in her chair. 'I'm almost an expert. I know how it goes.'

No, you don't, Molly wanted to scream, *you've no bloody idea.* Nothing she had ever read or seen on the TV had prepared her for being involved in something like this. But Amelia was trying to be kind and supportive, the way Jack should have been, so she merely shook her head and shut her eyes briefly to hide the fear she knew was lurking there. 'West End Central Station,' she said a moment later, attempting to sound amused. 'He said it as though I'd know where that was, as if I were acquainted with police stations. I've never been inside one before.'

Amelia stretched behind her for her iPad. 'We'll soon sort that out,' she said calmly. 'Okay, here it is. Fairly convenient, actually, it's on Savile Row.' She looked up. 'Easy, you get the Circle Line to Oxford Circus, then head down Regent Street, take a right on New Burlington Street and it's at the end of that road. Six minutes' walk. It'll only take you thirty to forty minutes max from here.' She tilted her head. 'Why don't you ring Jack and ask him to go with you?'

'No,' Molly said, wishing she could. 'Jack mentioned being really busy. I'll be fine. You're probably right, anyway, they're simply going through the motions.'

'I could go with you, if you like?'

'That's very kind,' Molly said, genuinely touched. 'But honestly, I'll be okay.'

'Well, at least let me make you a sandwich. I bet you didn't have any breakfast.'

Molly smiled her gratitude and sat back while Amelia bustled about in the kitchen. Molly had plugged her mobile in to charge and checked it for messages, hoping for one from Jack. He would forgive her eventually, but she wondered how long it would take her to forgive him for not standing by her when she needed him most. It was ironic when she thought of how much time she had spent in the last couple of weeks worrying about him.

She wondered what the police wanted to ask her. There was nothing she hadn't already told them. She'd been an idiot, but that wasn't a crime.

The sandwich Amelia made her was probably nice, but it tasted like cardboard in her mouth. She struggled to eat half, pushing the rest away with an apologetic shrug. 'I've got collywobbles, I'm afraid. But thank you, even that much was enough.'

At one, she unplugged her phone. 'I'll go now. I'd prefer to be early.'

Amelia gathered her in a hug. 'You stay strong, okay. Remember, you've done nothing wrong.'

There was light rain falling when she left Oxford Circus. Of course, she hadn't thought to bring an umbrella. She took it as an omen that the rest of the day was going to be a hellish one. Turning down New Burlington Street, she saw the imposing grey building immediately ahead, police vans parked either side of its entrance. There was nothing threatening about the grey brick or the almost startling white window frames, but her insides spasmed with a fear that intensified as she approached. She could turn and run away but what then? 'I've done nothing wrong,' she muttered as she used the handrail to negotiate the nine steps to the front door. Another bad omen: lust was one of the nine circles of hell in Dante's Inferno and isn't that what had started this nightmare in the first place?

Inside the station, she gave her name to the bored counter clerk and took a seat to wait. It wasn't long before DS Carstairs arrived, his too-knowing eyes sliding over her, making her skin crawl.

'Morning,' he said. 'We're this way.' He headed off down the corridor without another word.

Instantly irritated at his attitude, Molly lifted her chin and followed.

He stopped at a door and pushed it open, indicating with a silent jerk of his head that she went inside. It was a standard cold interview room. The only thing that made it different to any number of small conference rooms she'd been in over the years was the table screwed to the floor. The chairs weren't, she was pleased to see, but they were light moulded-plastic ones that wouldn't cause much damage if smashed against the side of someone's head.

Not that she was planning on doing any smashing, despite the look on the detective's face that said, as clearly as if it had been written there, that he didn't think much of her. She met his gaze straight on, her eyes never wavering as she sat on one of the chairs. There was only one way to deal with people like him – show them you weren't afraid. She guessed she did an okay job as he immediately looked away and told her he'd be back in a few minutes. But if he thought she wasn't afraid he was a poor judge of people: she was terrified.

The room was warm. When he left, she took off her dark-blue coat and hung it over the back of the chair beside her, dropping her bag on the seat rather than a floor that looked as if it only ever had a faint relationship with a mop.

It was after two. She was wondering how long she'd be kept waiting when the door opened and DS Carstairs returned, DI Fanshawe close behind. Neither thanked her for coming in. DI Fanshawe took the chair opposite and put a slim file on the table in front of him before looking at her, his eyes assessing.

His expression, unlike his colleague's, didn't appear to be condemnatory, his grey eyes a little warmer than she remembered. Or maybe that was wishful thinking. Tension made her shoulders ache.

Without a word, Fanshawe opened the file, withdrew a photograph and slid it across the table toward her. 'Is this the man you met on the canal?'

Grateful that he had said *met* rather than any of the words he might have used, and certainly one of the words Carstairs would have chosen, she looked down at the photograph. Her initial reaction was *no, it wasn't him*. This man had blue eyes, his skin was pale, hair tousled. But there was something... 'It might be,' she said, 'but his eyes...'

Fanshawe took a sheet of acetate from the file and laid it over the photograph. 'What about now?'

Molly gasped, reaching out and pulling the photograph closer. How well she remembered those fabulous turquoise eyes. Too fabulous; like a lot of that encounter, they weren't real. She looked at the DI. 'He was wearing coloured lenses.' It wasn't a question; she'd been fooled, but she wasn't stupid.

He nodded. 'When you mentioned his eye colour more than once, it reminded me of a case about a year ago where a witness spoke about a man's amazing brown eyes. I pulled the case file.' He tapped a stubby finger on the edge of the photograph. 'His real name is Lucien Pleasant. He's been implicated in a number of cases where people, usually women, have been conned out of a lot of money. He's a slippery individual, we never managed to nail him down until last year when one of his alleged victims was found dead. He was arrested but unfortunately' – Fanshawe's lips narrowed – 'the case was thrown out on a technicality and he disappeared.'

Molly's eyes dropped to the picture and a wave of sadness swept over her. She'd been foolish, ripe for plucking. Her cheeks flushed with colour that was part embarrassment, part anger. 'He was a con man,' she said, gritting her teeth.

Fanshawe shook his head. 'A very clever and slick operator which was why he was able to evade prison for so long.' He sat back, his hands clasped over the hint of a belly and tapped his thumbs together. 'Pleasant was way too clever an operator to be sitting by the canal on the off-chance that someone worth targeting would wander by.' He waited for that to sink in before continuing. 'Did you get any sense that he was waiting for you?'

She shook her head slowly, thinking back to that morning. 'No, I didn't. I had slowed to a walk and was thinking about turning to go back to the hotel when I saw him.'

'Okay,' he said, looking down at his notebook. 'Then

Pleasant said hello, you said the same and he asked the time. Is that it?'

'Yes.' She had been over this so often. There were few words spoken between them during that first encounter. Her indrawn breath was sudden and loud. Eyes wide, she stared across the table. 'He asked me the time.'

Fanshawe waited.

'After I sat beside him, he pointed to where he'd seen a kingfisher.' She met the inspector's eyes. 'He was wearing a watch. It didn't register with me then, but now...'

'Pleasant was waiting for you specifically.' He nodded as if it was what he'd surmised. 'And you still maintain that nothing happened between you?'

'Nothing.' Molly's hair had fallen forward, she brushed it back behind her ears. 'I was carried away by the romance of it all. It was like something from a movie, you know.' She avoided looking at Carstairs, guessing he'd find what she said amusing, maybe even pathetic. 'Had he wanted more, that second morning, I think I might have been tempted. For a moment, I felt young and desirable but it wasn't what he wanted from me.'

'Then what was?' Fanshawe said, a frown appearing between his eyes. 'You mentioned that you thought he'd gone to your house with the intention of blackmailing you. Are you very wealthy, Mrs Chatwell? If he had succeeded, how much could he have hoped to achieve?'

Molly had made an error of judgement; would she have paid up to stop Jack finding out? She remembered his stricken face, his anger. Yes, she'd have paid anything to prevent that. 'We're not wealthy but I suppose I could have got my hands on twenty thousand,' she said quietly.

Fanshawe tapped his thumbs together again and his frown deepened. 'I doubt he'd have settled for that. He knew where you lived, he'd know there was more.'

'But how did he know where I lived?' Her voice cracked.

'That's something we'll be trying to find out,' he said, taking the photograph and slipping it back into the file.

'There was something else,' she said, her lower lip quivering. 'It may be nothing, but I've been going over and over the encounter.' She saw Carstairs' raised eyebrow and ignored him, keeping her eyes on the inspector. 'Although he'd looked appalled when I tried to kiss him, when I went to run away I had to wrench my T-shirt from his hand. Why was he holding on so tightly? And why did he run after me for as long as he did? I'm fast and I soon left him behind, but I could hear him shouting after me. Why?' She shook her head. 'I'd embarrassed myself, but he'd done nothing. Why not just leave it?'

'You couldn't hear what he was shouting?'

Molly shook her head. 'I was moving too fast and my feet were crunching noisily on the stony path.'

'Probably called you a tart,' Carstairs suggested.

She shot him a look. 'He would have had no reason to, would he? As I have said, more than once, nothing happened. I only heard one of the words he was shouting,' she said, looking back at Fanshawe. 'It was, *understand*.'

18

Molly went through it again, every action or word she remembered, every nuance and tone until she was sick of the sound of her own voice going over and over the details of such a short period of her life.

Short but devastating.

Finally, when she wanted to scream that there was nothing more, Fanshawe told her she could go.

His words were sudden and unexpected, and she looked at him in confusion, wondering if this were some kind of trap for the unwary. It wasn't until he and Carstairs stood and Fanshawe said they'd be in touch that she realised her ordeal was over.

It was a few seconds before she got to her feet, knees trembling, head swimming. She kept her hands flat on the table for support, unable to move. But when she felt tears well, she knew she had to get out of there. Following the exit signs, she was soon on Savile Row, stepping out onto the street with a feeling of relief. The rain had stopped, but ominous grey clouds reflecting her mood, drew her eyes upward and made her shiver.

She didn't want to go home yet. Instead, she wandered down

Regent and Oxford Street, swept along with crowds of shoppers and groups of tourists, trailing along aimlessly with them, wandering, backtracking, uncaring as to where she went, trying to exhaust herself so that she wouldn't have to think.

Her legs were aching by the time she decided to go home. It was after six, Jack would be waiting. Going into automatic mode, she didn't remember the journey home, catching the tube without much thought.

It was six thirty before she opened her front door and stepped into the hallway. She listened. It was an old house; if there was someone home, floorboards would creak, water would gurgle in the pipes. But the silence was telling. If Jack had come, he'd gone again without waiting to see what the police had wanted with his beloved wife. Bitterness twisted her mouth for a moment. She should be glad, shouldn't she? It was sleep she needed, not an argument; a confrontation that would be difficult, painful and undoubtedly nasty. She knew it would come eventually; wounding words that would slice through what little self-esteem and pride she had left, but she didn't want it now. Her heart wasn't in a state to fight back.

What a price she was paying for those foolish moments. She checked her mobile, saw nothing from him and dashed off quick messages to Remi and Freya, making a joke about misplacing her phone and having to use one of their rejects.

Her feet feeling like lead, she trudged up the stairs to her bedroom where she undressed and climbed under the duvet. From outside, she heard a car's engine start, another passing by with a swoosh of tyres on the rain-wet road, the high-pitched laughter of a child – everyday sounds, a reassuring lullaby to remind her that not everything had changed. She lay exhausted, willing herself to fall asleep, for temporary release from the mess she'd made.

In her dreams, turquoise eyes gleamed with malice and brought her to the edge of wakefulness each time. Finally, after tossing and turning for what felt like hours, but what a glance at her watch told her was less than one, she gave up and went downstairs. She curled up on the sofa, switched on the TV and found a romcom she knew would be candyfloss for her brain and might, if she were lucky, help her to relax.

Tucking her feet under, she tried to concentrate on the movie, but her mind had already drifted when the house phone rang, startling her. It rarely rang, their friends and acquaintances usually called their mobiles. A cold caller, she guessed, staring at it, willing it to stop.

When it did, her eyes flicked back to the movie which she had to admit was excruciatingly bad. Reaching for the remote, she channel-surfed for a few minutes, settling on the rerun of a property programme she'd watched before.

Then the phone rang again.

She stared at it, eyes wide, her heart beating a little faster, a little louder. Even when the ringing stopped, she continued to stare at it until, with a frustrated shake of her head, she reached to take the handset off the hook. Her hand was on it when it rang for the third time. Maybe it wasn't a cold caller. They weren't normally this persistent.

She held it to her ear. Unable to hear anything, she muttered, 'Hello.'

'Thank goodness.'

It was a voice that sounded vaguely familiar, but she struggled to remember. Shifting in her seat, sliding her feet to the ground, as if the position gave her more authority, she spoke firmly. 'Who is this?'

'It's Stuart. Stuart Mercer. I've been trying to get hold of you.' He sounded relieved.

Shutting her eyes in disbelief, she was tempted to hang up without another word. Instead, she gripped the handset. 'I'm sorry, I'm not interested in meeting you.' She heard a quick indrawn breath on the line before he spoke. This time his voice was sharp, irritated.

'I've gone to a lot of trouble to get your home number,' he said. 'I've tried your mobile, but I must have the wrong number–'

'I blocked you,' she interrupted him without compunction. 'I think you might have misunderstood my friendliness at the party and assumed it was something more. So, let me make this quite clear... I do not want to meet you.' There was silence for so long that Molly thought he'd hung up, but then she heard the slight rasp of his breath. She was about to repeat herself when he spoke.

'I think it's you that have misunderstood,' he said. 'I'm not sure why I'm bothering except you always seemed like a nice woman, and there's something I thought you should know.'

Know?

'I'm taking a big risk contacting you,' he continued. 'I'd be in trouble if it came out. Listen, forget I rang.'

'No wait,' Molly said quickly. 'You can't ring up, tell me there's something I need to know, then bugger off. What is it you want to tell me?'

'I can't do this over the phone. Meet me. Tomorrow at one, in the coffee shop on the corner of Ebury Street and Lower Belgrave Street. You know it? Casper's?'

It was ten minutes' walk from Jack's office; she had been in it a couple of times in their early months together when they couldn't bear not to see each other for a whole day. How long ago that seemed. How long ago it *was*. She couldn't believe the café was still there. 'Casper's. Yes, I know it. Okay, tomorrow at one. Here's my new mobile number, just in case.' She reeled off the number and dropped the handset back on the stand.

Maybe Stuart would be able to tell her what was bothering Jack. It would be one worry off her mind.

19

When Jack still hadn't arrived home by midnight, Molly headed to bed where exhaustion closed her eyes and she drifted into a restless sleep. But turmoil wasn't a good bedfellow and after only a couple of hours she was wide awake.

The silence in the room was oppressive, uneasy. She felt pinned to the bed by the weight of all that was hanging over her and, panicking, she struggled to her feet and felt along the wall for the light switch. The sudden brightness swept the shadows and shades from the room. Her breathing, fast and rasping, slowed and quietened. There was no bogeyman hiding in the dark. She sank onto the bed and checked her watch. 3am.

She hadn't heard Jack come in. He'd not wanted to wake her; she'd have preferred if he had. A sudden need to see him sent her barefooted to the spare bedroom, turning the doorknob and easing the door open. The curtains weren't pulled, and streetlights lit the room... and the empty bed. He hadn't come home.

Her eyes filled and she slumped against the wall. He had several friends; he could be with any of them. She returned to her bedroom and picked up her mobile, expecting to see a message from him. There were three: from Remi, Freya and Amelia, but nothing from Jack.

She crawled back under the duvet and shut her eyes. For the next few hours, she dozed, waking each time with a pounding in her chest and the faint hope that he had come home. Each time she swung her feet to the floor and crossed to the spare room, each time desolate to find it empty.

At six, she gave up, pulled a robe on and went down to make coffee and something to eat. Apart from half a sandwich she'd had at Amelia's the day before, Molly had had nothing to eat since the hotel.

She made toast and sat at the table nibbling it while she drank her coffee and waited for the world to wake up. Finding the quiet of the house depressing, she switched on the TV. She didn't look to see what was on, it didn't matter; all she wanted was the sound of voices to keep her company.

It wasn't until eight thirty that she heard a key in the lock. She kept her eyes on the kitchen door, waiting for it to open. When it did, Jack stood looking at her, one hand on the doorknob, a curious expression on his face. He was still wearing his suit, but it was creased, his tie loosened, the top button of his shirt undone. A five o'clock shadow shaded his jaw. It added an air of menace as he stood without speaking.

The silence dragged out. Molly got to her feet and went to switch the kettle on, hoping that a hot drink might cure the chill that gripped her belly.

She watched him take off his jacket and hang it carefully on the back of a chair, struck once again by how thin he'd become. The yearly annual check-up his company insisted upon had only been two months before. She'd seen the report, she knew he was in perfect physical health. Or, at least, he had been. 'Are you okay?' she said into the silence before spooning coffee into two mugs.

'Okay?' he snorted. 'Gosh, why wouldn't I be?' He hit his forehead so hard with the heel of his hand that she heard the sound across the room. 'Oh yes, I remember why I wouldn't bloody well be okay, why I'm a million miles from being even remotely near okay, because my wife got herself involved with a stranger, a stranger who was murdered, and now I have the police calling to the damn office because my wife... *my wife* is under investigation.'

She added milk and shoved his mug across the counter. 'I wasn't *involved* with him, Jack, and I'm not under investigation,' she said, hoping she was right. 'I'm simply helping the police with their enquiries.' She allowed the bitterness in her voice to spill out. 'Thanks, by the way, for giving them my phone number and not bothering to tell me.'

Without responding, he picked up his coffee and took it to the sofa. He sat, crossed his legs and switched the TV to a news channel.

She clasped her hands around her mug and lifted it to her lips. It would be nice to throw it across the room and watch the arc of coffee shatter his composure. 'Where have you been, anyway?' She knew it would have been with one of his friends, but she couldn't resist saying, 'Did you find yourself a pretty shoulder to cry on?'

He moved so suddenly that she was startled even before he threw the mug. It missed her head by inches, hot coffee splashing her skin, causing her to jump up with a yelp of fright. In all the years she'd known him, she'd never seen him lose his temper. The man standing glaring at her with his hands clenched in fists was a stranger. Brushing away the splashes of coffee with a tea towel grabbed from the rail, she stared at him. 'Have you lost your mind?'

'Me? It's you that's lost your mind. How dare you accuse me? Just because you've the morals of an alley cat, don't put that on me.'

The mug had hit a cupboard and crashed onto the floor where it had smashed into shards of china. She looked at it in confusion. It felt like her life. Trying to get her thoughts in order, she used the tea towel to mop up the coffee that had streaked the countertop, the wall behind her and the floor. She mopped it slowly, conscious of Jack's heaving body standing a few feet away. With a final sweep across the counter, she threw the cloth on top of the broken china, moved to the sofa and sat.

'You didn't come home.' Her voice sounded broken, pathetic.

His temper gone as quickly as it had come, he ran a hand through his hair, and took a step towards her. 'I've never cheated on you, Molly. I always thought we had something so precious, so special, I wasn't going to risk destroying it.'

Guilt seared her. She wanted to say she felt the same, that what they had *was* special, and so very precious. Too precious to be destroyed by her stupid moment of weakness, a meaningless nothing. She wanted to grab him, scream at him until he listened, until he acknowledged the stupidity of risking what they had for something that never happened. Instead, keeping her eyes on his, she asked quietly, 'So, where did you go?'

He took a step closer. 'I cadged a bed at a mate's.'

She wanted to ask which mate, but she didn't because she'd known him too long and she knew, without a doubt, that he was lying.

20

Molly could see the lie in the way Jack's eyes were unwilling to meet hers, and in that slight restlessness that had him shuffle from foot to foot. She wanted to challenge him, but a wave of weariness swept over her and took all concern for him with it. Perhaps he'd stayed overnight in the office, trying to iron out whatever problems he was having. Maybe, despite his protestations, he had been with a woman.

Too tired and numb to deal with any more grief, she pleaded exhaustion and went back to bed. As she lay trying not to cry, she heard Jack moving about, the hum of the shower and the opening and closing of doors. Exhaustion, both mental and physical, had seeped into her bones and when the house quietened, she drifted off to sleep, waking confused a short while later. Checking her phone, she saw it was after nine. Using the same throaty voice she'd used before, she rang her office to say she was still unwell, hanging up before they could query when she'd be back. It wasn't something she knew.

She lay staring at the ceiling, thinking. What did Stuart want to tell her? His voice had sounded worried, concerned even. It had to be something important; something to do with Jack's troubles at work. The two men weren't friends as such, but they were friendly in the way that work colleagues often were.

Colour rushed to her cheeks when she remembered thinking he was making a play for her. He and that stranger; she'd been wrong both times. A stupid self-deluded fool, desperately clinging to a version of herself that no longer existed.

Restless, she threw on a robe and went downstairs for coffee. She'd need her wits about her when she met Stuart Mercer, for whatever it was he was going to tell her.

When the doorbell chimed, she put her mug down and headed to the front door, hoping it wasn't the police with yet more questions. She pulled the door open and immediately relaxed when she saw Amelia standing there. 'Thank goodness it's you,' Molly said.

'I did text you to ask how yesterday went but you didn't reply. I was going to ring and then decided, what the hell, I'd come over.' Amelia stepped inside and enveloped Molly in a hug. 'I can't stay long.'

Molly led the way back into the living room. 'Have a seat. There's coffee, or I can make tea?'

'Coffee is fine.' Throwing her coat on the back of a chair, Amelia sat and looked at Molly. 'Tell me everything.'

Molly took another mug and poured coffee, placing it carefully on the table before sitting back against the cushions and telling Amelia about her visit to the police station the day before and Jack's behaviour earlier that morning.

'I don't know what to say.' Amelia shook her head slowly. 'The man on the canal, the police think he was waiting for you?'

'It looks like it,' Molly said. 'He has form for duping gullible older women. Pathetic women like me who were seeking something that doesn't exist. I was an absolute fool.'

Amelia picked up her mug and took a drink. 'It's your friend with his amazing brown eyes who's at fault, Mol, not you. You must stop blaming yourself.'

Moll's fingers tightened on her coffee. *Amazing brown eyes?* Where had she heard that before? Then she remembered. During her interview at the police station, DI Fanshawe had mentioned a witness who'd commented on Lucien Pleasant's amazing brown eyes. 'Turquoise,' she said softly. 'He'd turquoise eyes, not brown, and they weren't real. He wore tinted contact lenses and changed the colour to confuse his victims.'

'I told you nobody really had turquoise eyes,' Amelia said. She lifted her mug. 'Is there more coffee?'

'Of course.' Molly stood and fetched the cafetière from the counter. She brushed the eye-colour error aside. It wasn't important. After all, it wasn't as if Amelia had seen his eyes. If she had she'd have remembered the colour. Molly filled both their mugs, wondering how much caffeine she'd need to ingest before she felt in any way alert.

'You have to stop blaming yourself,' Amelia said, adding milk to hers. 'Eventually it will all blow over. Jack won't stay mad with you, he's not that sort.'

He's not that sort. Molly picked up her mug and took a long drink to hide her annoyance. Since when had Amelia become an expert on her husband. For goodness' sake, they barely knew one another. Over the years, they'd met maybe a handful of times and only on a couple of occasions since Amelia and Tristan had returned to live in London.

Molly lifted her eyes from her coffee to regard her friend suspiciously, remembering how pleased she was to see Jack mixing with her female friends at their party. Maybe it was only one he had mixed with, Amelia tossing her damn hair around and laughing at something he had said. And what was it she had said later... oh yes, that Jack was one of the sexiest men she'd ever met. Molly had thought she'd imagined the expression of lust on her friend's face. Maybe she hadn't.

'Is Tristan still away?' Molly asked, having a vague recollection he'd said he was flying somewhere after the weekend.

'Yes, he's in Berlin for a couple more days, endless meetings about something or other. I would have gone but Berlin isn't my favourite city. And anyway,' she said, 'I've a lot on here.'

Jack never had said where he'd spent the night, could he have gone to Amelia, maybe to question her about the weekend, staying for the comfort she would have happily given? That Jack was her friend's husband wouldn't have stopped Amelia from taking what she wanted, especially if it wasn't the first time.

Molly shut her eyes on the tears that had begun to gather as if it would stop them falling. It didn't work, she could feel them squeeze their way out to tremble a moment in the corner of her eyes before gathering momentum and careering down her cheeks.

'Oh, don't cry, Mol!'

Amelia did *sincere entreaty* so well, Molly thought, opening her eyes. She brushed the tears away with her fingers and looked at her friend. She looked sincere too. But suspicions, once aroused, were hard to put to sleep. Amelia and Jack. Was it possible? And what about that *amazing brown eyes* remark? What was it the police had said, something about Lucien Pleasant liking rich, vulnerable women?

Vulnerable like her; rich like Amelia.

If Amelia had been one of his victims, Molly knew she'd never have told anyone. She'd certainly never have gone to the police to expose herself as such a fool. She'd have paid up and shut up.

Molly put her mug down and dragged a smile into place. 'Tears come easily these days. I've an appointment myself at one,' she added, looking at her watch. 'I'd better go and get ready.'

'You look worn out,' Amelia said, 'you should get a taxi to wherever you're going.'

'No, I'll be fine. I'm meeting a friend in Casper's, it's only a few minutes' walk from Victoria station. A taxi would take forever.' She stood and gathered the mugs, hoping Amelia would take the hint. It would be a relief when she was gone. Molly was probably being ridiculous, but the life she had considered as mundane, almost boring, had become a crazy rollercoaster that sent her thoughts churning. Apart from Freya and Remi, who thank goodness, were away from it all, there appeared to be nothing solid, nothing reliable left in her life.

She swallowed the lump in her throat. Maybe the sudden inexplicable suspicion of her friend was crazy but when was it that she'd started worrying about Jack? Wasn't it around the time that Amelia and Tristan had come back to London?

'Okay,' Amelia's voice interrupted Molly's thoughts, 'I'll head off.' She looked at Molly with concern in her eyes. 'You should try to get some rest when you get back, you look shattered.'

'Always good to know,' she said with an attempt at humour. 'I'll try to sleep later.'

Amelia put an arm around her, gave her a quick hug and picked up her coat and bag. 'Why don't we meet later for a glass of wine in O'Dea's? Maybe around six?'

O'Dea's? Why not? She could text Jack and get him to meet her there. 'Good idea.'

'Great, I'll let myself out.'

There was a sharp clip-clip as Amelia's stilettos crossed the wooden floor of the hall but it wasn't until Molly heard the front door shut that she let out the breath she'd been holding and stumbled to the sofa where she sat and shut her eyes. It was over an hour before she moved. She didn't want to meet Stuart. Any more complications and her brain might explode. But maybe, whatever it was he wanted to tell her, would clarify whatever was going on in Jack's life. If she could be convinced all his problems were work-related and nothing to do with a woman, she might be able to think straight.

On that slim hope, she stood. She'd enough time to have a quick shower and dress.

Twenty minutes later, wearing heavier make-up than she'd normally do during the day, she pulled on her coat, grabbed her bag and headed out.

The rain had stopped, the day was blue-sky bright, but it didn't lift her mood. She walked, eyes down, mind swirling with conflicting thoughts, one minute sure Amelia was having an affair with Jack and involved somehow with Lucien Pleasant, the next castigating herself for her crazy paranoia.

Molly reached South Kensington station in a daze, waited for the Circle line tube and ten minutes later was making her way through the crowds at Victoria station. Outside, the pavement was a heaving mass of people; fast-moving Londoners intent on their destination, dawdling, gawping tourists stopping abruptly to take photographs, selfie-sticks wielded like dangerous weapons forcing passers-by to duck and dive.

As a veteran London commuter, she weaved and dodged without much thought and with little attention to what was going on around her. Strange notions chased through her head and befuddled her brain. Nearer to the café, the crowds thinned. She stood at the roadside waiting for pedestrian lights to change, throwing a sympathetic glance at the woman beside her who was trying, unsuccessfully by the sound of the cries, to soothe a fractious child. When Molly looked back to the crossing lights, it was turquoise eyes she saw, and she closed her eyes briefly on the stupidity of it all. Maybe her sudden suspicion of Amelia was trying to deflect attention from her own idiotic behaviour. Tears welled as she watched the lights, waiting for them to turn.

A blow to the small of her back made Molly cry out as she was pushed forward into the moving traffic. She sought desperately to regain her balance, arms flailing, twisting her body so she was at an angle to the car that was bearing down on her. That one movement saved her from the full brunt of the collision but the contact was enough to send her flying.

Witnesses, she was told later, said she'd landed with such a thud they thought she was dead. She thought so too as she lay unable to move, shouts and screams swirling above her, darkness creeping around the edges of her vision until it was all gone. Later, she remembered there had been a millisecond of relief that she'd no longer have to worry about anything.

For the next twenty-four hours, she was vaguely aware of voices; some were reassuring, some demanding, others questioning. She ignored them all, choosing consciously or not to stay in the comforting darkness, the steady beep-beep of a monitor close to her right ear telling her all she needed to know. She was in a hospital and she was alive.

It was curiosity that finally opened her eyes. She was alone. Turning her head slightly, she could see the monitor; she thought the squiggles that raced across the screen looked okay. On the other side of the bed, tubing ran from a bag of fluid into her left hand. She watched it closely for a few seconds; it was dripping very slowly. She decided that was a good sign. Squeezing her eyes shut, she tried to remember what had happened. Had she stumbled into the traffic! There had been a scream, then a blow that had sent her sailing through the air, a faint memory of feeling weightless before she hit the ground and the world dissolved into pain. A car, she guessed, although she wasn't sure; she felt like she'd been trampled by a herd of elephants but unless there was a serious problem in London Zoo, she doubted there were many of them on the streets of London. She distinctly remembered being confused about the lights; hadn't she seen turquoise eyes? Maybe she'd stupidly walked out onto the road at the wrong time.

Panic started to build then, how badly hurt was she? She didn't seem able to move. Nor was she in any pain. Oh God, she couldn't feel anything, maybe she was paralysed. The beeping of the monitor increased in speed and escalated her fear, a spiral that might have gone on if the door hadn't opened and a kindly face appeared looking down at her from what seemed to be a great height. A soothing hand on her arm gave instant relief, she could feel it. She swallowed the lump in her throat.

'You're going to be fine,' the woman said, her voice soft and calming. 'I'm Edel, your nurse. Are you in pain?'

Molly gave the question some thought. 'No.' The word came out a husky croak.

'Good. You've had some pain relief, but we can give you more if needed. You're in Guy's Hospital, Molly, okay?'

Guy's. A good one. 'Am I paralysed?' Better to know than keep guessing.

'No, you were very lucky,' Edel said with a smile. 'A broken rib where you collided with the ground and a lot of bruising. You were unconscious for a while and then semi-conscious for the last several hours, so you'll be kept in for observation. That's standard with any concussion, but all going well, you'll be fine.'

Molly's lips were dry and her tongue felt too big for her mouth. 'Can I have a drink?'

Edel used the bed control to sit Molly more upright, pushed a bed table within reach and put a glass of water in her hand. 'Take it slowly,' she advised.

Even a little drop made a difference. 'How long have I been here?'

'Almost twenty-four hours. It's Saturday afternoon.' The nurse fussed around the monitor for a while, then fiddled with the intravenous line in Molly's left hand. Finally, she wrote something on the clipboard that hung on the end of the bed and looked at her with a serious expression. 'If you're up to it, a couple of policemen arrived a few minutes ago. They've been in and out a few times since yesterday hoping to have a word with you. I said no, but perhaps now you're awake you would prefer to speak to them.'

It was the last thing Molly wanted. 'Absolutely n...' She stopped. 'Yes, okay.' If they wanted to speak to her about the accident it was probably better sooner than later. 'Is my husband here?'

'He was here yesterday evening holding your hand for hours and again this morning. When you didn't wake, he said he had to leave and would be back later.' The nurse refilled the water glass and left.

Molly couldn't remember Jack being there and tried to rationalise his absence; he'd probably gone for something to eat. Perhaps she should have insisted the police waited until he came back before speaking to her.

She was debating ringing the call bell to tell the nurse she'd changed her mind when the door opened. When she saw who entered, she groaned.

DI Fanshawe, about to speak, stopped and stared at her, his forehead creasing in what she guessed might be concern. 'The nurse said you weren't in pain, that you agreed to speak to us.'

'She didn't tell me it was you,' Molly said, uncaring if she sounded rude. 'Are you the only two coppers in London? Why are you looking into an accident? Shouldn't you be looking for the man who killed...' She searched for the man's name, shaking her head when it wouldn't come to her. '...what's his name?'

'Lucien Pleasant,' Fanshawe provided calmly. 'We are, Mrs Chatwell. That's why we're here.' Fanshawe pulled up a chair and nodded to DS Carstairs to do the same. 'It looks very much like someone tried to kill you.'

21

Molly had told the nurse she wasn't in pain but a dull throb started in her head. She reached up and slid her hand across her forehead as if she could wipe it away. 'You'll have to forgive me if I sound a little dopey,' she said. 'Did you really tell me that someone tried to kill me?'

'It's a line of enquiry we're following,' Fanshawe said. 'There was a woman with a pushchair beside you. She said you seemed distracted, but that you were waiting patiently for the lights to change when suddenly you went flying in front of a car.'

The dull throb in Molly's head ratcheted up a notch. She didn't need it to be spelled out. 'Someone pushed me.' She nodded slowly. 'Yes, I remember. I felt a blow to my back.'

Fanshawe leaned closer, his eyes meeting hers. 'The car that hit you was a four-by-four with bull bars; if you hadn't managed to turn as you did, if it had hit you full on, chances are we wouldn't be talking now.'

A wave of nausea swept over her. She grabbed a kidney dish that had been left within reach and held it in front of her mouth. It was almost amusing to see how fast the two policemen moved out of the line of fire. A few deep breaths and the feeling passed.

Her head was pounding, she needed the nurse to give her something to take it away. 'Why would someone try to kill me?'

Fanshawe drew closer again. 'They probably hoped it would look like an accident. There was a crush of people waiting; but the woman with the baby is one of us, a copper, she was quite clear about what she saw.' He sat back and shook his head. 'In the ensuing chaos, nobody saw anyone running away but there's a CCTV camera on that corner and we've had a look at the footage. Directly behind you in the crowd waiting to cross was a hooded figure. They kept their head down so we couldn't see their face, nor could we see the assault but as you went flying forward, he... or she... pushed through the crowd and hurried away. Trawling through footage from various CCTV cameras in the area didn't show us where he went which is itself suspicious.' Fanshawe nodded. 'So, to answer your question, Mrs Chatwell, yes, we think someone tried to kill you. And as we don't believe in coincidence, we think it must have a connection somehow to the murder of Lucien Pleasant. What we're struggling to understand is what that connection could possibly be.'

Still in shock from the accident, reeling from the knowledge that it had been deliberate, Molly couldn't handle any more. A sob started deep inside, a few hiccups before it came loud and pathetic. And she couldn't stop.

She saw Fanshawe's expression turn from sombre to sympathetic to helpless in a series of slight facial movements that she normally wouldn't have noticed. She did now because in her whirling, swirling world, he seemed to be the only thing to anchor her.

He poked the unaffected Carstairs in the arm and whispered something Molly didn't catch, but whatever it was made him leave the room. Moments later, he returned with the nurse in tow.

'That's enough,' Edel said, holding the door open. She stood there with one hand on it, waiting for them to leave. 'Any further questions will have to wait.'

Fanshawe stood and with a brief sympathetic smile for Molly, he and Carstairs left the room. Edel shut the door firmly behind them, took a handful of paper tissues from a box and put them into Molly's free hand. 'I'll be back in a jiffy,' she said and vanished.

When she returned, there was a metal tray in her hand. 'This will help,' she said, putting it down on the bedside locker and injecting something into the intravenous bung in Molly's left hand. 'There you go,' Edel said, soothingly, adjusting the drip and standing back. 'You'll feel better in a minute.'

Molly hoped the nurse was right.

When Molly woke, the hypnotic beep from the monitor was once again reassuring. She opened her eyes slowly and glanced around the room, half-expecting to see Jack, unsure whether to be relieved or upset to see she was alone. A sigh made her wince slightly and reach a hand to hold her chest. Ah yes, she'd a vague memory of being told she'd broken a rib. She moved all her limbs one by one, feeling a lot of aches especially on her right side, but no severe pain. Whatever the nurse had given her had worked. Apart from the monitor, the room was quiet. Molly felt calm and drifted back to sleep.

When she woke again, she lay with her eyes shut, wondering if she could stay where she was until everything was sorted and her life had returned to normal. Expecting the room to be empty, she was surprised when she eventually opened her eyes to see Jack sitting in a chair beside the bed. He was slumped down, tie askew. She took in the pallor, the dark circles under his eyes, the angles on his cheek that were becoming more noticeable.

He looked worse than she felt.

When she saw the stubble on his chin, she wondered how long she'd been there and looked around for the time. It was on the bottom right corner of the monitor screen. 7am. She'd slept the afternoon and night away. Whatever the nurse had given her had worked; she wished she could take it with her, she hadn't felt so good in a long time. Drug-induced euphoria, it probably wouldn't last for long. She frowned. Everything was a blur, but she had a vague idea that the police had called to see her yesterday. She was still trying to puzzle it out when Jack opened his eyes and saw her awake.

'Thank God,' he said, moving over and taking her hand.

She squeezed his fingers and managed a reassuring smile. 'Have you been sitting there all night? I'm okay, Jack, honest. A broken rib, and lots of bruises, that's all.'

Lifting her hand, he planted a kiss on the back of it. She could feel the warmth of his breath on her skin as he struggled to control tears. 'The police said someone tried to kill you,' he mumbled, his lips still against her hand.

Of course! She remembered now. She reached her hand up to caress his head, brushing a lock of his hair back. 'That's what they're saying.' She smiled. 'Whatever drugs they're giving me are great, because I can't seem to care.'

His eyes bored into hers. 'Do they have any suspects? Witnesses must have seen something.'

'I don't know, I really can't remember much of what was said.'

'They're taking it seriously anyway. There's a uniformed officer outside your room.'

'Really?' Her eyes widened.

'That's why you're in this spacious private room too. The police insisted for security reasons. Normally, you'd still be on a trolley in A & E.'

'Something to be thankful for.' Her eyes were heavy, she shut them as Jack continued to hold her hand. 'I was supposed to be meeting Amelia,' she mumbled. 'She called around Friday morning.'

'Amelia?' His tone startled her into opening her eyes.

'What is it?'

He pressed his lips together for a moment before tightening his grip on her hand. 'Your life seems to have become a disaster since that weekend in Semington.'

Molly looked at him in dismay. Hadn't she been a little suspicious of Amelia? She tried to remember why, but her head was fuzzy.

Jack leaned closer. 'You go away for the weekend with her and get involved with a man who is then murdered. She calls on you and someone tries to kill you. It seems clear to me what the common denominator is.'

The fuzziness in her head cleared a little. Amelia. *Amazing brown eyes*, she'd said. That's what had started her suspicions. 'Yes,' Molly said vaguely.

'You have to tell the police,' Jack insisted, running a hand through his hair, his eyes bleak. 'They said they were coming back today. I gather you were still in shock yesterday when they tried to speak to you.'

Molly had a vague memory that she'd collapsed in a sobbing mess, but shock sounded better. They were coming back; she'd tell them her suspicions about Amelia.

There was a soft knock on the door, a nurse peered around the edge and came in when she saw Molly awake. 'I'm Jane,' she said, 'do you feel up to some breakfast?' She checked the monitor as she spoke, writing information on the clipboard as she waited for an answer.

'Coffee would be great.'

'And a slice of toast?' The nurse smiled. 'You'll feel a lot better if you eat something, you know.'

Smiling at her insistence, Molly agreed to try.

'Good, I'll go and get that sorted. Do you need pain relief? No, okay, let me know if you do. The police,' she added, 'said they'd be here to speak to you at ten. The consultant does his rounds about eleven, and we're anticipating he will discharge you home at that stage.'

'Discharge?' Jack looked at the nurse in disbelief. 'She was knocked down; she's got a broken rib for Pete's sake. There's no way she's ready to go home.'

Molly tried to grasp his arm, but he'd stood to confront the nurse. 'Jack, it's okay, I'll be better at home.'

The nurse spoke soothingly. 'Your wife is doing fine, Mr Chatwell. There is nothing to be done for broken ribs, except to take pain relief as needed and to be careful until they heal. She would be better off in the comfort of her home.' She threw a smile towards Molly, gave Jack a guarded look and left.

'Ridiculous,' Jack said when she'd left. He paced the room restlessly.

Molly was tired already. 'Why don't you go home and get some rest. I'll be depending on you to be alert later.'

He frowned. 'You sure you don't want me to be here when the police come?'

'Positive. Go home, get some sleep, then come back like a knight in shining armour and rescue me.'

It made him smile. 'I'll ride to your rescue, fair maiden.' He leaned down and planted a gentle kiss on her cheek. 'Stay safe until I get back.'

It was peaceful when he'd gone. She lay trying to think of nothing, slightly annoyed when the door opened.

The young man, who came through carrying a tray, introduced himself as Geoff. He put the tray on the bed table and pulled it within her reach. 'Can you manage everything?' he asked, fussing with the position of the cup and knife.

The aroma of coffee drifted toward her; she nodded gratefully and reached to pick up the cup. It was surprisingly good. The toast was freshly made; she spread butter and marmalade awkwardly with one hand and despite thinking she wouldn't, she ate the two slices.

She had almost finished the coffee, her mind once again wandering, when she was brought back to earth by a knock on the door. 'Come in,' she called, guessing it would be the two detectives she was starting to refer to in her head as *hers*.

DI Fanshawe smiled at her. 'You're looking a little better than yesterday at any rate,' he said, pulling a chair over to sit. 'You feel up to talking?'

'Yes,' she said, 'in fact, I have something interesting to tell you.'

'Oh?' he said, raising an eyebrow. 'Go ahead.'

DS Carstairs, sitting slightly behind, took out a tatty notebook and cheap pen and looked at her expectantly. She would have preferred to speak to Fanshawe alone. There was something about the sergeant that made her squirm. It was the way his eyes were constantly assessing her and finding her wanting.

Trying to ignore him, she took a steadying breath and told them about Amelia, the remark about the brown eyes that had started her suspicions, the fact that she'd called to her house on the very day she'd been knocked down. She debated adding her other worry; that everything had started going wrong in her life not, as Jack had suggested from the weekend in Semington, but from when Amelia and Tristan returned to London. It sounded so crazy, she decided against mentioning it. She didn't want to sound paranoid.

'She knew where you were going on Friday?' Fanshawe

asked.

'Yes, she suggested I should get a taxi and I remember saying that Casper's was only a few minutes' walk from the station.'

'Who else knew where you'd be?'

Molly picked up her empty coffee cup to delay answering until she gave it some thought. She'd forgotten all about Stuart and wondered how long he had waited for her. 'The friend I was meeting,' she said slowly, anticipating their next question, a slight colour already rising in her cheeks.

'And this friend is?'

Her hesitation made it look as if she'd something to hide, as did the stumble as she told them his name. 'Stu... Stuart Mercer, he's an old friend.'

'Friend?' Fanshawe looked at her. 'Or lover?'

Her cheeks flamed. She'd have loved to be able to use the phrase *what kind of woman do you think I am*, but unfortunately they already had a fair idea. 'A friend. To be precise, he's a work colleague of my husband's.'

'And Mr Chatwell knew you were meeting him? He knew you'd be in that café?'

'No, neither. I'd gone to meet Stuart because I'm worried about my husband. Jack is a very private man when it comes to his work, he wouldn't confide in me if he were having problems, so I thought I'd ask Stuart.'

Fanshawe looked at her with sudden interest. 'What kind of problems?'

Molly huffed in exasperation. 'I don't know, do I? I never got to meet Stuart thanks to whatever idiot tried to push me under that damn car.'

'So only two people knew where you were going to be?' Fanshawe said. 'Amelia Lovell and Stuart Mercer.'

Molly looked at him in horror. 'Stuart would have absolutely no reason to harm me.'

'That you know of,' Fanshawe said, unperturbed. 'Your suspicions of Amelia Lovell are based on a simple slip-up, brown eyes instead of turquoise. And that she happened to call upon you on the morning you were knocked down.' He held a hand up when he saw she was going to argue. 'I've been a detective for a long time, I've heard more preposterous ideas. I'm not ruling anything out yet.'

'You'll speak to her?'

'To her, and to Stuart Mercer.' Fanshawe stood. 'You're being discharged today. We don't have the manpower to post an officer outside your home, but I will ask for a car to pass down your street as often as possible.' He gave a quick smile. 'Which won't be often, I'm sorry to say. Go home, keep your house alarm on, don't go out alone, don't let anyone in. I assume your husband is collecting you?' When she nodded, Fanshawe handed her his card. 'This is my direct number. If you see or hear anything suspicious, ring me immediately.'

She looked at the card. Somebody wanted to kill her. It was a chilling thought. It was even more chilling to remember that somebody *had* murdered Lucien Pleasant.

'Will they try again?'

Fanshawe kept his eyes fixed on hers. 'We are working hard to pin down some connection between you and Pleasant. If it's there, we'll find it.'

'If it's there?' She put his card down on the bed table. 'If it's not, if it is some weird coincidence, then despite what that woman... that copper said... maybe my accident was simply that, an accident.'

'Maybe,' he said and with a final nod, he and Carstairs left.

'Maybe, my ass,' Molly muttered as the door clicked shut after them. A connection between her and Pleasant. Once again, she faced the only truth she could see, it had to be something to do with Amelia.

22

When the nurse returned to check she was comfortable, Molly asked about her phone. 'Was it damaged in the accident?'

Jane checked the monitor, updated her notes and moved to the small wardrobe in the corner of the room. 'Everything you had was put in here. Would you like me to have a look?'

'Please.'

'Here you go,' the nurse said, returning with a handbag. 'It's not in the coat pocket so maybe it's in here?'

'Thanks.' Molly took the bag, opened it and looked inside. Everything was as she'd left it, just as if someone hadn't tried to kill her. There was the usual glut of rubbish; old receipts, three lipsticks, a few old bills, and, finally in the bottom, her phone.

'There you go,' the nurse said with a smile. 'If you're okay, I'll leave you in peace. Professor Ludlow will be around in an hour or so. As soon as he gives the go-ahead, we can disconnect the monitor and the intravenous line.'

Molly checked her phone. There were several messages from Freya and Remi; she read them quickly and sent off a message to both with a lame excuse about letting the phone go flat and misplacing the charger to explain her unusual absence. They wouldn't question it.

There were a couple of missed calls from Stuart shortly after one o'clock on Friday and a text message sent at one thirty. *Assume something has come up, surprised not to be able to get hold of you. Hope all is okay, will try to ring again later.*

She sent a brief answer. *Sorry. Something unexpected happened. Will explain in a day or two.*

Throwing the phone on the bed, she stared across the room. Not one text from Amelia, not one call to ask why she hadn't turned up in O'Dea's. The police were going to speak to her. Maybe she'd confess that she was responsible, it would all be over, and Molly could go back to her mundane existence. After the last few days, she'd never knock mundane and conventional again.

She shuffled in the bed. There was no pain really, but everything ached. Including her head. Amelia might have been mixed up with Lucien Pleasant, she might even be having an affair with Jack, but did Molly really think she was capable of trying to kill her? And anyway, why would she want to? 'Arrgh,' she groaned, resting her head back. Perhaps it would be best if she left the detective work to the detectives.

She managed, despite everything, to fall asleep.

She was woken by the sound of the door opening, followed by footsteps and the nurse's voice asking if she was okay.

'Yes, I'm fine,' she said automatically. She shook off a momentary disorientation, her eyes flitting over the faces of the group of people who surrounded her bed. Junior doctors, she guessed, as an older man stepped forward to introduce himself.

Professor Ludlow was a small chubby man with a round, smiling countenance that made him look like a children's party entertainer rather than an eminent consultant. He spoke with her for a few minutes, his voice barely above a whisper. 'We are happy that you've made a complete recovery from your concussion,' he said. 'You may go home whenever you wish.' With a final polite smile, he and his entourage swept out of the room, leaving a nurse behind to remove the intravenous line, leads and monitor. Molly instantly missed its reassuring beep.

With the nurse's assistance, she walked to the bathroom and to the wardrobe. What was left of the clothes she'd been wearing hung there. 'I don't think I want to wear these,' she said with a shudder.

She sat in a chair with her hospital gown wrapped around her and listened as the nurse gave her a list of instructions before handing her a prescription for pain relief.

'You can get it filled downstairs,' she said. 'If you need more, you'll have to go to your GP.'

Molly blamed the medication she'd been given for making her feel woozy and disconnected. She'd get the prescription filled but hoped she wouldn't need to take them. There was paracetamol at home, that should be sufficient. As soon as the nurse left, she rang Jack. 'Come and get me and bring me something to wear, please. Something stretchy and comfortable.'

It was over two hours later before she stepped into the hallway of their house, Jack with his arm around her waist, refusing to move from her side until she was sitting on the sofa. He hovered around, insisting on lifting her feet onto the couch, taking off her shoes, tucking a blanket around her, plumping a pillow to put behind her head.

All she wanted, was to be left alone.

'I'd love a cuppa,' she said, hoping that if she gave him something to do, he'd leave her be.

In what seemed like seconds, he was putting a mug of tea on

the table beside her. 'Here you go, and I'll put your tablets here within reach. Make sure you take one when you need to.'

'Thank you.'

'It's going to take a while to get over the shock.' He perched on the arm of the chair.

'That someone tried to kill me?' She pulled up a smile that wavered and died. 'Maybe a little while.'

'You told the police about Amelia?'

'Yes, but I'm not sure they were convinced.'

He reached down to pat her leg. 'They'll find whoever is responsible.' He looked at her ruefully. 'Do you think you'll be okay on your own for a few hours? I know it's Sunday but I've an appointment to meet an investor. It was the only day he could meet.'

She'd been surprised when he'd turned up at the hospital in a suit rather than casual clothes. Now she understood why. Despite being relieved he was going, she was hurt that he wouldn't have cancelled his meeting. 'I'll be fine, I'll probably fall asleep in a while. Go. I'll see you later.'

As soon as she heard the door closing, she put the tea down and stood. She still felt a little woozy, but she'd do. Ignoring the pain medication she'd got from the hospital pharmacy, she went to the kitchen and found a packet of paracetamol. While she was on her feet, she got her handbag, took out her phone and plugged it in to charge. The inspector's card was tucked beneath it. She slipped it into her pocket.

Back on the sofa, she swallowed two pills with a sip of tea and leaned back. Her ribs hurt. They would do for a few weeks, according to that pleasant nurse who'd discharged her. But at least she could fool. If that car had hit her full on, she'd be lying in a morgue.

Pushing the cushion into a more comfortable position, she rested her head against it and closed her eyes. Some of the medication they'd given her in the hospital was probably still in her system because she felt incredibly tired. Her eyes drifted closed, and she felt herself falling into a deep sleep when the doorbell chimed, startling her awake. Immediately, her heart began thumping and a nervous tremor ran down her legs.

She wasn't expecting anyone. Whoever it was would soon go away when they saw no sign of life. But it rang again, for longer, stopping, then chiming again. Swearing softly, she struggled to her feet, wincing as her ribs complained. For a second, her head spun, and she thought she was going to faint. With a loud gulp and a deep breath, she crossed the room in her bare feet.

At the front door, she put her hand to the doorknob, then stopped. Someone had tried to kill her, maybe she shouldn't open it. She gave a quick look back to the living room, wishing she had her phone, wondering if she should ring the police. She was still trying to decide what to do when the sound of someone hammering the door knocker made her yelp with fright.

It was loud enough to alert the person on the other side of the door to her presence. 'Molly? Mol, are you there? It's me, Mol, Amelia. I've only just heard about your accident.'

Despite her suspicions, despite everything, all Molly could remember was the friend she'd known for so many years. Were her suspicions as preposterous as the inspector thought? Anyway, Amelia was hardly going to try to kill her in her own home. On that positive thought, she opened the door.

Amelia's concern seemed so genuine Molly felt tears well. 'Oh, Amelia,' she said, stepping back to let her inside, 'it's been awful.' Back in the living room, she made an attempt at hospitality. 'Would you like tea or coffee?'

'Sit down, for goodness sake, before you fall down,' Amelia said, throwing her coat across the back of a chair. 'Where's Jack?'

Almost embarrassed at his absence, Molly shrugged. 'He's

had to go to a meeting – just for a couple of hours. He didn't want to go,' she lied, 'but I insisted.'

Amelia raised an eyebrow. 'Odd,' she said, and waved towards the kitchen. 'I'll make some tea.'

'I'm feeling a little groggy, actually. I think it's the after-effects of the medication I had in the hospital.' Happy to leave Amelia to it, Molly sat and watched, weighing her up. Her fingers slid into her trouser pocket and felt for the inspector's card, flicking the edge of it rhythmically. Like a worry stone, it gave her a certain amount of relief.

Amelia bustled about the kitchen finding everything she needed and a few minutes later, carried a laden tray over to the coffee table. 'Tea, biscuits, cake that's a couple of days past its best before date but looks okay.' She smiled and took the seat beside her.

Molly didn't want anything, but she accepted the tea and biscuit that was handed to her, shaking her head at the cake. Taking a sip of the tea, she leaned forward and put it on the table. 'The police came to see you?'

Amelia nodded. 'A rather pleasant inspector, name of Fanshawe, and a rather creepy little man, whose name I can't recall.'

'Carstairs, I bet. He is creepy, isn't he? I thought it was because he didn't like me. He didn't approve of my seduction attempt.'

'Sanctimonious hypocrite.' Amelia reached for a slice of cake, looking at it suspiciously for a moment before taking a bite. 'It's okay,' she said, holding it up, 'you should have a piece.' When Molly shook her head, she reached out her free hand and rested it on her arm. 'Darling, what an ordeal you've had.'

'What did the police say?' Molly was curious as to what her friend knew.

'That you'd been in an accident. A hit-and-run, they said.'

She shook her head. 'Shocking. I did wonder why you hadn't turned up in O'Dea's, but I assumed you'd forgotten. You have been a bit absent-minded recently. Anyway, I met some friends, so I was okay.' Putting the empty plate down, she picked up her tea. 'The police wanted to ask me if I knew anything about this man you'd met, and if I'd told anybody you'd be running that morning.' She put her tea down, untouched, and looked sombre. 'They wanted to know if I knew of anyone who wanted to cause you harm. It's so odd, you know, you hear that question asked in crime dramas all the time. There was something so unreal about it.' She shook her head. 'Of course, there was nothing to say. You're probably the most inoffensive person I know. I told them you were almost strait-laced and that it was totally out of character for you to come on to any guy never mind some stranger you'd bumped into while out on a run.'

There was silence for a moment. Molly felt her friend's eyes on her, inquisitive, puzzled. She picked up her tea and drank it, waiting for her to speak.

'They don't really believe you were involved with his death, do they?'

'They might have done before someone tried to kill me, but I don't think they do anymore.' Molly smiled as her friend's mouth sagged. 'It wasn't an accident, you see,' she explained. 'Someone deliberately tried to push me under a car. It was lucky that I wasn't killed.'

'Someone tried to kill you?' Amelia looked at her in horror. 'Seriously? But why?' She got to her feet, paced the room and turned to look down on Molly. 'This is crazy. Why on earth would anyone want to murder you?'

Bizarrely, Molly almost felt insulted, as if in Amelia's estimation she wasn't important enough to be murdered. A wave of weakness rushed over her. She really couldn't handle any more. 'I'm sorry, I'm going to have to ask you to go, I need to lie down.'

Amelia rushed in with apologies. 'Of course, I shouldn't have stayed at all. I only wanted to make sure you were okay.'

Right at that moment, Molly wasn't sure of anything except she felt weak, she needed to go to the loo and she wasn't sure she'd manage on her own. 'I need to go upstairs,' she said, her words slurring slightly. 'We don't have a downstairs loo and I'm not sure I'm able to get up without help.'

'Oh, Molly, you poor thing!' Amelia took her arm and helped her to her feet.

Molly swayed, feeling an arm snaking around her back to support her as they moved across the room into the hallway. She wasn't sure she was going to make it. Jack had been right, she should have stayed in hospital.

'Hang onto the banisters,' Amelia said as they climbed the stairs. 'Hold on tightly, or we'll both fall.'

When Molly staggered out of the en suite a few minutes later, Amelia was leaning against the door frame. 'There's no point in going down again,' she said. 'You look exhausted. Get some sleep, I'll head off.'

Molly took the few steps to her bed and sat heavily.

'They were strong drugs the hospital gave you,' Amelia commented.

'They'll be out of my system soon.' Molly looked across the room at her friend. 'Why did you say the man I met had *amazing brown eyes*?'

Amelia frowned. 'What?'

'The other day… you mentioned them.' Molly felt worse than she had earlier; weaker, fuzzier. Her eyes widened in alarm as Amelia kept swimming in and out of focus.

Amelia. Had Jack been right, was she the key to everything? Molly had let her in and had drunk the tea she'd made. It was getting harder to stay focused. Amelia seemed very far away, her voice fading. But her eyes were still sharp; Molly could see them peering at her, assessing.

If Jack was right, Amelia wouldn't want to fail at this second attempt on Molly's life.

23

There was a heavy weight on Molly's chest. Panicking, she tried to push it off but she was caught under it and couldn't free herself. Gasping, she made one last effort, gave a firm push and felt the weight move. And then she was free – and immediately cold.

Opening her eyes, she saw the duvet she'd pushed to the floor. She'd been dreaming. How long she'd been asleep, she'd no idea, but it was almost dark, the room lit only by the street lights outside. She remembered thinking that Amelia had poisoned her and shut her eyes, opening them quickly when she realised, she'd still been there when she'd... what? Fallen asleep or collapsed?

Pushing up onto her elbows, Molly listened. There wasn't a sound to be heard. She reached for the lamp and clicked it on to look at her watch. Almost six. It would have been easier to stay where she was, but with a grunt she swung her feet to the floor and stood, keeping her hand on the bedhead until she was sure she wasn't feeling dizzy.

Letting out a breath, she rolled her shoulders. She felt better. Whatever they'd given her in the hospital had obviously worked its way out of her system. The idea that Amelia had tried to poison her, had been involved with Pleasant, surely it was all a product of her overtired and overstressed mind. Molly switched on the landing light and headed down the stairs. The door to the living room was shut but she could see a rim of light around the edges. Maybe Jack was home. Molly took a deep breath before she twisted the knob and quietly pushed open the door.

Amelia was sitting with her back to her. She had a magazine in her hands, legs crossed, one foot bouncing lazily.

'Hi,' Molly said.

The magazine went flying and landed on the floor with a loud smack. 'Bloody hell, you scared the wits out of me.'

'Sorry,' Molly said automatically even as she thought *there you go again with that bloody useless word*. 'I fell asleep.'

Amelia picked up the magazine and threw it onto the coffee table before going over to her. 'You didn't fall asleep,' she said, 'you passed out. There's a difference.'

'The medication the hospital gave me obviously didn't agree with me.' Molly dredged up a smile. 'I feel better after that sleep.'

'Well, you look awful. Come and sit down. I'll make you a cup of tea.'

Molly sat and listened as the kettle was filled and switched on. She seemed to be drinking a lot of tea and coffee these days.

Minutes later, a mug was put on the table in front of her.

'I really need to go,' Amelia said, checking her watch. 'I'm way overdue at a meeting.'

'Go, please, I'll be fine.' The suspicion of Amelia still lurked; Molly didn't want whatever was in the mug, and certainly wasn't going to drink it, but picking it up allowed her to switch her focus to it and hide her mistrust.

'Jack will be back soon, won't he? So, you *will* be okay.'

Looking up, Molly gripped the mug more tightly. 'Yes, of course.'

Amelia didn't look convinced. 'Maybe I should wait until he's here?'

'No please, go. I'm sure he'll be home soon. I'm going to finish my tea, then lie back and probably sleep again.'

'If you're sure.' Amelia picked up her coat and slipped it on.

Molly listened as Amelia's footsteps crossed the hall, the front door opened then closed. Finally, silence. Standing, Molly took the tea and threw it down the sink. What if she'd been right, that Amelia, for whatever reason, was trying to kill her? It was preposterous, ridiculous, but the truth was someone *had* tried. They'd failed. Wasn't it logical they'd try again?

Molly turned the tap on to wash all traces away. Rinsing out her mug, she spooned coffee in and filled it from the kettle.

'Damn,' she said, turning to stare into the sink. She should have kept it and given it to the inspector to have analysed. It would have confirmed her suspicion or set her mind at rest. Either would have been good. He'd probably have thought she was barking mad, but she wouldn't have cared. But it was too late.

She was considering whether she should ring the inspector and keep him up to date when the sound of the front door opening startled her, eyes wide and staring as she listened to the sound of heavy footsteps approaching the kitchen door. Panicking, she looked around, her hand reaching for the biggest knife attached to the magnetic strip on the wall. As she grabbed it, her hand slipped and the knife clattered onto the counter.

'Hi.'

Jack's voice. Of course, it was Jack. Letting her breath out in a whoosh, she turned and almost ran to him, feeling his arms close around her. Ignoring the twinge from her broken rib, she snuggled deeper into him as if to burrow for safety.

'You're okay,' he whispered into her hair. Resting his chin on her head, he continued to hold her.

In the safe circle of his arms, the trembling eased and the fear faded a little. After a few minutes, she pulled back and looked at him. 'Can you ever forgive me?' She kept her eyes fixed on his; she could tell so much from the light that glinted in them, sometimes baby-blue soft, sometimes almost steely-grey. When they turned soft, when he bent his head and planted a gentle kiss on her lips, she felt a release of the tension that was wound so tight it hurt more than her broken rib.

'What choice do I have?'

She'd have preferred a straightforward *yes,* but she wasn't in a situation where she could be picky. 'Thank you,' she said, resting her head on his shoulder.

'Are you feeling okay?' he asked, pushing her away gently. He took off his coat and draped it over the back of a chair. 'You look so pale.'

'I was feeling awful. Amelia had to–'

'Amelia?' he interrupted. 'What the hell was she doing here?'

Molly moved to the sofa and sat, her movements slow and laboured. Her side was painful, she needed to take more painkillers. 'She called around when she heard about the accident. We had tea and talked. Afterwards, I was feeling so weak, she had to help me up the stairs.'

There was no point in telling him that Amelia had made the tea and that she was afraid she might have put something in it. He'd think she was crazy.

'You look pale and tired,' Jack said. 'How about we go out somewhere for something to eat? A nice meal would be good for you.'

She put her hand over his. 'The police said I should stay indoors to be safe.'

He pulled away and shook his head. 'How long are we going

to have to live like this? It's crazy. Why would anyone want to murder you? I'd say you were in the wrong place at the wrong time. The police are making a huge leap in connecting your accident to the death of that man.'

She shut her eyes for a moment, trying to get her head clear. 'They said they don't believe in coincidences,' she said eventually, but Jack had gone to the fridge.

'Hang on,' he said, as he peered inside it. Shutting it, he took out his mobile. 'The fridge has milk, beer, and not a lot else. I'll order a takeaway. What would you like?'

'Indian, the usual dishes,' she said automatically, wondering why he bothered to ask. In all the years, they'd never ordered anything else. He rang it through as she sat staring at him, a slight frown between her eyes, her concerns about her own predicament fading a little as she took in his pallor.

He took the seat beside her again. 'Now, what were you saying?'

What had she been saying? She shook her head in frustration. 'I can't remember.'

He leaned forward and planted a kiss on her cheek. 'Try to stop worrying. Have you heard from the kids today?'

'Just messages.' She smiled. 'They're really busy. I'm going to try to Skype them tomorrow, it would be nice to see them. They seem to have settled down, both mentioned friends they were meeting.'

'Good,' he said, echoing her smile. 'I'm going to get out of my suit. The meal will be here in ten. If the doorbell rings, leave it, and I'll come down, okay?'

She reached a hand out, felt it clasped in his. 'I won't move.'

He raised her hand to his lips and gave it a kiss. 'Good, I'm going to spoil you until you're better.'

She was still smiling as she heard his step on the stairs. They'd be fine. Whatever was going on would be sorted and they'd get back on track. As for her suspicions, either the meds they'd given her in the hospital or the bang to her head were making her imagine things and jump to ridiculous conclusions.

The police would do their job and things would return to normal. Then she remembered something. Before she'd passed out, she clearly remembered asking Amelia why she'd mentioned Pleasant's *amazing brown eyes*. She'd never answered.

Maybe Molly was overthinking it all. Or maybe she was right, maybe Amelia and Lucien Pleasant weren't strangers at all. Taking out the inspector's card, she took her phone and put his number in under a speed dial key. With one stroke she could contact him.

She wished it made her feel safer.

24

Molly didn't say anything to Jack. There was no point in worrying him about her suspicions, especially since, she admitted with a shrug, they were so changeable. In the morning, she'd ring the inspector. Maybe by this stage he'd have more information to put her mind at ease.

They sat at the table to have their meal. Molly pushed food around her plate, trying to hide the fact that she'd no appetite. Looking across the table, she realised Jack had eaten even less. She opened her mouth to plead with him to tell her what was wrong but closed it again. Her brain was still too fuzzy, she couldn't deal with any more. 'I'm really not very hungry,' she said, pushing her plate away. 'I think I'll head to bed.'

Jack pushed his barely-touched plate away. 'I'm going to watch TV for a while. I'll sleep in the spare room so's not to disturb you when I come up.'

She stood and leaned down to kiss him on the cheek. 'Goodnight,' she said, unable to stop the grimace as she straightened.

'You should take one of the painkillers the hospital prescribed. Where are they? I'll go and get one for you.'

She shook her head. 'I put them in the bathroom cabinet. I'm not keen on taking them, Jack, they made me feel quite disconnected. The pain isn't that bad, really, I'll take a couple of paracetamols.'

He didn't look convinced. 'Promise me you'll take the stronger ones during the night if you need them.'

'I promise,' she said with a smile and headed off. He didn't need to know that she never wanted to take a tablet again, not even paracetamol. The pain would ease when she was lying down. It didn't, in fact, it was worse, but she decided she preferred the pain to the grogginess she remembered from earlier. She knew she was being silly, but her life was in such turmoil, she needed to keep as clear a head as possible.

Lying there, she listened to the distant murmur of the television, the sounds from the street outside, trying to concentrate on them rather than going over and over the events of the last few days. The fear had eased but she knew it was lurking, ready to strike. A smile curved her lips when she heard Jack's step on the stairs. He was trying to be quiet, but he never remembered the fourth step that squeaked despite several carpenters' attempts to fix it.

A hush settled over the house. From outside, there was still the muffled sound of the odd car passing that the triple glazing couldn't quite mute, a comfortable city sound that usually helped her drift off to sleep. But tonight it wouldn't come. Her brain might be mush, but it was restless mush. Had Amelia tried to poison her? She'd certainly felt worse after the tea, groggier, more disconnected. And there was Amelia's surely overdramatic reaction when she'd opened the door. Maybe, she hadn't expected her to appear.

Molly stared at the ceiling. Would Amelia really have risked killing her in her own home? Surely not. But a thought struck her as she closed her eyes. Amelia hadn't been expected. If she'd succeeded, nobody would know she'd been there and Molly's death would have been seen as a delayed reaction to the accident.

It was strange how perfect clarity seemed to come in the middle of the night as if, with all the external distractions gone, everything could slot into place. It was Amelia. Molly was sure of it.

An hour later, clarity had become fuzzy. After all, if they found her dead, they'd do a post-mortem and whatever weird drug she'd given her would show up, wouldn't it? Maybe there were drugs that didn't. She'd no idea. Anyway, what possible reason would her friend have for killing her? Exhausted, Molly fell asleep, unsure of anything.

She was surprised when she woke to find it was almost nine. There wasn't a sound in the house. Jack had probably gone to work. No doubt he'd looked in on her and saw she was asleep. He wouldn't have wanted to disturb her to say goodbye. Turning, moving very slowly, she slid out of the bed. She kept her right arm close to her damaged rib, relieved it was less painful. Pulling on a robe, she put her mobile in the pocket and crossed the landing to the spare bedroom. The door was open, the bed empty.

Downstairs, she found a note propped against the coffee jar. *I looked in on you and you were out for the count. Hope you have a good day. I'll ring later. Rest!*

Smiling, she crumpled it, threw it into the bin and reached for her phone. Two minutes later, after an embarrassing phone call to Dawson Marketing to explain that she had been in an accident and wouldn't be in for a few more days, she hung up and checked for messages. There were three: one each from Remi and Freya, and one from Amelia.

Her children sent the usual messages of reassurance. They were having a great time. Some part of her world was ticking by the way it was supposed to.

Over a breakfast of toast and coffee she read the one from Amelia. There was nothing worrying in the short message, *hope you're feeling a little better, I'm here if you need me.* Molly put the phone on the table beside her and sat a moment with her brow furrowed before reaching for it and pressing the speed dial key for DI Fanshawe.

'Fanshawe.' His voice was deep, calm. Reassuring.

Molly felt herself relax. 'Detective Inspector Fanshawe, it's Molly Chatwell.'

'Good morning, Mrs Chatwell. I hope you're recovering. What can I do for you?'

She took a deep breath and let it out noisily. 'Amelia Lovell came around yesterday,' she said, keeping her voice steady with difficulty. 'I think she may have tried to kill me again.'

Molly expected a quick response, horrified words, sympathy. Instead, there was a long silence. 'Inspector, did you hear what I said?'

Did she imagine it or was the tone of his voice less friendly? 'Yes, I heard you.' There was another brief silence before he spoke again. 'It's probably better if I come and see you.' There was the sound of muffled voices, the clunk as a drawer was shut, a rattle she couldn't identify, and a deep indrawn breath she certainly could. 'I'll call this afternoon, about four.'

He hung up before she could argue. She glared at her mobile and dropped it on the sofa. Four... a whole day to get through. She'd have a shower and get dressed, cling to the normality of routine. Her phone beeped as she reached the door. She turned with a grunt, wanting to ignore it, incapable of doing so. Then she was sorry she hadn't. It was a text from Stuart Mercer.

We have to meet. ASAP.

A long groan escaped her. This was too much to take on now. She tapped out a short message, *I'm afraid not,* then deleted it and wrote, *Meet you tomorrow in Casper's. At eleven?* She pressed send and stood waiting for a reply. It came within seconds. *See you then.*

She was probably crazy to go; she gave a quick laugh – certainly crazy to go to Casper's but it was the first name that had popped into her head. Or maybe it was a touch of bravado. She wasn't sure. Anyway, it would be good to forget about her mixed-up life for a while and focus on Jack's problems. He had been so understanding, she owed him. Hopefully, Stuart would be able to tell her what was going on.

If by sorting out whatever was troubling Jack would help him completely forgive her, that was okay too.

25

After her shower, she pulled on jersey trousers, baggy from years of washing, and a soft, well-washed cotton jumper. Comfortable staying-at-home clothes. She stretched out on the sofa, finished the book she'd been reading, then switched on the TV and found a movie to watch, following it with another. When the doorbell rang, she checked the clock. Five minutes past four.

The doorbell had rung a second time as she struggled to her feet and made the journey to the front door.

'You should check who it is before opening up,' DI Fanshawe said, stepping into the hallway, his eyes sweeping over her. He pointed at the security chain. 'You have one, why don't you use it?'

Ignoring him, she led the way back to the living room and sat. 'If you want tea or coffee,' she said, 'help yourself.'

'We're okay,' the inspector said, taking a seat beside her while DS Carstairs sat opposite. 'How're you feeling, or is that a silly question?'

'It's a silly question,' she said, then shook her head. 'Sorry, you were being polite, and I was being rude. I feel pretty crap if you must know although the pain isn't quite so bad.' She could feel her eyes filling and rubbed them roughly. She would *not* cry.

'Why don't you tell me what it was you wanted to tell me,' he said gently.

It was tempting to say, *no, you go first*, but her life had already descended into a farce, it didn't need any more help from her. Slowly, she told him about Amelia's visit, the tea she'd made for her, the weakness that had come over her shortly afterward and Amelia's surprised reaction when she'd come downstairs.

'You think she poisoned you?'

Molly rubbed her eyes again. 'I was so sure last night but today...' She looked at him. 'I've lived a very ordinary life, Inspector, it didn't equip me for coping with all that's been thrown at me.'

He smiled. 'You're doing okay. It's not surprising your mind is in a whirl and you're second guessing yourself the whole time. You've done the right thing, you've told us.'

She nodded, pleased that he appeared to be taking her seriously. She brushed away the small part of her that had hoped he'd say she was being ridiculous. 'You think I'm right, that she tried to poison me?'

He rubbed the back of his neck.

'You look as if you need coffee,' she said, and made to stand.

'Stay,' Fanshawe said. 'DS Carstairs is a dab hand at making coffee.'

He was, as it turned out, and also an expert in finding where the biscuits were. He didn't, she noticed, bring the out-of-date cake.

Once they had coffee in hand, Fanshawe explained what was happening in the investigation. 'We spoke to Ms Lovell yesterday. She appeared shocked on hearing about your accident.' He held a hand up when he saw Molly was going to interrupt. 'Yes, I'm aware she could have been putting on an act, but I'm a very good detective. We've found no link between her and our friend Pleasant.' Fanshawe gave her a sympathetic look. 'It might be because there isn't one there, Mrs Chatwell.'

Molly looked at him for a moment without speaking. 'Maybe,' she said, trying to make sense of the ideas swirling around her head, 'maybe they were partners, and when he didn't succeed with his blackmail attempt on me, she killed him and then, full of remorse, she tried to kill me as a kind of revenge.'

Colour rushed over her cheeks when she heard Carstairs chuckle. She threw him an angry look before concentrating on the inspector. 'It could have happened like that, couldn't it?'

Ignoring the repeated chuckle from the other side of the room, Fanshawe said, 'It is hard for you to remain objective; you've been through a lot the last few days. Remember, we'll be looking into every aspect.'

'So what happens now?'

'The investigation continues. We'll keep digging and hopefully come up with a connection between you and Pleasant that makes sense. Until then, stay inside, safe.' He stood. 'As soon as we have anything concrete, we'll be in touch.'

There was no point in telling him she was planning to go out the next day, to the very area where she'd been knocked down. He'd think she was crazy. Irresponsible. And he'd be right on both accounts. But she was worried about Jack. She had considered sending Stuart a message and asking him to come to Elystan Street. There was a time when she wouldn't have thought twice about it but that was before Lucien Pleasant. Her judgement had been called into question; she wasn't taking any more chances.

She insisted on getting up to show them out. 'It's good to keep moving around. Thank you for keeping me updated.' Ignoring Carstairs, she held her hand out to Fanshawe. When he shook it briefly, she added a smile. 'And thanks for listening to me.'

'Part of my job,' he said. 'Stay safe.'

She watched them walk up the street before shutting the door and returning to the living room. She'd been pleasantly surprised about how forthcoming they were with information. Her previous experience with the police was courtesy of TV shows, where victims were normally kept in the dark.

No doubt there were things they weren't telling her, just as she hadn't told them she was going to Casper's the next day.

She checked her watch. Five twenty. Jack would be home after six. She looked at the sofa. The pains and aches were starting to take over. If she sat, she wasn't sure she could get up again. A medicinal glass of wine might do the trick.

Gathering anything she might need: her laptop, phone and the remote control, she placed them all on the coffee table before fetching a large glass of wine and settling down onto the sofa, lifting one leg after the other and resting her head back on the cushion.

She took a mouthful of wine before opening her laptop. There was no need to check the local time. If Freya or Remi were available, they'd answer her Skype call no matter what time it was. Freya answered almost immediately.

'Maman!'

She was lying on her bed, her hair in a ponytail, looking wonderful. Molly's heart leapt. 'Hello darling,' she said, 'what time is it there?'

'C'est sept heure, Maman,' Freya replied.

Molly had enough schoolgirl French to understand that it was seven o'clock but she would be quickly out of her depth if her daughter continued to show off her language ability. 'Everything okay?'

Luckily, excitement required her daughter to revert to

English in order to perfectly explain what an amazing time she was having. Finally, she paused. 'You don't look too hot, Mum.'

Luckily, Molly had prepared an answer should either of her children enquire. 'I've the flu,' she said, 'almost over it, actually, so nothing to worry about.'

'Oh, that's okay then. Look after yourself.' Freya spoke to someone out of sight before turning back to Molly. 'I have to go, Mum, we're heading out for dinner.'

'Have a good time, don't forget to send a message every day so we know you're okay.'

'Mai oui, Maman,' her irrepressible daughter said before the screen went dead.

Molly sat back with a satisfied smile on her lips. Freya looked good, her eyes were bright, her mouth always ready to curve in a smile. She was one of nature's happy people; Molly would have liked to coddle her, to protect her from a world that didn't necessarily treat people well. Instead, both she and Jack had encouraged her to follow her dreams to the Sorbonne.

There was no answer from Remi. Scrunching up her eyes, Molly tried to remember what time it was in Boston. Five or six hours behind. He was probably in class. She left a message asking him to Skype when he was free, adding that she was home all day with the flu. It made it simpler to tell the same lie to both children.

Remi, she guessed, would send a quick message rather than Skype. It was enough.

She shut the laptop and slid it under the sofa, the movement causing her to wince. She was being stupid; she should take some damn painkillers. Instead, she reached for the wine. She switched on the TV, hoping to find something to divert her attention, pleased to find *Thor*. It was her guilty secret, she absolutely loved Marvel movies. She'd seen it before; they'd gone to Cape Town for a holiday and it had been one of five movies she'd watched on the twelve-hour flight while Jack snored quietly beside her.

It was complete escapism. She sipped her wine, relaxing for the first time. The police had her case in hand. The next day, she'd find out what Stuart had to say and hopefully, it would throw some light on Jack's worries. Until then, she'd say nothing. Tonight, when he got home, she'd ask him to order a takeaway again and they could relax and watch TV together. There was no point in bringing anything up until she had some facts. And anyway, she didn't have the energy. She'd find some before the morning.

26

If Jack objected to having a takeaway again, he said nothing. Apart from asking Molly if she was feeling a little better, he barely spoke the whole evening.

'How's Charlie?' she asked, searching for a safe topic of conversation and anyway genuinely interested in how he was coping with his break-up.

Jack pushed his plate away and shrugged. 'Charlie isn't the kind of man to let a little thing like his wife walking out on him interfere with his life.'

'Zara walked out on him? They seemed such a happy couple.'

'That's you all over,' Jack said, with a faint sneer. 'You see what you want to see. Everything in your garden is always rosy, always so damn perfect.'

Molly put her fork down and pushed her half-eaten meal away. 'You make it sound like a bad thing, Jack.'

He reached for his beer. 'No, I'm sorry. Sorry, okay, I've had a tiring day.'

While she'd been sitting around recovering from having

been pushed in front of a car. The unfairness of it all stung. If he was tired, she was physically and mentally exhausted.

'I'm going to bed,' she said abruptly, getting to her feet. She picked up her plate, then put it down again. Okay, he didn't want her to be perfect, she'd leave the damn thing where it was. It was childish, and it might have made her smile if she hadn't felt so miserable.

'You're obviously in pain, take some of the painkillers the hospital prescribed you,' he said, reaching out to caress her arm.

She took some comfort in his touch and put her hand over his. 'Yes, I might do. Goodnight.'

The tablets sat on one of the shelves of the bathroom cabinet. They'd probably help her sleep but she remembered the disconnected feeling she'd experienced after the pain relief she'd had in the hospital and shook her head. She was meeting Stuart in the morning, she wanted to be sharp. Instead, and with reluctance, she took a couple of paracetamols. They were enough to take the edge off the ongoing discomfort, but still she slept fitfully, waking finally at five, unable to drift back to sleep.

She lay quietly and listened as the house woke; the rattle and hiss of the central heating, the creak of the floorboards, and finally the hum of the electric shower that told her Jack was up. He'd slept in the spare room again. 'In case I might hurt you unintentionally,' he'd said. She'd not had the energy to argue with him.

Only when she heard the front door shutting, did she push herself gingerly from the bed, relieved to be feeling a little better. A peek through the window told her the weather, at least, was in her favour. It was a blue-sky day; she wouldn't need to battle with an umbrella.

By the time she'd showered and dressed, it was almost nine. She debated taking some more paracetamol but decided against. If nothing else, the aches and pains kept her focused. Unable to drag up any enthusiasm for food, she drank coffee as she watched the clock and wondered what it was that Stuart was so desperate to tell her.

At ten, she pulled on her coat. It wouldn't normally take her an hour to get to Casper's, but she needed to walk slowly, too many parts of her body ached to move with speed. She took a different road; crossed in a different place, but fear shadowed her from the moment she left Victoria station and she was almost in tears by the time she saw the café loom into view.

What an incredibly stupid idea this had been. There were thousands of places she could have suggested meeting Stuart. Stupid bravado, it would be the death of her. What on earth was she trying to prove? A tremor ran through her as she pushed open the door and stepped inside.

She was surprised that Stuart had agreed to meet her here. He must know about what had happened on Friday by now. Even if Jack hadn't told him, he'd have no doubt mentioned it to someone in the office and the story would have spread. Scanning the café, she saw he hadn't yet arrived. It wasn't quite eleven, she was early.

Early, but the café was busy and there was only one table free in the far corner with a minefield of tables and chairs to shuffle around before reaching it. Finally, she pulled out one of the chairs and used the edge of the table to balance her descent, grimacing as she settled down, wondering at the same time if she was going to be able to get up again.

A waiter appeared before she'd time to even look at a menu. It didn't matter, she knew what she wanted. 'A large Americano,' she said. She'd have liked, despite the early hour, to have ordered a large glass of wine but she needed to keep her wits about her – no medication, no alcohol.

She looked around as she waited. It hadn't changed much since her last visit several years before. Wooden tables of various sizes were still surrounded by an eclectic mix of old chairs, but with a nod to comfort that was new there were now floral-patterned chair pads on each. The cream painted walls were hung with art for sale; some very good, some not, the same as it had been then. It was like stepping back in time.

With a smile of reminiscence, she picked up the menu; the food had always been classic, and good. She scanned it and closed it with a snap. It too, hadn't changed much, perhaps more vegetarian options, and a lot of sourdough bread and avocado but otherwise much as it had been. But her appetite wasn't, and she wasn't tempted to order anything to eat.

Her coffee arrived and there was still no sign of Stuart. She checked her watch, sipped her coffee, then checked again. Ten past eleven. Where was he? It wasn't until fifteen minutes past, that he bustled in the door, a frown between his eyes, a grim tightness pursing his lips.

When he saw her, his expression relaxed and he rushed over to her table, bending down to plant a kiss on each cheek as if they were old friends. 'I'm so terribly sorry,' he said, taking the seat opposite. 'Something came up as I was about to leave.'

She indicated her coffee. 'I've kept myself company. And at least *you* turned up.'

He smiled. 'True.' He lifted a hand to attract the waiter's attention. 'A double espresso, and an avocado and brie sandwich on granary bread.' Stuart grinned at Molly's surprise. 'I never look at the menu, I have the same thing every time I come. Are you going to have anything to eat?'

'No, but another Americano would be good.'

The waiter nodded, reached for her empty cup and left.

Stuart sat back and looked at her with critical eyes. 'If you don't mind me saying so, you don't look at all well. And you've lost weight since the party.' He leaned closer and dropped his voice. 'Is everything okay?'

She frowned. He didn't know. 'I thought you'd have heard,' she said. 'Even if Jack hadn't had a chance to tell you, I would have thought the news would have spread around the office by now.'

He shook his head. 'You're talking in riddles, Molly.'

'The reason I didn't turn up the last time. I *was* on my way to meet you, but I was knocked down. The police think someone deliberately pushed me in front of a car.' As Stuart's eyes widened in horror, she attempted a smile that wavered on one corner of her mouth before fading. 'I broke a rib, have more bruises than I can count, and ache all over, but apart from that I'm okay.'

Stuart ran a hand over his mouth and shook his head. 'Seriously? Someone tried to hurt you?'

She wanted to correct him. Someone had wanted to kill her, but his disbelief brought a weary chuckle and she let it go. 'Seriously! I appear to have got mixed up with the wrong kind of people.'

The arrival of the coffees and sandwich gave Stuart a moment to recover. 'For goodness' sake,' he said, looking around anxiously. 'Should you be out?'

She shrugged. 'The police told me to stay indoors, but I don't feel any safer there. I thought meeting you would take my mind off things.' She leaned both arms on the table, the cup of coffee between her hands. 'Why did you want to meet me?'

Stuart, in the act of taking a bite of his sandwich, stopped, put it down and groaned. 'How can I tell you bad news, after what you've told me?'

Molly's fingers tightened on the handle of the cup. *Bad news.* Across the table, Stuart had picked up his sandwich again and was making inroads into the first half. Why had she never noticed his weak chin before, his rather watery blue eyes? 'Well,' she said, her voice sharp, 'I know there's something going on. Jack has been so stressed recently but he won't talk about it. Now you've told me there's bad news. It would be kinder to tell me the details, rather than leaving me guessing, wouldn't it?'

'Okay, let me finish this,' he said, picking up the second half of his sandwich, his eyes avoiding hers.

She wanted to grab it and throw it across the room. Worryingly, she wanted to grab *him* and throw *him* across the room. The thought made her smile briefly. She didn't know herself these days. Finishing her coffee, she waved a hand for the waiter and this time ordered a double espresso. It came as Stuart finished the last of his sandwich. Adding a few grains of sugar to her coffee, she stirred it before saying quietly, 'Tell me.'

He pushed his plate away. Picking up his coffee, he took a sip and put it down before he met her eyes. 'Jack couldn't have told me about your accident, Molly. He hasn't been in the office in over a week.'

She choked on her coffee, coughing and spluttering, her hand going automatically to hold her ribs. It was a few seconds before she was in control. Ignoring the eyes that had swivelled to stare, she took out a tissue, wiped her eyes, held her arm tightly against her ribs and gave another cough. 'Sorry,' she said, 'what do you mean he hasn't been in the office? He goes every morning.'

Stuart shook his head. 'I don't know where he's going but it's not into work. He was suspended.' He wiped a hand over his mouth, brushing away crumbs. 'The details are being kept hush-hush, but it has to be something pretty serious. The company doesn't suspend willy-nilly, it's bad for morale and makes investors nervous.'

A wave of dizziness swept over Molly, forcing her to shut her eyes. The coffee churned in her stomach and, for one awful second, she was afraid she was going to eject the lot.

'Bloody hell,' Stuart squealed, seeing her colour drain away. 'Don't faint on me!'

She dropped her head into her hands and took some deep breaths.

After a few minutes, when the churning had stopped and the dizziness eased, she lifted her head, reached for a serviette and wiped her face. She stared across the table with dislike. 'God forbid, I should embarrass you, Stuart. Now tell me the rest.'

'That's it,' he said.

He was lying. It was obvious in the shifty way he wouldn't meet her eyes. She wasn't in the mood to be polite. 'Don't lie,' she said bluntly and watched as he pretended to look outraged. 'You may as well tell me. If you don't, I'm going into the office. I'll ask to speak to the CEO, tell him what you've told me, and ask him to elaborate.'

His mouth turned down when he saw she was deadly serious. 'I should never have contacted you,' he muttered. 'I should have minded my own business.'

'Yes, but you did contact me, so finish it.' She pushed her empty coffee cup away, leaving her hand resting on the table. His pale-blue eyes darted around the café. She wasn't sure if he was checking to see if there was anyone listening or searching for the fastest route out. 'Oh, get on with it, Stuart,' she said, losing what little patience she had left.

He licked his lips nervously and leaned a little closer. 'Fine. You mentioned Jack's frequent business trips to Las Vegas.'

Was he going to tell her Jack had a mistress there? 'Yes, so?'

'The company doesn't do any business in Vegas, Molly. There were tentative enquiries, a few meetings, but it didn't work out.'

This wasn't what she expected. She laughed uncertainly.

'Don't be ridiculous. You've spent so long in Hong Kong you're out of the loop, Stuart, you said it yourself.'

He reached out and gripped her hand. 'We do business in New York, Boston and Seattle. Not in Vegas. After the initial talks fell through, the idea was shelved.'

She looked down at his hand. 'But he's been away several times–'

'He's been *sick* several times in the last year,' Stuart interrupted her. 'I'd take a guess that if I looked at the dates, they would coincide with the dates you said he was in Vegas.'

Pulling her hand away, she sat back and crossed her arms. 'This is all ridiculous.'

'I've heard rumours in the office. Does Jack have a gambling problem?'

A gambling problem? 'Of course not!' Her voice was firm. Jack didn't have a gambling problem. She'd know if he had. Wouldn't she? A little voice whispered nastily, *the way you knew he'd been suspended.* 'I don't know,' she admitted with a gulp. She wanted to add that she didn't know anything anymore, but she was afraid she would fall apart and never be able to put herself together again. 'I'll speak to him,' she said, standing abruptly. Too abruptly. She gasped at the sudden pain, putting a hand on the table to steady herself, hearing, as if at a vast distance, Stuart asking if she was okay. She rode the pain out, waiting until it eased before straightening slowly.

'I'll be fine,' she said. She should thank him, she supposed, but looking down at him, she saw a glimmer of pleasure in his eyes and knew that his motivation for telling her wasn't completely selfless. Jack had never liked him very much, she remembered. What was it he'd said, *Stuart had an ulterior motive for everything he did.*

'Maybe we could meet for a drink after work soon,' he said. 'Or dinner?'

When hell freezes over! 'That would be lovely. I'll give you a ring.' She almost ran from the café, only realising when she got outside that she hadn't paid her bill.

It brought a brief smile to her lips but then she considered what Stuart had told her.

Jack had been suspended. He was making multiple trips to Vegas for reasons that had nothing to do with work.

He'd been lying to her. For months. Maybe for years.

27

By the time Molly arrived home, she felt as if she'd been knocked down again. Despite walking slowly and taking care not to be crushed or pushed on the tube, every part of her ached. It would have been sensible to take some painkillers but even though she popped two paracetamols from the packet, she couldn't bring herself to swallow them and threw them into the rubbish with a groan of despair.

Too much coffee had made her jittery and given her heartburn. She took milk from the fridge, poured a glass and drank half straight off. Taking the rest, she lay down on the sofa, kicked off her shoes and tried to relax. There was no point in going over and over what Stuart had told her, she needed to speak to Jack.

Taking out her mobile, she rang his number. It wasn't a surprise when it went straight to answerphone and she was invited to leave a message. He went to so many meetings, his phone was frequently turned off. Except, according to Stuart, he wasn't going to meetings at all. Where the hell was he?

She composed a text asking Jack to ring her but deleted it

without sending. She didn't want him phoning and telling more lies. It was better to wait until he came home.

The feeling of weakness that had swept over her earlier returned. Unsurprising, since she'd hardly eaten anything recently. Struggling to her feet, she went to the fridge and peered inside. Almost hidden behind bottles of beer, she found some hummus only a day past its best-before date. She made tea and toast, took everything to the coffee table and lowered herself onto the sofa. The hummus was a good choice; she spread it on the toast and ate the two slices before sitting back with her mug of tea.

A ding from her phone told her she had a message. It was from Jack. He must have seen a missed call from her. *Meetings all day. You okay? Text if you need anything, x*

The lie made her stomach heave; she made it to the sink before vomiting all she'd eaten, the spasm causing her to flinch and clasp her ribs. She turned on the tap, closing her eyes as the undigested food swirled around the basin before being washed away. She scooped water from the tap with her hand, rinsed her mouth and spat. When the taste of vomit had been washed away, she splashed water on her face a few times before grabbing a towel to dab it dry.

Her head was thumping, her legs wobbly. She filled a glass with water and stumbled over to the sofa. A chill ran through her as she lay down, tired and worn out. She reached for a blanket that lay folded across the arm of the sofa, pulled it across and wrapped it around herself. Then, with a grunt of despair, she rested her head back and shut her eyes.

Exhaustion won over pain, and within a few minutes she'd drifted into a restless sleep.

When she finally woke, the room was in darkness. She reached for her phone, surprised to see it was almost seven. Jack was unusually late.

Especially since he wasn't working.

She checked for messages, but there were none. Pressing the speed dial button for him, she listened to his voice asking her to leave a message. Instead of hanging up, as she usually did, she said, 'Jack, it's Molly. Where are you? Ring me, please.' Her forehead creased in worry as her fingers flew across the keypad to send a message saying the same thing.

By eight o'clock, she was frantic, her mind working overtime. What if he'd had an accident? Horror coursed through her. Maybe whoever had tried to kill her had decided to go after him? There was no logic in it, but then there had been no logical reason for someone trying to kill her.

She looked at the speed dial number for DI Fanshawe and was about to press it when her phone rang. Startled, she yelped and dropped it to the floor, bending with difficulty and groaning as she scrabbled for it, finally picking it up and answering. 'Hello, hello?'

'Molly, it's me.'

A sob escaped before she could stop it. 'Jack! Where the hell are you? I've been going crazy worrying.' He didn't reply for a moment. In the background she could hear voices, noises. Wherever he was, it was busy.

'I'm sorry,' he said, his voice almost lost in the noise. 'I'm in the Hyde Hotel. Can you come here?'

'What? Jack, what on earth's going on? I can't go haring off to a hotel. I've been injured, remember; I ache all over. Why on earth can't you come home?' There was more commotion on the line. Pressing the phone as closely as she could to her ear, she was still unable to make out what was happening.

'Please come here, Molly, ask for me at reception. I'll explain everything.'

The line went dead. Staring at it, she pressed redial. It went straight to answerphone. This was crazy. She had no intention of going. Where on earth was the Hyde Hotel anyway? She did an internet search, finding it within seconds. Not simply the Hyde Hotel.

He'd left out the Casino bit. The Hyde Hotel and Casino.

Gambling. It appeared Stuart was right.

28

Molly tried Jack's number again but as before it went to answerphone. Perhaps, bringing her to a casino was his way of showing her what was going on. It didn't look as if she'd much choice, she had to go.

One thing was certain, she wasn't going to take the tube and risk getting pushed and shoved by revellers. She wasn't sure there was much point in trying to get a taxi, not at that hour, but she dialled a number she knew on the off-chance she might be lucky. In two hours, she was told, hanging up with a grunt of frustration.

It looked like she'd no choice here either, she'd have to take the car. She slipped on the shoes she'd kicked off a few hours before, picked up her coat and keys and headed out, wondering if she'd make it. The car was further away than she remembered, either that or her laboured gait made every minute seem longer. Finally, she was there, lowering herself into the driver's seat. Luckily, the BMW was an automatic, so it made driving a little easier. She'd have to make sure she parked near the hotel.

She'd written the satnav co-ordinates on her hand, she inputted them and groaned when she saw the hotel was on

Eastbourne Mews, near Paddington station. The traffic would be manic. Gripping the steering wheel, she took a deep breath, indicated and pulled out.

It didn't take long to discover she'd grossly underestimated the situation. It wasn't merely manic; it was mayhem and madness. Added to that, the satnav directions were confusing, and she went the wrong way several times, almost crying with relief when it eventually told her she'd *reached her destination on the left*. The hotel and casino loomed large on the relatively narrow street. There had been no expense spared on neon lights, it looked garish and tawdry.

To the left of the hotel, a smaller neon light pointed out a downward ramp to the underground car park. Unfortunately, a large sign standing dead centre of the entrance told her bluntly it was *full*. She swore loudly and reversed, almost hitting a car behind. A hand raised in apology, she moved forward again, hitting the sign and knocking it flat. It seemed like an omen. She drove over it and headed down the ramp into the car park.

The sign hadn't lied, every row was indeed full. Desperate, she parked in front of a door marked *maintenance.* Ignoring the *no parking* signs, she got out and moved away as fast as she could before someone arrived to take her to task. She pushed open a door into the hotel and followed signs for reception down narrow, brightly-lit corridors until she reached a large bustling lobby.

She'd never been anywhere like this before; it was heaving with people, most of whom appeared to be laughing uproariously, the noise level deafening. Numerous neon arrows in garish colours pointed towards the far side of the lobby where a rainbow of flashing lights arching over a door advertised the casino entrance. In case anyone was in any doubt, the word itself was written in strobe lighting on each side of the double doors.

Standing with her mouth slightly ajar, her eyes scanned the

raucous mass of people that stood between her and the reception desk. Going through them wasn't an option. Instead, she took the longer route, sliding around the side of the room.

Reaching the desk, she leaned against it.

A tall, dark-haired woman with striking cheekbones smiled at her. 'Can I help you?'

'I'm looking for Jack Chatwell.'

'Ah, yes, Mr Chatwell,' the receptionist said as if the name was well known to her. 'Is he expecting you?'

'Yes.'

The receptionist checked her computer and immediately dialled a number. 'There's someone here to see you, Mr Chatwell.'

Molly wanted to point out that she wasn't *someone*, she was his wife. But the woman's smile was friendly and her eyes kind, so Molly kept quiet and waited.

'He asked if you'd go up. Room 353, third floor. The lift is behind you.'

With a nod of thanks, Molly turned, waited while a very loud group of women crossed in front of her, and made her way to the lift.

There was a second, standing outside room 353, when she didn't want to knock, didn't want to find out the truth. She knew it was going to come with pain. But there wasn't much point putting it off, it was going to come whether she liked it or not.

Jack answered the door on the first knock, reaching for her and pulling her inside. He'd obviously forgotten about her ribs, his arms squeezing far too tightly and making her cry out.

'Oh God, I'm sorry,' he said, pulling back to look at her, concern in his eyes. 'I forgot. I've hurt you.'

She pushed his hands away and walked further into the room, her eyes widening when she saw its size. 'Bloody hell,' she said, 'this must be costing a fortune.'

Instead of answering, he strode to a seat by the window and picked up a drink. 'Have a whisky,' he said, taking a sip.

She shook her head. 'I'm driving. I didn't want to travel by tube, and you know how impossible it is to get a taxi at this time of night.'

'Of course,' he said, swirling his drink before raising it to his lips.

She stared at him. How much had he drunk? His expression was set, his eyes steely. With sudden intuition, she knew whatever he was going to tell her it was bad. He didn't seem in any hurry, but she wanted it over. 'I met Stuart Mercer today,' she said. 'In fact, it was him I was going to meet on Friday.'

His eyebrow rose at that. 'I'd assumed it was Amelia.'

'No, Stuart. He'd asked to meet me then, and again this morning. So, I went.' She walked to the bed, her hand moving automatically to test the mattress. 'Comfortable,' she said before turning and sitting on it. 'Why didn't you tell me you'd been suspended, Jack? Why did I have to hear it from him?'

'You know, I never liked Stuart,' Jack said, 'he always was a smug bastard.' He finished the whisky and put the glass down with a clatter that told her he'd had quite a bit to drink. 'I didn't tell you because I didn't want you to worry. It's a storm in a teacup. It'll be sorted.'

'Stuart said it's been over a week.'

'These things take time.'

If he was going to keep speaking in clichés they weren't going to get anywhere. 'Tell me what's going on,' she said, trying to keep the note of pleading from her voice. 'Why did you bring me here?'

He waved both arms around the room. 'Isn't it nice? I thought you'd like to get out of the house for a while. We can go for dinner, maybe pay a visit to the casino.'

She ran a hand through her hair in frustration. 'What? You

brought me here to have fun? I told you how badly I felt, Jack. I only came because I thought you were going to...' She wanted to say *confess* but thought better of it. 'Stuart has heard rumours, he said you might be gambling.' She saw Jack's lips tighten.

'Stuart said, Stuart said,' he mimicked before standing and moving to a console that held an array of bottles. 'You don't want whisky, how about I make you a non-alcoholic cocktail?'

She didn't want one. She didn't want anything except to know what was going on. 'Jack–'

His back was to her. 'Have a damn drink,' he said quietly without turning around. 'We'll have a drink together, then we can talk.'

Once more, it seemed as if she didn't have a choice. 'Fine.'

'Pineapple juice,' he said, pouring some into a glass. 'A splash of lime juice and fill it to the brim with tonic water.' He spooned some half-melted ice cubes in and stirred before turning and handing it to her.

He poured whisky into a glass for himself. A very large measure, she noted, frowning.

'Cheers.' He lurched across the room to the chair and sat heavily before draining a quarter of the whisky in one mouthful. 'Drink up,' he said, raising the glass toward her.

She took a sip. It was good, and probably the closest she was going to get to food that evening. Remembering the crush of people in the lobby, she'd no intention of going down to the restaurant. Anyway, Jack had always been hopeless when drunk. She sipped some more and waited, deciding it was better not to push.

Finally, he took another mouthful of his drink, and stared into the amber liquid as if looking for the right words. 'I've been playing the tables a bit, I suppose, but it's under control.'

Whatever he was reading in his whisky, it wasn't the truth. Molly heard denial in every word. The unexceptional *playing the tables* instead of the more insidious *gambling* was bad enough, but the overemphatic *it's under control* meant it was anything but. A frisson of fear swept over her. How bad was it?

'Is this why you were suspended?' She sipped her drink again, hoping the sweetness would give her the energy she needed to get through this.

He slammed his glass on the table, startling her. 'It's got nothing to do with it,' he said, raising his voice and glaring at her. He picked up his glass, realised it was empty and got to his feet. 'D'you want another?' he asked, slurring his words.

She shook her head, watching as he moved unsteadily to the console to fill his glass, unable to resist saying, 'Haven't you had enough?'

Ignoring her, he raised his glass. 'Cheers!' His mouth downturned when she didn't raise hers. 'Don't you like your cocktail?'

'It's fine,' she said, lifting it to drink. She finished it and stood. 'I'm going home, Jack. Are you coming?'

He waved his arms around the room again, whisky sloshing from his glass. 'That would be a waste, I've paid for the night.'

'It doesn't matter, Jack,' she pleaded. 'I want you to come home.'

He grinned, an inebriated twist of his mouth. 'I want you to stay. Stalemate.'

She stood looking at him for a moment. Maybe she should stay. She felt dreadful, the day beginning to take its toll. They could get room service, maybe talk some more. Maybe, if they talked enough, the truth would come out. Because she knew she hadn't heard it all yet. 'You lied about the police visiting your office,' she said.

He waved his free hand dismissively. 'They rang to speak to me; the office gave them my mobile number. Does it matter?'

It was one of many lies he'd told her. She wanted to ask

about Las Vegas, but in the state he was in, there didn't seem much point.

'Anyway, forget about all of that,' Jack said, swirling his whisky. 'Come to the casino, have some fun.'

'I don't want to go to the damn casino,' she said, frustration in every word.

'Stalemate again, 'cos I do.'

She refused to stay and watch him gamble. 'I'm going home. Maybe, when you've sobered up in the morning, you'll give me a ring.'

He got to his feet, stumbling a little. 'I think I may have had one too many,' he slurred, staggering and falling onto the bed.

She waited for him to sit up, but he didn't, then he was snoring the loud stertorous snore of the very drunk. One after the other, she lifted his legs onto the bed, unlaced and removed his shoes and dropped them to the floor. He'd probably sleep until the morning. She picked up the pencil and pad from the bedside locker, wrote, *ring me when you wake, xx,* put it on the bed beside him and bent to place a kiss on his cheek, her nose crinkling as the waft of alcohol-laced fumes hit her. He was going to have a massive hangover. She loved him, but the thought gave her a tiny bit of pleasure.

With a final ruffle of his hair, she left the room, a yawn escaping as she made her way toward the lift. Becoming disorientated, she stopped halfway along the corridor and retraced her steps, convinced it was the other direction. When she found herself outside Jack's room again, she wondered if perhaps she should stay after all. She had her hand on the door handle before she realised, she'd no way of getting back inside. There wasn't much hope of being able to wake him; that drunk, he'd sleep through the hotel falling down around him. Voices drifting toward her from further along the corridor made her move. At least she could ask them where the damn lift was.

It was, as it happened, just around the corner. She stood waiting for the doors to open, her head beginning to thump. It wasn't helped by the raucous voices of the group of men who were waiting alongside. When the lift arrived, she stood back, ignoring their wolf whistles and invitations to join them and waited until the lift had gone before pressing the button again, relieved, seconds later, when one of the other lift doors opened. It was empty and, inside, she propped herself against the wall as it dropped to the ground floor.

When the lift opened, she was taken aback by the noise and the crowd. She eased around groups of people until she reached the door she'd come through earlier. It seemed an awful long way to the neon exit sign that flashed ahead of her. Sliding her hand along the wall, she started to walk, feeling the floor sway under her feet. She was so very tired.

In the car park, she stood a moment looking across the brightly-lit but deserted space feeling suddenly anxious. It was safe, of course, there'd be security men. She hadn't convinced herself, but she also couldn't stand in the doorway all night. She wanted to get home, get into bed and sleep forever. Halfway to her car, she got the distinct impression she was no longer alone. *Stop and look around or run like hell*. She didn't do either, afraid to look around, too weak to run. Instead, she kept walking, one shaky foot in front of the other.

She almost gasped with relief when she saw her car, pulling out her keys and rushing towards it. When she saw the yellow wheel clamp that said her car wasn't going anywhere, her squeal of anguish echoed around the car park. There were instructions as to what to do, phone numbers to ring, fines to pay. Ignoring the lot, she walked away, and exited the car park onto the street. She was in luck, a taxi pulled in and four noisy and already inebriated passengers climbed out. Despite the taxi driver's complaint that he had a fare to pick up, she jumped in. 'I'll give you a fifty-pound tip,' she said, giving him her address and resting her head back. 'You might have to wake me when we get there, I'm wiped out.'

She fell into a sound sleep, woken by a rough hand shaking her with more force than she thought necessary. 'Okay, I'm awake, for goodness sake you don't need to be so brutal.' Glaring at the driver, she rubbed her arm.

'I've been trying to wake you for about two minutes,' he said calmly.

'Sorry, sorry,' she said, taking a deep breath. 'I have to go inside to get your money.'

To her surprise, he got out and followed her to the front door. 'No disrespect, miss,' he said with a rueful smile, 'but I've learned not to trust people too much.'

She needed to trust him; her head was spinning so much she couldn't get the key in the door. Inside, he gave her back the key and she slid her hand along the wall to the living room.

Her bag was where she'd left it. 'Help yourself,' she muttered, pointing towards it.

With an audible *tut,* he picked it up, took out her purse and opened it. 'The fare is twenty-five plus the fifty tip.' He showed her three twenties and a ten. 'We'll leave it at seventy, okay?'

She didn't care if he took every penny as long as he went away.

'Do you see?' he persisted, holding the notes up.

'Yes, yes, fine.'

Pocketing the cash, he looked at her with concern in his eyes. 'You sure you'll be all right?'

She opened her eyes wide and attempted a smile that she knew came out askew. 'I'm exhausted,' she said, 'shut the door after you, please.'

He took the hint and left.

Hearing the front door shut, she closed her eyes and

groaned. She couldn't remember the last time she felt so wretched. She'd overdone it. With difficulty, she swung her legs up onto the sofa and slid her shoulders down, pulling the cushion under her head.

And then, everything went dark.

29

It was the light shining through the windows that woke Molly the next morning. Opening her eyes briefly, she thought she was going to die. Every single part of her body ached. Her mouth was dry, her breath rancid. Even her eyeballs hurt.

Very slowly, she moved her legs to the floor and used the arm of the chair to pull herself upright. Immediately, her head spun. It was a few minutes before she was able to move to the kitchen where she filled a glass of water and drank it slowly, filling it and taking it back to the sofa.

She lay down again, pulled a blanket over herself and shut her eyes, opening them with a groan when she remembered her car. Her mobile was in her pocket, she pulled it out. It was only five. Jack wouldn't have surfaced yet. She sent him a text. *Car clamped in hotel car park. Got taxi home. Sort it out.*

He'd have a thumping headache, and it was the last thing he'd want to do, but she never doubted that he would do it anyway. He'd be feeling guilty, so would be pleased to be doing something for her and would never think of it as being his fault in the first place.

Sometime today, when they both felt better, they'd sit down

and discuss the gambling. Stuart was an insufferable prig; he'd probably exaggerated everything to make himself sound more important. She'd sit down with Jack and find out exactly what was going on. The decision made, it helped her relax and within minutes, despite the aches and pains, she fell asleep again.

When she next woke, the first thing she noticed was that her head didn't ache. It was a relief, because she was beginning to wonder if the doctors in the hospital had missed something. It wasn't unheard of. Sitting up, she was glad to find the dizziness too, had gone. Her ribs still ached; her bruises were still a lovely shade of green but all in all she felt much better.

She'd feel even better after a shower. It was almost nine. There were no messages, but she didn't really expect one from Jack. He'd arrange to have the car released and drive it home. 'Oh, hell!' she groaned. He'd have to come home first. Since he rarely drove, he refused to weigh down his key ring with a cumbersome car key. The spare was in a bedroom drawer.

A brief thought that she could bring it to the hotel was brushed away without hesitation. She'd done too much running around yesterday. Today, she wasn't leaving the house, and going upstairs was as far as she was moving.

After her shower, intent on a day at home, she slipped on a pair of pyjamas and tied her wet hair up in a loose knot. She thought it might be a good idea to have a pot of coffee ready for when Jack eventually arrived home and went down to put on the kettle.

She wasn't hungry but she needed to eat. Taking a bowl of cereal and a mug of coffee over to the table by the window, she sat and ate as she looked out at the garden. It was raining, the window streaked with rivulets of water. Perfect staying-at-home weather. She might even catch up with programmes she'd recorded and books she'd planned to read.

At ten thirty, Jack still hadn't made an appearance and she was beginning to worry. She'd parked her car in front of maintenance doors, the hotel might need access. They might decide to have her car towed; that would be a nightmare and cost a fortune.

Picking up her mobile, she rang Jack's number. It went straight to answerphone. Of course, if he were in the car park, there may be no signal. She sent him a text, *ring me,* and waited, tapping the phone against her chin.

When he hadn't rung by eleven, she stood and paced the room, wondering what she should do. She'd almost decided to go to the hotel when the house phone rang. It was such an unusual occurrence that she stared at it for a moment. Then she smiled. Of course, Jack probably hadn't charged his mobile.

'Jack?' she said, picking up the phone.

'Hello?'

It was a female voice. Frowning, Molly said, 'I'm sorry, can I help you?'

'This is Harriet Summers, I'm the manager of the Hyde Hotel. I'm hoping to speak to Jack Chatwell.'

Join the queue, Molly wanted to say. 'I'm sorry, he's not here. May I take a message?'

There was silence for a moment before the manager said quietly, 'Is that Mrs Chatwell?'

'Yes, Molly Chatwell.'

'Mrs Chatwell, I'm in a difficult situation. Your husband wrote a cheque to cover his...' There was a long hesitation before she continued. '... expenses. Unfortunately, it was returned. When we tried to use the credit card number he left to secure his room, it was rejected. Mr Chatwell is a good customer, we are obviously keen to get this error sorted without any problem, or delay, but we've been unable to contact him.'

'He's not in his room?' Molly said, trying to think, but finding it a struggle to make sense of anything.

'He was seen leaving his room before 6am, Mrs Chatwell. He hasn't been seen since.' There was silence for a few seconds, then in a firmer tone, the manager said, 'In light of the returned cheque and the declined credit card, we've been left with no alternative. Your husband's belongings have been packed up and are awaiting collection in our luggage room. If you would come and collect these, and settle your husband's account, we would consider the matter closed and not involve anyone else.'

Molly took a deep breath before saying as calmly as she could. 'I can settle the account now with my credit card.'

'I'm afraid we will need you to attend in person, Mrs Chatwell, to sign for his belongings.'

'Fine,' she said, letting her frustration show in the one blunt word. She thought about the car. 'My car is in your car park; my husband was supposed to arrange for the clamp to be removed. I don't suppose you know if that's been done.'

'Ah,' the manager said, 'did you park it in front of the maintenance door?'

Molly wanted to say she was desperate, that she'd been injured, that she was, in fact, fast approaching the end of her tether. She settled for, 'Yes, I'm afraid I did.'

The manager sounded genuinely sympathetic. 'Unfortunately, it was necessary to have your car towed. The maintenance team needed access to that doorway.'

'Of course, I understand,' Molly said, squeezing her eyes shut. 'I'll have to sort that out later.' Once more, she was left with no choice. 'I'll be there as soon as I can.'

'Thank you, it makes it so much easier; we don't like to involve the police unless we have to.'

Molly gave an uncertain laugh. 'The police! For non-payment of a hotel bill. Surely that's a bit excessive. What are we talking about, a few hundred?'

'Ah, I'm sorry, Mrs Chatwell, you don't seem to understand. It isn't only the hotel room, it's also his casino debts.'

Molly felt her heart skip a beat. 'How much?'

'Just under seven.'

'That's not too bad,' she said, relieved it wasn't more. When there was silence from the other end, she knew she'd made a mistake. There was a definite tremor in her voice when she asked, 'You mean seven thousand?'

'Six thousand, nine-hundred and twenty. Perhaps you can understand now why we were concerned.'

Yes, Molly could. It was a colossal amount of money. 'Yes. Yes. But it's not a problem. I'll be there in about an hour and we can get this sorted.' She hung up, put the handset back on its stand and collapsed into the chair behind. Seven thousand pounds! She held a hand to her forehead. The headache had returned.

Picking up her mobile, she tried Jack's number again but, once more, it went straight to answerphone. With a frustrated shake of her head, she stood and went upstairs to dress.

Casual clothes would have been easier, but she had fences to build. Looking smart and professional would give her more leverage. She pulled on black trousers, a white silk shirt and her black Armani three-quarter length coat and slipped her feet into black kitten heels. Her hair was still damp. Instead of spending time drying it, she brushed it out and pinned it up in a smarter French pleat.

With her make-up applied, she looked a little less like she was a vampire's latest victim. Before she left, she checked her mobile. No message from Jack. There were messages from Remi and Freya that she read and quickly answered, also messages from Amelia and Petra, both asking if she was okay. She sent a *yes, fine, don't worry* in reply to each.

She felt a quiver of guilt for having been suspicious of Amelia, for jumping to such a terribly wrong conclusion. What a fool she had been.

A final text to Jack asking him to ring her, and she left the house for South Kensington station. It was only a short distance on the Circle line to Paddington station and no more than five minutes' walk to the hotel from there. Less than an hour after speaking to the manager, Molly was entering the Hyde Hotel.

She stepped up to the reception desk with her chin held high. 'The manager is expecting me,' she said in response to the receptionist's pleasant *may I help you.* 'Molly Chatwell.'

'Please, take a seat, Ms Chatwell and I'll tell her you're here.'

In contrast to the evening before, the lobby was quiet with only a few people sitting in seats reading papers or drinking coffee. With the garish neon lights switched off, the décor was pleasant without being outstanding. There were empty seats near the window, Molly walked over, kitten heels click-clacking on the tiled floor.

It was impossible to sit still and she jumped to her feet when she saw a tall, smartly-dressed woman crossing towards her, a hand extending as she drew close. 'Harriet Summers.'

'Molly Chatwell.'

'I'm so sorry you're having to go through this,' Harriet said. She held Molly's hand a moment longer.

The sympathy brought tears that Molly quickly brushed away. 'Thank you for giving me the opportunity to sort it out,' she said, 'my husband will appreciate it too. He's going through a difficult patch.' She met the manager's eyes, saw the steel behind the kindness and knew she'd seen it all before.

'Come to my office. We'll get everything taken care of.' The manager led the way past the reception desk, veering towards a door on the right. Opening it, she indicated that Molly enter. 'Can I get you some coffee or tea?'

Molly shook her head. She wanted this done and to go home to where she hoped she'd find Jack waiting.

The manager took her seat behind the desk and smiled at her. 'Sit down, Mrs Chatwell, it will take a minute or two.' She opened the folder before her and withdrew a sheet of paper, her eyes skimming over it before sliding it across the desk.

Molly picked it up and read the details. The bedroom wasn't hideously expensive considering how spacious it had been. However, Jack had knocked back a fair amount of alcohol and at London hotel prices, this mounted up. But it was the casino bill that had her eyes widening. Trying to maintain her professionally cool façade, she reached into her bag, withdrew her wallet and took out her credit card. She handed it and the invoice back across the table.

'Thank you,' Harriet Summers said before taking a credit card machine from her drawer. She slid the card in, tapped in the amount and handed the machine over.

With an unsteady finger, Molly put in her PIN number and handed it back.

'Thank you. Oh, and by the way,' the manager said as they waited, 'I took the liberty of finding out where your car was taken. It's in the Wandsworth pound. They're open until five.' She took a notelet and passed it across. 'That's their number.'

Molly took the slip of paper and put it into her bag. She'd worry about the car tomorrow. 'That was kind of you, thank you.'

Looking down at the credit card machine, the manager frowned. 'I'm sorry,' she said, meeting Molly's eyes, 'this card has been declined.'

'That's ridiculous. I have a 10K credit limit.' Molly saw the woman's impassive face, took back the proffered card, and opened her wallet again. 'Use this one, please.'

There wasn't a word spoken as the machine beeped, their eyes focused on it, waiting.

The manager gazed at it for a moment before looking at Molly with a grim expression and a firm set to her mouth. 'This has been declined too, I'm afraid.'

Molly laughed in disbelief, the sound fading quickly as the implication hit her. There was a 10K credit limit on both. 'Will you try five?' she asked, keeping her voice steady but unable to meet the manager's eye.

A few minutes later, with both cards being declined yet again, she put them away and clasped her hands in her lap. 'I know how bad this must look, but I promise I will get this sorted.'

Harriet's eyes were sympathetic, but her lips were firm. 'As I've said, we try our best to avoid involving the police, Mrs Chatwell, but as I'm sure you can understand, no hotel can afford to absorb such losses. I do appreciate your predicament, however, and your efforts to settle this. I am willing to give you until midday tomorrow to find the funds. After that, I will have no option, but to bring in the police.'

30

Feeling like her world was collapsing around her, Molly managed to say, 'I appreciate that, Ms Summers.' Dizziness swept over her, pinpricks of darkness blurring her vision. 'I think I'm going to faint,' she muttered, and proved herself right by keeling over onto the floor.

She wasn't out long, coming to with the horrified manager kneeling beside her and gently tapping her cheek. 'So sorry,' Molly whispered, struggling to sit up. She was helped into the chair and handed a glass of water which she sipped gratefully.

'You've had a terrible shock,' Harriet said, sitting back into her chair. 'Is there anyone I can ring for you?'

Molly managed to drag up a smile. 'I think the fewer people who know about this the better, don't you?'

'It will certainly make it easier to get your lives back on track,' Harriet agreed. She opened her drawer and took out a leaflet. 'This might be something worth looking into too.

Molly took it. *Gamblers Anonymous.* It was time to acknowledge the truth. She folded it, put it into her bag. 'Thank you. Now, I'd better go.'

'You sure you'll be okay?'

Molly stood and straightened her shoulders. 'I'll have to be,' she said, then trying to look efficient, added, 'There were belongings I had to collect.'

The manager shook her head and stood. 'No, that was a ruse to get you to come in; we find it's safer than trying to deal with this kind of thing over the phone.'

'Just as well, as it turned out,' Molly said, relieved not to have to carry anything. 'Before midday tomorrow, I'll have it sorted. Thank you, you've been very kind.' With a grateful smile, she turned and left the office.

Outside, the rain had returned, heavy and cold. It was perfect weather for the mood she was in. The head office of her bank was in Bayswater. Walking as briskly as she could, feet splashing heedlessly through puddles, she made her way to Paddington station. Minutes on the Circle line and she was back out on the street.

There were only a few people in the bank, and none were at the customer service desk. 'Good afternoon,' Molly said. 'I'd like to speak to the manager please.'

The assistant looked at her with a helpful smile. 'Do you have an appointment?'

Molly clenched her fists. 'No, but this is an urgent matter which has come up. It's vital that I see him.'

'Mr Victor, the manager, is always happy to see customers,' the assistant said, in a well-rehearsed line, 'but unfortunately an appointment is necessary.' Her smile was forced, insincere.

Glaring at her, Molly put both hands flat on the desk and leaned forward. 'I need to see him. If you can't make that happen, get me someone who can.'

Her expression must have mirrored her thoughts because the young woman's smile vanished to be replaced by a slightly anxious stare. A hand went to the phone, and without taking her eyes from Molly, she picked up the handset, dialled a two-digit number and asked for assistance.

Hoping it wasn't a secret code for *call the police*, Molly stood back from the desk and waited.

Only seconds later, a well-dressed man came through a door behind. He glanced at the anxious assistant who nodded slightly to where Molly was standing, and immediately approached her. 'You've a problem?' he said, without bothering with pleasantries.

A problem? Her life seemed to be collapsing around her – did that count as a problem? She swallowed and took a shuddering breath that echoed loudly in the quiet bank.

'Come with me,' the man said, putting a hand on her elbow and leading her through the door and down a long, narrow corridor. He guided her into a small, neat office and pointed to a chair. 'Sit,' he said before going to the other side of the desk and taking a seat.

Molly opened her bag, took out a tissue and dabbed her eyes. 'Thank you,' she said, looking across at him. 'It's been a nightmare of a day.'

'I can see that,' he said gently. 'I was afraid you were going to pass out on me.'

She managed a shaky laugh. 'If I had, it would have been the second time today. Are you the manager?'

'No, not the general manager, if that's what you mean,' he admitted with the merest hint of a shrug. 'My name is Spenser Roberts, I'm the customer service manager. Perhaps, if you tell me what the problem is, I'll be able to help you.'

She would have preferred the general manager, but she wasn't in a position to make demands. The frown between her eyes deepened and she reached into her bag for her purse. Taking out her two credit cards, she put them on the desk and pushed them forward. 'I tried to use them this morning to settle a bill, and they were declined.' She couldn't stop the quiver in her voice when she added, 'Both of them.'

There was no change in Roberts' expression as he picked the cards up. Without a word, he turned his chair slightly to face the computer screen on his desk. One-handed, he tapped a few keys, picked up one of the cards, tapped some more. A single crease appeared between his eyes. Picking up the second card, he tapped the keys and stared at the screen. Apart from the single crease, his expression didn't change.

He put the cards back on the desk, then using both hands he tapped keys, his focus on the screen in front of him.

Molly watched as his lips tightened and his eyes narrowed slightly; whatever he was reading there, it wasn't good.

It was another minute before he turned to look at her.

'It's not good news, is it?' she asked, hoping he'd laugh and disagree.

Instead, he looked at her for a moment with calm assessing eyes as if trying to decide how much he should say.

'It's better to tell me,' she said, lifting her chin. So much had been thrown at her recently, she was almost getting used to it.

'I'm afraid it's not good.' Roberts reached out and tapped the two cards. 'These access a joint account with your husband. Both have reached their maximum limit. What I shouldn't be telling you, is that your husband also has two more, in his name only.' He took a deep breath before continuing. 'They also have reached their maximum limit.' As if he knew she was going to ask, he added, 'That's ten grand per card. Forty grand, in total.'

Forty thousand pounds. Molly blinked and gulped.

Roberts' eyes flicked to the computer screen before coming back to meet hers. He lifted a hand and rubbed it over his mouth.

Molly didn't need a psychology degree to know what that meant – the fear of speaking because what you were about to say was going to cause pain or distress. She wanted to beg him to get on with it. To throw whatever it was into the maelstrom that was whirling around her. It couldn't make it much worse.

It could.

'Are you aware that you're also behind in your mortgage repayments?'

Molly stared at him for a moment then gave a confused laugh, stopping abruptly when she saw his face. Whereas before it had been expressionless, now, with downturned mouth, he looked sympathetic, almost pitying.

'I think you must have made a mistake,' she said, raising her voice a little. *A mistake, that's what this was. A customer with a similar name, maybe. It would be sorted, they'd apologise, then they'd all laugh about it. It would be a story they could tell for years to come to entertain their friends.* 'We don't have a mortgage on our home, it was cleared a few years ago.'

Roberts looked back to the screen then slowly shook his head. 'Six months ago, you remortgaged it.'

Not a mistake then. Molly stood, paced the room from wall to wall and sat again. 'How much for?'

'Two hundred and fifty thousand.'

A quarter of a million pounds. Molly fought to keep her expression neutral. 'And you say we're in arrears?'

'Two months. A letter was sent after the first repayment was missed.' He hesitated, then shook his head. 'You are obviously unaware of all of this, Mrs Chatwell but' – he waved toward the computer screen – 'we have the remortgage application on file, you have signed it.'

'Yes, yes, of course, I remember now.' She managed a shaky smile that she held despite his eyebrows rising in disbelief. She had to keep it together until she got out of there. 'So how much are the arrears?'

'You took it out over ten years. The repayments are three

thousand a month. Currently, you are six thousand in arrears.' He held up both hands. 'The interest rate on the arrears are high, Mrs Chatwell, you'd be advised to clear it as soon as possible.'

Her eyes widened. Between credit cards and the arrears, they owed almost 50K, so she wondered how they were supposed to do that. They had used almost all their savings to pay for Freya and Remi's university fees. She remembered being surprised that Jack had insisted they paid the full amount up front. Now, she knew why. At least the children wouldn't suffer for his stupidity, or for hers. Because, of course she'd signed the damn remortgage application.

She remembered distinctly; she was in the middle of cooking when he had come in with a sheaf of papers.

'I'm changing our insurance,' he'd said, tapping the papers with his fingers. 'I want to make sure Remi and Freya's belongings are covered while they're away.'

She'd been touched that he'd thought of it. 'I'll sign later,' she'd said, lifting fingers that stank of raw onion. But he'd insisted, and she'd given in and signed each page beside the X he'd so considerately marked. And no, of course, she hadn't read what she'd signed.

Her eyes were bleak as she looked across the desk at the customer service manager whose sympathetic expression made her want to cry... no, howl... she wanted to howl for the perfect life that was slipping from her grasp with such speed she was stunned. From somewhere deep inside, she managed to drag up anger that strengthened her. 'We may need time to get this sorted,' she said, meeting his eyes.

He nodded slowly. 'Please be aware, Mrs Chatwell, that the next mortgage repayment is due in two weeks. If you can make some payment towards that. Any payment,' he added, seeing her tightened look. 'It would be viewed kindly by the bank.'

They didn't have money saved anywhere else. They were both well paid, but even their combined salaries wouldn't clear the arrears and the next payment. She closed her eyes. She still didn't know why Jack had been suspended. If he lost his job? She gulped again and met the manager's worried look with a shake of her head. 'I'd better go and see what I can do, Mr Roberts,' she said and stood.

He got to his feet. 'I'll walk you out.' With his hand on the doorknob, he turned to her. 'Do what you can to make repayments,' he said, 'keep the bank informed, if you can't. We'll be able to work out some form of repayment schedule.'

In a daze, Molly headed back to the Underground. She remembered Jack's blasé statement that he played the tables. At a rough estimate, he'd done so to the tune of over three hundred thousand pounds.

31

Outside the bank the rain still fell, heavier now, a deluge that pounded Molly's head and ran down her set face, rivulets running down her neck to slip under the collar of her coat and soak into her shirt. Passers-by glanced at her from under their umbrellas or as they ducked under the shelter of storefronts, but nobody stopped to ask if she was okay as she walked robotically, arms rigid by her sides, feet heedlessly splashing through puddles, kitten heels slipping and sliding so that she jerked from side to side.

She should have felt pain but all she felt was numb... too numb, too shocked for thought, her feet automatically taking her back to the station. On the busy, noisy platform, waiting for her tube, her brain swirled, trying to make sense of everything. It took a few seconds before she realised her phone was vibrating. Hoping it was Jack, she took it out, her eyes widening when she saw it was DI Fanshawe.

'Hi,' she said, holding the phone to her ear. She tried to shut out some of the noise that surrounded her by pressing her free hand against the other ear. Unfortunately, being deep on an

Underground platform meant the signal was poor anyway and being jostled by impatient commuters didn't help.

'Hi, it's DI Fan... I just... to... that we've...'

'Inspector, I'm in the Underground, I'm losing you.'

'We'll call... this aft...'

She pressed the phone more tightly to her ear, knowing it wasn't going to make any difference. 'Did you say you're coming to see me this afternoon?'

'Yes, I'll fill...'

The line went dead. When he didn't phone back, she sent a short text to say she'd see him that afternoon. Maybe he had some news for her. She couldn't rustle up any interest. If it weren't for Freya and Remi, she didn't think she'd care that someone was trying to kill her. The numbness and the soul-destroying emptiness lasted until she was almost home. She walked down Elystan Street and stood outside their house for several minutes. It was a lovely house, on a beautiful street. Anger broke through the numbness, rushing up, white hot. She gripped the gate as it doubled her over, a scream of rage and frustration erupting, the sound lost in the growl of traffic behind her.

Anger was quickly overlaid by sorrow. She didn't want to lose her home. It was brimful of memories. Jack had proposed to her in the kitchen. In the garden that stretched behind, they had made love, had moonlight drinks and daytime picnics. Freya and Remi had taken their first stumbling steps in the living room, she and Jack on their knees cheering them on. Jack had put together a climbing frame in the garden for the children and Molly had sat on a rug on the grass and watched them, Jack taking photo after photo, she laughing at their antics, her heart swelling with love for all three.

Molly had danced around the kitchen with Freya when she'd been accepted to the Sorbonne, remembered running up the stairs with Remi's letter from MIT, waiting while he'd opened it before gathering him into a hug where tears of happiness mingled on their cheeks.

It had been a home filled with love and laughter, a home fit for the perfect life she thought she'd been living.

She opened the front door, the beep-beep of the alarm telling her that Jack wasn't home. Where was he? Fear settled in her chest. He'd probably guess that the hotel would contact her, so he'd know she knew the full extent of the trouble he was in. He'd be feeling guilty, maybe even desperate. She took out her mobile and left him a voicemail. 'I know everything, Jack. Ring me, we need to talk.' She added, 'I love you. We can get through this.' In case he was ignoring voice messages, she quickly sent a text.

She stood looking at it for a minute, willing Jack to reply. Then, with a grunt of frustration, she peeled off her wet coat and hung it over the newel post, kicked off her water-stained muddy kitten heels and padded into the kitchen leaving wet footprints behind her on the wooden floor.

The collar of her shirt and bottom of her trousers were wet through but she ignored both, lowering herself onto the sofa and looking around the room. She would have to sell some stuff. The car. They'd paid cash for the BMW, using both their Christmas bonuses and some of their savings over a year ago to buy it. The mileage was very low, she might get 30K for it and be able to pay off the arrears and reduce some of the credit card debt. She shut her eyes, remembering she'd yet to arrange to get the car back.

She considered what else she could do. There was some jewellery she could sell. Her eyes dropped to her diamond engagement ring. That too would go. Whatever it took to keep the house from being repossessed. They could manage the three grand a month repayment on the mortgage, if they cut back on everything. No more weekends away in expensive hotels, no more five-star holidays. No more designer clothes.

If Jack lost his job? She still had no idea what that was all about. She wasn't a fool, it had to be linked to his gambling. If it were, if he lost his job, then it would be a struggle. She could almost cover the mortgage with what she took home, but it left nothing for bills, food. She really needed to talk to Jack. Picking up her phone, she checked for messages before ringing him. As before, it went straight to answerphone.

With a grunt of frustration, she dropped it onto the table and swung her legs up onto the sofa. The stress, the pain, everything was wearing her down. She was exhausted. Closing her eyes, she fell into a restless sleep where burly men broke down her door shouting that *they* owned the house.

It was the doorbell that woke her, and panic shot through her until common sense kicked in. Burly bailiffs wouldn't be calling quite yet. Checking the time, she realised she'd slept for a while. It was four, the doorbell was probably the police. She pushed up from off the sofa and walked into the hallway like a decrepit old woman; although the pain wasn't as severe, every part of her continued to ache. But she'd suffer the pain, she needed her wits about her.

The doorbell rang again, the sound resonating as her hand reached for the knob. She turned it and pulled the door open. As she guessed, it was DI Fanshawe and his less-than-welcome sergeant. Standing back, she waved them inside. 'Go straight through,' she said, shutting the door.

They stood watching her as she made her way back. She was trying her best to move normally, but knew she was failing dismally when she saw Fanshawe's eyes narrow.

'You look dreadful,' he said bluntly. 'Have you seen a doctor?'

She lowered herself back onto the sofa. 'I'm fine, honestly.

The painkillers they recommended make me woozy, so I haven't been taking them.'

'Is your husband here?' he asked.

With a slight smile, she shook her head. The question he wanted to ask, she knew, was why her husband wasn't there to look after her. She could have told him, and if he had been there alone, she might have done. He might have been able to advise her on what to do. It was tempting, and she was about to blurt it all out when she caught Carstairs' mean eyes looking at her. No, she'd given them enough ammunition to think badly of her, she wasn't going to give them more to think the same of Jack. 'He'll be home soon,' she said instead. 'Please, if you want something to drink, help yourselves.'

'We're fine,' Fanshawe said, taking the seat opposite her. Carstairs, meanwhile, stayed standing, leaning a shoulder against the wall. His eyes never left her, she could feel them boring into her. She had to keep reminding herself that she was the victim.

'Have you news for me?'

Fanshawe shook his head slowly. 'The investigation is ongoing. Lucien Pleasant, like most people who use blackmail as a means of extorting money, kept a low profile, but he wouldn't have been invisible. We're working our way through his contacts. We'll find something, eventually.'

Molly gave a bark of laughter. 'You're no closer to knowing why someone tried to kill me.' For a change there was no sneering grin on Carstairs' lips. 'Tell me,' she said, looking straight at Fanshawe. 'Do you still think the person who killed Pleasant, is the same person who tried to push me under a car?'

Fanshawe shrugged. 'So far, we've not turned up any links between you, or to anyone you have in common.'

'But you do still think there's a link.'

It looked as if he wasn't going to reply and then he rested his elbows on his knees and leaned towards her. 'You meet Pleasant. A day later he turns up on your doorstep. The next day he is murdered and two days later, someone tries to kill you. So yes, bizarre as it is, I think there's a connection. But as yet, we've no idea what that could be. We're still checking a number of people. Stuart Mercer, who you were heading to meet the day you were knocked down, and your husband, of course.'

'You're checking out Jack? Why? Jack would never harm me.' She saw Fanshawe exchange glances with Carstairs. 'What is it you're not telling me?'

The inspector sat back and tapped his index finger on the arm of the chair. Then, as if making a decision, he leaned forward again. 'We are aware that Mr Chatwell has been suspended. The CEO was cagey as to why, but we are aware of your husband's gambling problem.' His eyes softened. 'We've no proof, but we assume the two are linked.'

There was a question in his words. Molly wished she knew the answer. 'I don't know,' she said, turning to glare at Carstairs who'd given a grunt of disbelief. 'I didn't know Jack was suspended until yesterday; I didn't know about his gambling and certainly didn't know the extent of it...' She broke off, aware she was telling the police what they wanted to know.

'The extent of it?' Fanshawe prompted. 'And what is that?'

Her eyes watered as she stared at him. What did it matter now? It was all going to come out. A great big unholy mess. 'The credit cards are maxed out. We owe about 40K on those and he has remortgaged the house for a quarter of a million. He hasn't paid the last couple of months so we've arrears of 6K.'

'And you didn't know?'

She shook her head, then held her hands up. 'Oh, don't worry, he didn't forge the documents. He was too clever, and I was too stupid. I signed them thinking they were something else.'

'Do you have life insurance?' Carstairs' cold, gravelly voice startled her. She'd almost succeeded in forgetting he was there.

'Of course,' she said, then shook her head vehemently as she turned to look at him. 'No, no you're not going down that road. There's no way Jack would have tried to kill me. That's ridiculous. That's not the kind of people we are.' She turned back to Fanshawe, still shaking her head. 'You don't really think he's involved, do you?' She couldn't read his expression and, stretching a hand towards him, she repeated, 'Do you?'

He looked down at her hand before saying slowly, 'We wouldn't be doing our jobs if we didn't look at every angle.'

It was a politician's answer. Molly felt a solid lump of fear lodge in her throat. 'That's crazy,' she said, her voice trembling. Meeting the detective's eyes, she saw doubt in them, and something else, sympathy. 'Jack loves me, he'd never harm me.' She refused to lower her eyes. Despite his gambling, despite his drunken behaviour the previous night, she knew the man she married would never hurt her. Or was she fooling herself? After all, she'd been doing a lot of that recently.

'We're keeping every avenue of investigation open,' Fanshawe said. 'We would like to speak to Mr Chatwell, however. Do you know where we could find him?'

Molly wanted to say yes, wanted to say, he'd be home any minute. But they were the police; lying to them would achieve nothing. 'I haven't seen him since last night. In the hotel. The Hyde Hotel. But he's left there now.'

'You said he'd be home soon,' Carstairs replied.

'Well, I lied,' she snapped at him. 'I don't know where he is. He left the hotel early this morning–'

'Without paying his bill?' Fanshawe interrupted.

'Without paying his bill,' she said, her voice thick. 'A seven-thousand-pound bill, if you want the gory details. I have until noon tomorrow to find a way to pay that, or they'll be forced to act. By that' – she gave a grim smile – 'they mean bring in you lot. Our credit cards are maxed out, so I'm really not sure what I can do.'

'I know the manager of the Hyde Hotel,' Fanshawe said, surprising her. 'Harriet Summers. She's a reasonable woman, I'll have a word with her, tell her you need a bit more time.'

That would be one thing off her mind. 'Thank you,' Molly said, genuinely grateful. 'I'm going to sell the car, it'll bring in enough cash to sort out a few things including the hotel, but I have to organise getting it back first. It's in Wandsworth pound.' She held a hand up. 'Don't ask!' He'd hear the story from Harriet, she'd no doubt, but she didn't want to have to tell them and see Carstairs sneering at her stupidity.

'If you're going to sell it to a garage,' Fanshawe said, 'do a deal with them, get them to pick it up themselves.'

'Good idea, thank you, I'll do that.' That would make things easier; she could ring the BMW dealership where they'd bought it and get that process started. The sooner she had money to pay off some of the debts, the happier she'd feel. *Happier?* At least she was still able to kid herself.

Fanshawe looked at Carstairs and tilted his head slightly towards the door.

Molly's heart fell as they stood. Despite the obnoxious Carstairs, she found their presence reassuring. When they left, she'd be alone, and she had no idea where Jack was or when he'd come home. Trying to keep the fear from her voice, she said, 'Until you find whoever it is, I'm still in danger, aren't I?'

Fanshawe looked down at her. 'When I rang you earlier, it sounded like you were in the Underground, Mrs Chatwell. We did, if you remember, suggest that you stay indoors. Obviously, you didn't take heed, so I'll say it again, until we find out what is going on... and we will... stay inside where you are safe.' He jabbed a thumb towards the hallway. 'And please, put the chain on the door and check who it is before you open it.'

Molly struggled to her feet and walked to the front door after them.

Fanshawe rattled the chain. 'Put it on as soon as we leave,' he said. 'Be careful. You have my number, ring me if there's any problem and when you hear from Mr Chatwell, persuade him to contact me, okay?'

She nodded because it seemed the thing to do.

After they'd gone, she rang the garage where they'd bought the BMW and asked to speak to the manager.

Ten minutes later she hung up. She'd got less than she'd expected, but he'd offered to check the car over at the pound and if everything was as promised, have the money transferred immediately, so she wasn't going to complain. She took the car key off her set of keys, found the spare, got the paperwork he'd need to take the car from the pound and left everything on the hall table. He said he'd be over in forty minutes to pick everything up. The pound closed at five so it would be the morning before he'd be able to access it.

The twenty-five thousand he'd offered for the car would pay the money owing to the hotel, the arrears on their mortgage, plus the next month's payment and a couple of thousand off each credit card. It would give her breathing space.

Now all she needed to do was find Jack.

32

Pete Randall, the garage owner, arrived almost an hour later. When the doorbell rang, Molly's heart leapt, hoping it was Jack. Her disappointment must have been obvious when she opened the door. 'Have you changed your mind?' Randall asked.

'No, no sorry, I've lots to think about,' she said, stepping back to let him in. 'Thank you so much for doing this. I have the documentation you need, plus the keys.'

Randall looked through the paperwork carefully. 'Okay. First thing tomorrow, I'll head over and check it out. If everything is as you say, I'll have the money transferred into your account.' He took a document from his pocket. 'I need you to sign this.'

Molly led the way into the living room. 'Would you like some coffee while I read it?' Never again was she going to sign something without examining every single word. Randall seemed to think it was normal. He declined the coffee, said nothing and stood with his hands in his jacket pockets watching as she read.

Finally, Molly took a pen and signed. 'There you go,' she said, handing it back. 'And thank you again, you've got me out of a bit of a hole.'

Randall shrugged. 'It happens,' he said dismissively, as if it was an everyday occurrence. Maybe it was, Molly thought as she shut the front door. She never thought *her* life would go into such a spiral.

Easing herself back onto the sofa, she picked up her mobile. Still no word from Jack. She tried ringing him again, but once more it went to voicemail. There didn't seem any point in leaving another message.

There were several messages. One was from her line manager in Dawson Marketing hoping she was recovering. He didn't say outright but she knew he was wondering when she was returning to work. She sent a brief reply thanking him for his good wishes and saying she'd be off at least another week. They had a good working relationship; she'd make an appointment to see him when she went back and explain everything.

More heartening, there were messages from Freya and Remi. She read them, could almost hear the sound of their cheerful enthusiastic voices and yearned to have them nearby, at the same time relieved they were spared the trauma of the current situation. They would be horrified, appalled. They'd want to leave and come home to help. But they were entitled to a life full of hope and promise; she'd do anything... anything... to make sure they got it.

She sent them short cheery messages about how busy she was, how much she missed them, how happy she was that they were doing so well, and she threw the phone on the sofa beside her. Resting her head back, she shut her eyes. Where was Jack? He wouldn't be able to use the credit cards to check into a hotel. Should she start ringing around their friends to ask if he was staying with them? Tears gathered and she rubbed them away roughly. It was not the time to cry, it was a time to plan her next step.

A painting over the fireplace caught her eye. It had been a fortieth birthday present from her to Jack. It was only right that she sold it to pay off some of their debts. Luckily, the value of art tended to go up rather than down; she'd spent a ridiculous sum on it, almost twenty grand, she might get more for it now. It would go towards paying off more of their debts. She'd give the gallery a call in the morning.

Pushing slowly up from the sofa, she headed to the kitchen. She needed to eat something, but the fridge didn't hold anything tempting. Taking out the milk, she checked the date, relieved to see it was still okay. A bowl of cornflakes was better than nothing. Sitting back on the sofa, she ate slowly, her ears pricking between crunchy mouthfuls for the sound of the front door opening. Surely, he would come home.

A flicker of anger shot through her worried mind. He knew that someone had tried to kill her, that she'd been hurt. He should be with her, taking care of her. The sympathetic look in Fanshawe's eyes came back to her. Did he really think Jack was capable of an attempt on her life? Gambling was an addiction, had it become more important than her? Suddenly there was a smidgeon of doubt in her mind, and that worried her even more.

She meant what she'd said to the police. Jack, the man she had married, wasn't capable of hurting her. But this man, this gambler willing to risk everything, she wasn't sure about him. They, each of them, had very healthy life insurance; the death of either would pay out over a million.

There had been a fanatical light in Jack's eye when he'd said he wanted to go back down to the casino in the Hyde. Was that all it was about now, his next gambling fix? She gulped, and a shiver ran down her spine. From desperately wanting Jack to come home, she was suddenly aware she was scared he would. Anger surged through her. Fanshawe had told her to stay indoors where she'd be safe – if he really suspected Jack was guilty, she wasn't safe there at all. Her mind whirled. Did that mean he didn't really suspect him?

'Aaargh,' she said, the bowl dropping from her hand to bounce from the sofa to the floor in a messy stream of milk-sodden cornflakes. She no longer knew what to think. Fanshawe had been adamant that she put the safety chain on the door, maybe that was a hint that she should keep Jack out? But if she were in danger, shouldn't he have suggested she go somewhere safer? Perhaps, that's what she should do, go and stay with one of her friends. Her brain was whirling, she couldn't make a decision, not even to save her life.

She remembered she hadn't put the safety chain back on, and choked back a half laugh, half cry as she struggled to her feet. The aches and pains were making themselves felt with a vengeance, forcing her to hobble and slide a hand along the wall in the hallway for support. She was halfway to the front door when, without warning, it opened. She squealed in fright, stumbled backwards and would have fallen if she hadn't caught hold of the banisters, clutching at them frantically.

'Jack?'

But it wasn't her husband who pushed open the door.

33

Molly stared at the pasty-faced man who stood on the doorstep and shook her head, confused.

'What are you doing here? Where did you get the key to our house?'

'Are you going to ask me in or leave me standing here? It's raining in case you hadn't noticed,' Charlie Forster said, smiling beguilingly.

Molly frowned. She was wary of beguiling smiles these days. 'Of course, come in.'

She stood back as far as she could, but he still brushed against her as he passed, drops from his raincoat wetting the front of her silk blouse. He was close enough that she could smell the nose-crinkling acrid smell of sweat and caught Forster's eyes sliding down her. Why was he here? She wanted to tell him to leave, but panic robbed her voice and before it returned, he'd walked through to the living room.

Taking a sharp steadying breath, she followed. 'What do you want?' She didn't ask him to take a seat, she didn't need to; he'd already taken his coat off, hung it across the back of a chair and flopped onto the sofa. Molly wrapped her arms around her waist and watched in annoyance as his coat dripped onto the floor. 'Charlie, what are you doing here?'

He took a crumpled tissue from his trouser pocket and wiped rainwater from his face. 'Awful evening, I didn't want to come but Jack insisted.' Charlie threw the sodden tissue onto the coffee table.

'Jack!' As if the name released her, Molly moved forward, took the seat opposite and looked at him. 'He's at your place?'

Charlie screwed his mouth up. 'He was desperate, Molly. After he left the hotel, he didn't know where else to turn. He knew he could trust me.'

'He could have come home!'

'He couldn't face you, not yet. Guilt is tearing him apart. I was afraid to leave him for a while, to be honest, I was afraid he might do something stupid. He's a bit calmer now, but he wouldn't settle until I came over to make sure you were all right.'

'You make him sound like a child. I think it's best if I go back with you and talk to him.'

Charlie smiled and shook his head. 'Go out in that rain? Have you looked in a mirror recently, Molly, you look like death. And you're flinching when you move. Sit, for goodness sake, before you fall down.' He stood abruptly. 'Jack was right, he said you wouldn't be taking your painkillers.' He held a hand up. 'Don't worry, he told me exactly where you keep them, I'll go up and get a couple for you. Sit. I'll be down in a second.'

She was thrown by his audacity and stared after him as he left the room. Swaying from fatigue as much as the mental exhaustion, she sat on the sofa as she heard his heavy step head up the stairs, the dull sound of doors shutting and his noisy descent. Then he was standing in front of her, two capsules on the palm of his hand.

'Jack said I was to make sure you took them,' he said.

She was going to argue that she didn't like taking them, that they made her feel worse, not better, and looked up at him with the words ready. But there was something unsettling about his sympathetic smile, something worrying about the rigid determination of the hand held only inches away so, instead, she said, 'I'll need a drink.'

He filled a glass of water, handed it to her and tipped the two capsules onto her hand.

She looked at them warily, then tossed both into her mouth, drinking half the water to wash them down. 'Thank you.'

He sat opposite, his eyes fixed on her. 'You'll feel much better soon. Then I can go back and reassure Jack. He's going to look for help for his gambling, I think he has come to his senses.'

Molly felt weary. It wasn't going to be that easy. She closed her eyes briefly, hoping Charlie would get the hint and leave. When she heard nothing, she opened her eyes to see him staring at her with a strange expression. It vanished when he saw her eyes open.

'You feeling a bit sleepy?' he asked.

Sleepy? She was mentally and physically exhausted. Too tired to explain, she simply nodded and saw a satisfied smile appear. 'You can leave now, if you want,' she said, wishing he would go. 'I'll probably fall asleep. Tell Jack that I'm doing okay. Ask him to come home tomorrow, will you?'

Charlie shook his head slowly. 'No, I won't go yet. I want to make sure everything is okay this time.'

This time? Molly didn't have the energy to ask what he meant.

A wave of exhaustion and dismay washed over her, making her feel faint. Closing her eyes, she rested her head back on the sofa, wishing she could stay like that, in the dark. She heard Charlie move and opened her eyes to see him leaning forward and staring at her, his mouth a tight, pinched line.

'What's wrong?' she said, her words slurring slightly.

'For a change,' he said cryptically, 'I think everything is going right.' He sat back onto his seat and leaned forward, elbows resting on his knees and his hands hanging. 'Those tablets seem to be working. I think this calls for a celebratory drink.'

Molly didn't think there was any reason to celebrate but she gestured towards the fridge. 'Help yourself,' she mumbled.

The faint sound of him opening and pouring wine were background to the thoughts that were screaming in her increasingly befuddled brain. What did he mean everything was going right? Something was very wrong, but she couldn't figure out what. Reaching under the cushion, she pulled out her phone.

'I don't think it's a good idea to ring anyone,' he said, sitting down, a full wine glass in his hand.

She shook her head. 'I agree, I was checking to see if there were any messages from our children, Freya and Remi. They're supposed to contact us every day, they know I worry if I don't hear from them.' She looked at it for a second before dropping it on top of the cushion with a resigned shrug. 'Nothing from them yet. You remember, they're abroad. Freya is in...' She shook her head and gave a half laugh. 'D'you know, I can't remember where she is, but Remi is definitely in... the States, somewhere in the States.' Her brow furrowed as she tried to remember exactly where they both were, then shrugged. 'It doesn't matter, they're really enjoying themselves. At least our mess won't have any impact on them.'

She closed her eyes briefly before bringing a trembling hand to her forehead. 'I feel terrible. I might go up to bed in a minute, but first, tell me, do you know why Jack was suspended?'

Charlie sipped his wine. 'I suppose it will do no harm to tell you now. Unfortunately, some busybody in the office noticed a discrepancy in the finances. Money was being creamed off a few accounts. Not much, you understand, and only from people who really wouldn't notice the loss.'

Her jaw dropped. 'Jack embezzled?'

'Such an ugly word,' he said, 'but probably appropriate. Except it wasn't Jack.'

'You!'

'It was easy to persuade people Jack was to blame. I simply dropped a casual word into the right ears, told people I was worried about him, that his gambling problem seemed to be getting out of hand.' He gave a casual wave. 'It was really very easy.'

She frowned. 'But they didn't fire him outright or call the police.'

He swirled the last drop of wine around the glass. 'Don't be silly, I knew that wasn't going to happen, it would have worried investors. Being on suspension is a much more subtle way of getting rid of someone. People are already saying Jack who? Another week or two on suspension, it will be as if he'd never worked there, and once the investigation is finished and they've found the proof they need, he'll be quietly fired and arrested.'

Molly felt like the room was spinning and the ground falling from under her. Her mouth was dry, her tongue sticking to the roof of her mouth. It was hard to get the words out. Squeezing her eyes shut, she shook her head, trying to clear the fog that seemed to be engulfing her, but when she opened them again nothing was clearer. She felt a shiver of fear; this man with his cruel calculating eyes bore little resemblance to the smiling cheerful Charlie she'd met socially over the years. 'But they'll find Jack wasn't to blame, won't they? They'll find out it was you.'

'Oh no, before that happens, I'll have put the money back. Once they discover the figures balance, they won't investigate much deeper. But they will be suspicious, and Jack will still be fired.' Charlie shrugged dismissively. 'A casualty of war, I'm afraid.'

'I don't understand. If you have the money, why can't you put it back now and save him.'

'Because, you stupid bitch, thanks to you, I don't have the damn money yet!' He stood and paced the room, running a hand through his hair and looking increasingly wild.

While he had his back to her, Molly looked toward the open door to the hallway. It seemed so near, but she knew she couldn't make it. Even if every bone in her body didn't ache, her head felt increasingly woolly. None of what Charlie was saying made much sense, but she couldn't ignore the warning bells that were clanging in her ears.

She closed her eyes, opening them quickly and meeting his, only inches away. 'Thanks to me? I don't understand.'

Charlie flopped onto the sofa beside her. 'Lucien Pleasant. Does the name ring a bell?' When Molly gasped, he laughed. 'When Jack told me about your trip to Semington and mentioned that you liked to go running early in the morning, I knew I could organise something effective.'

It was getting harder and harder to make sense of anything. She tried to focus. 'I don't understand. What do you mean *effective*?'

He scowled. 'He was supposed to kill you, you stupid cow. I hired Pleasant to kill you.'

34

Molly looked at Charlie, speechless.

'It was a simple plan, and it would have worked if I'd hired someone better than that young gigolo,' Charlie said, frowning. 'It should have been easy. All he needed to do was push you into the damn canal, maybe hold your head under for a while. Instead, he rang me to tell me he hadn't been able to do it.' Charlie's top lip curled. 'He said he'd tried the second morning, but you'd been startled and ran off before he could stop you.' Reaching across, he picked up her hand and dropped it. 'You should be sleepier,' he muttered.

Molly remembered Pleasant shouting after her. The one word she'd caught, *understand*. Had he been trying to warn her, was that why he'd wanted to meet her? Maybe he'd discovered it was too big a leap from seducing vulnerable rich women to killing them.

She felt her skin crawl when Charlie picked up her hand and knew she was on dangerous ground when his words sounded frustrated. Her eyes drooping shut, her chin dropped onto her chest; she struggled to lift it and opened her eyes to stare at him. 'There was something in those capsules you gave me, wasn't there?' Her words were slurred.

'Jack said they made you sleepy. I told you I was going to make sure this time. You are the luckiest woman, but third time lucky is what I say.'

Third time. 'It was you who pushed me under the car?'

'It should have worked,' Charlie growled, 'and this would all be over.'

'I don't understand. Why are you doing this?'

He pushed a hand through his hair. 'I suppose telling you why you need to die is the least I can do. That moronic husband of yours persuaded me to invest a quarter of a million in some foolproof scheme of his. I borrowed the money from the company. If it had worked, we were going to be very rich. I could have returned the money, and nobody would have been any wiser. But his scheme went belly-up, taking all our money with it.' Standing, Charlie paced the floor restlessly again. 'He said he'd get my money back and gambled even more, but he was on a losing streak.' He stood over her. 'You're starting to look paler, about bloody time.'

She knew she was repeating herself, but the only words she seemed able to say were, 'I don't understand.'

Reaching a hand down, he brushed back a lock of her hair. 'You are quite beautiful, you know, it seems a shame.' He patted her cheek and moved away. 'Money, Molly. Your life insurance. Once you die, Jack will get it, and he'll be able to repay me.' Charlie smiled unpleasantly. 'He'll have no choice; I won't let him out of my sight until he signs it over.'

It was almost a relief to know everything. Almost everything. 'Lucien Pleasant, did you kill him?'

Charlie shrugged. 'He insisted on meeting me to explain what had gone wrong. Then he wanted 10K to keep quiet.

Luckily, I never go unprepared, and caught him off-guard when I rammed that knife into his belly.'

Molly stared at the pleasant, unremarkable face of a monster. There was one more question she had to ask, one thing she had to know. 'Does Jack...?' She couldn't continue.

Charlie turned and gave a short laugh. 'Does Jack know what I'm planning? Is that what you want to know?' He sat beside her again, staring at her the way a lab technician would stare at a specimen. 'He was really cut up about you and Lucien, you know, convinced the two of you had done the horizontal mambo. And of course, I couldn't tell him the truth because, no, he doesn't know. He'd never have played along. For one thing, he really loves you, and for another, apart from his gambling habit, he's a pretty decent guy.'

'I thought *you* were,' she said, her voice thick.

Charlie shook his head. 'People see what they want to see, haven't you learned that by now?' Standing, he reached for her hand and pulled her to her feet, ignoring her whimper of pain. 'It's lovely to sit here chatting with you, Molly, but it's time for the next phase of my plan. A nice hot bath. When they find you, they'll assume you got weak and slipped under.'

'Of course,' she muttered, swaying as she tried to stay on her feet. 'It has to look like an accident, doesn't it?'

He dragged her along. 'Yes, clever girl, it does. But don't worry, it will.'

In the hallway, Molly grabbed hold of the banisters with her free hand. She was damned if she was going to make it easy for him. He merely laughed and yanked her away, laughing harder when she squealed with pain.

Then she heard it, distant but unmistakeable. The sound of sirens. Charlie was too busy trying to get her up the stairs to notice. Every time he got one hand free, she'd grab onto the banisters with the other. His expression was growing more frustrated, angrier. He was resisting the temptation to hit her, she guessed that wouldn't last much longer. She needed to keep him occupied until the police got there.

The sirens were growing louder. Charlie's head jerked up and he gave a grunt of disbelief before looking down at her face. Whatever he saw there released his rage and with a growl of fury, he raised his hand and punched her.

She staggered from the blow. Already unsteady, she slipped and tumbled down the stairs, landing in a heap at the bottom. He jumped down beside her and fired a kick at her head, missing when she rolled away and curled up. The sirens were deafening, the police had to be outside. With a vicious yell, Charlie pulled his foot back again and took aim.

Molly had only one weapon left; she opened her mouth and screamed, a blood-curdling sound that echoed around the hallway.

It worked. Instead of kicking her, he turned away and looked frantically around. There were shouts from outside the front door. Panicked, he bent down, grabbed her hair and yanked it. 'Is there another way out?'

'Yes,' she said, gritting her teeth as he wrenched her head harder. 'Go out the patio door. At the end of the garden there's a gate that'll take you out onto the road behind.' She was lying. The garden was long and narrow and surrounded by a high wall. But it was dark, it would take him a while to discover she'd lied and by then the police would have broken through the front.

Unfortunately, Charlie wasn't a fool. His hand still gripping her hair, he dragged her to her feet. 'Show me,' he said, pushing her towards the living room.

Another shout from outside distracted him for a second, and Molly broke free. But she was too slow, he grabbed hold of her shirt and pulled her back, catching hold of her arm and twisting it painfully as he pushed her into the living room, his eyes darting towards the patio door. She yelled out, dragging her feet both from pain and a determination that she would not be taken with him.

A loud crash was followed by the sound of voices. Charlie, with a final jerk of Molly's arm, gave up the idea of taking her with him. He shoved her away and ran for the garden.

Molly lay dazed on the floor as heavy feet came running in, passing her to follow Charlie, shouts and calls fading as they chased after him.

'Where can he go?' a quiet voice asked, and she looked up to see Fanshawe bending over her.

She managed a satisfied smile. 'Nowhere, it's a walled garden. He can't escape.' The pain in her arm easing, she struggled to sit up. Fanshawe put an arm around her waist and helped her to the sofa. 'You heard everything?' she said, indicating her phone.

He nodded. 'Every word, that was very clever, and very brave of you.'

'It was lucky I'd put your number in speed dial,' she said, hugging her injured arm to her chest.

Fanshawe sat in the chair opposite, ignoring the shouts coming from the garden. 'What about those pills he gave you? Should you go to the hospital?'

Molly slid her fingers down the side of the sofa, felt around for a few seconds, then pulled up the two capsules Forster had handed her earlier. 'I don't like taking pills, so I palmed them. The ones the hospital gave me made me feel very woozy.' She rolled the capsules on the palm of her hand. 'I wouldn't have taken them anyway, but I'm almost certain these aren't the same ones.'

Fanshawe pulled an evidence bag from his pocket, opened it and held it out. She knocked them into it. 'Where do you keep the remainder?' he asked, holding the bag up to look at the two capsules.

'In the en-suite bathroom cabinet, top of the stairs, first on the left.'

'I'll get them before I leave, forensics will be able to compare them.'

'He'll be put away, won't he?'

'We have him for attempted murder,' Fanshawe said, 'and I have no doubt that when we search his home and check his phone and computer, we'll find enough evidence to prove he murdered Pleasant.'

Molly gave a long sigh of relief and turned when she heard raised voices and heavy steps.

Charlie was looking pale and subdued, handcuffs on his wrists, a police officer gripping each arm. He didn't look at her as they passed by and left through the front door.

'You'll need to get the Yale lock fixed,' Fanshawe said, staring after them.

'It's not a problem, we normally use the sash lock for security anyway.' She rubbed eyes that were prickling with tiredness and tears.

'We'll need you to write a statement.' Fanshawe got to his feet and looked down at her. 'The sooner you do so the better, but I think tomorrow will be time enough. You look done in.' He stood a moment more. 'We would still like to speak to your husband, Mrs Chatwell. He'll be able to corroborate some of what Mr Forster said.'

'Charlie said he was staying at his place.' She saw the detective's surprise. 'He must have told me before I pressed the speed dial for you.'

'We'll have a warrant to search Mr Forster's apartment within an hour. If your husband's still there I'll fill him in on what's happened. I'm sure he'll want to come home.'

When Fanshawe left, Molly turned the key in the lock, slipped the security chain in place and hobbled back to the sofa. When Jack heard what had happened, she was sure he'd rush home, there was no point in dragging herself up the stairs.

Her head ached where Charlie had wrenched her hair. She put a hand up to it and rubbed it gently. She supposed she should feel horror and disbelief that a man she knew had tried to kill her, but all she could seem to feel was intense relief. Jack's gambling problem, their precarious financial state, they paled into insignificance in comparison.

Exhausted, she lifted her legs onto the sofa and relaxed back. With her mind whirling, she didn't think she'd sleep but she did, a restless sleep where Charlie chased her and caught her again and again.

35

It was the sunlight filtering through the window that woke Molly and made her push up with a groan of pain. Her phone was on the coffee table, she checked the time. Seven. There was no message from Jack. Perhaps the police had taken longer to get the warrant than they'd expected.

Carefully and very slowly, she got to her feet. The few hours' sleep had served to clear her head a little, but they'd made no impact on the pains and aches that seemed to have doubled overnight. It wasn't surprising considering she'd been dragged, yanked, punched and pulled by a maniac. What was surprising was that she could move at all. She was lucky; her broken rib hadn't sustained further damage. Reluctantly, she headed to the kitchen, found a packet of paracetamol and swallowed two.

Later, she'd ring Fanshawe and see what the story was. She had a mug of coffee while she waited for the pills to take the edge off the pain then dragged herself up the stairs. She pulled off her clothes and examined the damage in the mirror. Her body was a mass of old and new bruises. She ran a hand over them; they hurt and probably would for a while.

A long hot shower eased some of the aches and she felt more herself an hour later as she came back downstairs.

There was still no message from Jack. She tried ringing, left a voicemail, left a text and threw the phone on the table in frustration. Finally, she could wait no longer and at eight thirty she rang DI Fanshawe. The call was answered immediately, the detective's voice brisk and alert. At least, she hadn't woken him. 'Jack hasn't come home,' she said, dispensing with any preliminaries.

There was a moment's silence before he answered. 'We went around to Charlie Forster's apartment around three,' he said, 'there was nobody there. The spare bedroom had obviously been used. I left an officer there, and he reported back about twenty minutes ago. Mr Chatwell hasn't turned up.'

Molly's heart fell. 'He isn't answering the phone. Oh God, you don't think he's done something stupid, do you?'

She heard a heavy breath on the line before Fanshawe answered. 'I'll have one of my men make some calls, Mrs Chatwell, but I wouldn't start worrying. There are any number of places he could be, there are far more places to gamble in London than people are aware of. If it's suitable, I'd like to call around later and get that statement done.'

'Yes, yes, of course,' she answered, her mind on Jack. How could he gamble, he'd no money? 'I'll be here whenever you want to come,' she said and hung up. She tapped the phone against her lips, then did an internet search for casinos. Far more than she expected. Twenty something in central London alone. She tried the first on the list, hanging up moments later with a frustrated grunt. Unsurprising, they weren't giving out any information. She'd have to rely on DI Fanshawe.

Restless, she sat on the sofa and switched on the TV for company. A minute later, she switched it off and reached for a book, only to put it down without opening it. What were they going to do? Her eyes drifted around the room, lingering on the furniture, the ornaments, all the lovely things they'd acquired over the years. She'd been wrong; it wasn't the house or the stuff that was important, it was all the memories attached to them.

They could make new ones elsewhere. They'd sell up, move out of London and buy something smaller. They'd have a spare bedroom where Freya and Remi could visit. *Visit.* With a sad smile, she decided it was time she accepted the truth; they were unlikely to ever live at home again. But, if they were happy, that was okay.

Now Molly knew what Jack's problem was, she could help him. Gambling... it was a disease; she'd help him recover and they'd get back their lives and be more solid than ever. They weren't like Amelia and Tristan; they'd always been enough for each other.

She was debating which part of the country they should move to when she heard a knock on the door. Jack! As fast as she was able, she got to the door, slid back the safety chain and turned the key in the lock. Everything would be all right now.

The clunk of the lock turning was loud, the sound barely faded before the door was pushed open, almost knocking her off her feet. Staggering backwards, she stared at the bedraggled man who came through the door. 'Jack, where have you been?'

He pushed past her. Shutting and locking the door, she followed him; he was home, safe, suddenly that was all that mattered. He was standing in the middle of the living room when she followed him in, his clothes wrinkled, coat ripped. Had he been mugged?

She went to him, put her arms around his neck and pressed up against him, ignoring the dampness, the smell of cigarette smoke and alcohol that came off him in waves. 'Oh Jack,' she said, burying her face in his neck. 'It's been so awful, and I've needed you so desperately.'

'Awful?' he said, pushing her away and taking a few steps back. 'What in your cushy overindulged life, could be classified as awful?'

Shock kept her silent for a few seconds. 'Of course, you don't know it all,' she said slowly, 'but you do know someone tried to push me under a car.'

Ignoring her, he pulled off his coat, flung it onto the sofa and went to the kitchen to switch on the kettle.

'It was Charlie,' she said, waiting for Jack's shocked reaction, for him to come to her and take her in his arms, for the reassurance, the comfort she needed. Instead, he continued to ignore her, standing and staring at the damn kettle. 'Did you hear me?' she said, a note of desperation creeping into her voice. 'Jack... it was Charlie who tried to kill me by pushing me under a car, then last night, he came here and tried again. He tried to kill me again, Jack... for the insurance money. He wanted to kill me so you could get the damn insurance money to pay back the money you owed him.' She was almost panting by the time she finished. 'The police arrested him,' she added quietly.

Finally, Jack turned to stare at her. 'I wondered what had happened to him,' he said before spooning coffee into a mug and adding water.

Molly stared at him. Was that all he had to say? Was it shock that was making him behave so oddly or maybe, she hadn't made it clear? 'He was going to drown me,' she said. She was pleased to see this had some effect. Jack lifted his eyes from contemplating the coffee and stared at her.

'Yes, Charlie went upstairs for those painkillers the hospital gave me. He said you'd mentioned they made me sleepy and he was waiting for them to take effect before putting me into the bath and drowning me. But I fooled him,' she said with satisfaction. 'I didn't take them.'

36

Molly waited for Jack to congratulate her on her cleverness, to voice horror and disbelief at Charlie's evil game, but he stayed motionless, expressionless, once again staring into his coffee.

'Jack?' She moved closer and rested a hand on his shoulder.

'Charlie, eh?' he said. 'Who'd have thought?'

Stunned by his response, the lack of concern for her and for all she'd been through, Molly took her hand away.

'You were clever not to take those tablets,' Jack said. 'They didn't agree with you anyway. I'll get rid of them.'

'No, it's okay, the police took them. To compare,' she added, seeing his odd expression.

Anger narrowed his eyes and mouth. 'The police took them?'

'To compare,' she said again, puzzled as to why he was angry. 'I told the inspector that I wasn't convinced the two capsules he gave me were the ones the hospital had prescribed.'

Jack ran a hand through his uncombed, greasy hair. 'I need to get away,' he said. 'Money. I need money. Have you any?'

She blinked in confusion. 'You know I don't,' she said, letting her irritation show. 'You maxed out all our cards, Jack. I've sold the car, and that's freed up money to pay some of the debts.'

He was pacing the floor. Hearing this, he stopped and turned to stare. 'How much?'

'Not as much as the car is worth,' she said. 'Twenty-five grand.'

Some of the tension left him. 'Where is it?'

Molly frowned. 'Pete Randall, remember, we bought the car from him? He's going to Wandsworth this morning to have a look over it, he said he'd transfer the money to my account as soon as he checked it over and got back to the office.' Her eyes flicked to the clock. Eleven thirty. 'It's possibly there now.'

'Can you check?'

His voice was overeager. For the first time, Molly noticed his eyes. The pupils were pinpointed. He was unable to stand still for a moment. Horror swept over her. Gambling was bad enough, but it seemed it wasn't Jack's only addiction. 'You've taken something,' she said.

'Can you check?' It was more an order than a question this time.

She shook her head. 'Why do you need money so badly? Please don't tell me you owe money to some drug dealer?'

Instead of answering, Jack stepped up to her and grabbed her by her arm. 'Do it!'

She picked up her phone and tapped a few keys. 'Yes, it's there.' She thought it might be a good idea to press the speed dial key for Fanshawe, there was something terribly wrong here, but before she could, Jack grabbed the phone from her hand.

He stared at it, then reached into his pocket for his wallet. He opened it, took out a card and handed it to her. 'Right, transfer it to this card,' he said, handing her back the phone.

'What?' she looked at him in dismay. 'I need it to pay off the hotel where you ran up that ridiculous bill, and for the arrears on the mortgage.'

'Transfer the damn money,' he shouted, startling her.

Throwing the card back at him, she put all the energy she had left into one word. 'No!' Desperately, she tried to press the speed dial button for Fanshawe, but as she looked down to see it, she felt a blow to her cheek. It sent her reeling, the phone flying across the floor. Her hand went to her face. 'Jack! What's happened to you? To us?'

His laugh was hateful. 'To us? You didn't give us much thought when you were coming on to that stranger, did you?'

She shut her eyes. Was this the way it was going to be? He'd put all the blame on her, on that one crazy moment of weakness. How convenient for him. She felt anger bubble and pushed it away; it wasn't going to help. Reaching a hand towards him, keeping her voice soft, she said, 'We can get through this, Jack. We'll get help for your addic–'

'It's too late,' he snapped. 'I have to get away. Transfer the damn money.' His mouth contorted with anger when she shook her head. She watched with a dart of fear as his hands curled into fists. Maybe it would be safer to give him the money. But it was too late. With a growl, he grabbed her arm and flung her across the room. She landed hard against the edge of the granite worktop and heard the sickening crack as her arm broke seconds before excruciating pain shot through her. 'Jack,' she pleaded, seeing him approach with a raised fist. She was wasting her time, this drug-fuelled person wasn't her husband.

The pain in her arm was agonising, the edges of her vision going fuzzy, shock trying to bring her down. She fought against it and staggered away from him, one hand clutching her arm, but he was right behind her and grabbed hold of her hair, jerking her back against him. She lay there unmoving, a lover's embrace from a different time, and moaned from pain and absolute terror. Then she felt his hands around her throat, squeezing.

His drug-fuelled rage had given him strength and taken

away any rational thought. She tried to plead with him, but all she could get out was a mangled wheeze. Her broken arm was useless, her one good hand making no inroads on prying the tightening fingers. Fighting for breath... for her life... she jabbed her nails into his hands, digging them in, feeling skin break under the force of her desperation. He shoved her away and stared at his bleeding hands in disbelief.

'You bitch,' he growled, lifting a clenched fist. She backed away, clutching her bruised throat and gasping as she searched for something she could use to defend herself. Knives were out of reach, there was nothing... as he swung his fist, she ducked away and grabbed the only thing on the counter, a giant Perspex salt cellar, swinging it wildly, aiming for his clenched fist and missing. As he drew his arm back, she swung it again, this time aiming for his body. It hit Jack squarely on the side of his head. She brought her hand back, prepared to strike again, fighting against her body's desire to shut down.

Jack sneered at her and took a step forward, then without warning, he dropped to the ground.

Panting, she leaned against the worktop. Horror coursed through her as she saw a bloody smear on the end of her makeshift weapon. 'Jack,' she whimpered, looking to where he lay on the floor at her feet.

Dropping the salt cellar with a cry of disgust, she hung her head for a moment as a wave of weakness washed over her. When she was sure she wasn't going to faint, she straightened and looked at the man she loved. He hadn't moved and a circle of dark-red blood surrounded his head. With a moan of despair, she took a step towards him, letting go of the worktop. She was almost next to him, when his hand snaked out and grabbed her ankle. Screaming, she pulled away and kicked out at his hand, but there was no strength in his grip, and it fell away easily. She leaned against the cupboard and stared at him, tears pouring down her cheeks. When he didn't move again, she shuffled back, gingerly laid a hand on his wrist, feeling for his pulse, sobbing when she didn't find one.

Too weak to walk, she slid to the floor and crawled to the living room to find her phone. She could have dialled 999, but she didn't, she pressed the speed dial for DI Fanshawe. To her relief, it was answered immediately. Words? She couldn't find any. Dropping the phone into her lap, she sobbed. She could hear the tinny sound of the detective's voice fading into the distance as she did what she'd wanted to do for several minutes and passed out.

When she came to, she was lying on a gurney in an ambulance. Twisting her head around, she saw Fanshawe sitting on the seat beside her. 'I killed him,' she said.

'Yes,' he agreed. 'But you'll be okay. We'll need to go through due process but it's a clear case of self-defence, Mrs Chatwell. There won't be any case to answer.' He sat forward and patted her arm reassuringly. 'A clear case, Molly. Those capsules that Charlie Forster wanted you to take, they were in fact the ones the hospital gave you, but they'd been opened, emptied and refilled with a very pure grade of heroin. One capsule would probably have killed you, two would certainly have done.'

Molly gulped. 'Charlie wanted to make certain I died, didn't he?'

Fanshawe shook his head. 'Not Forster, Molly. I'd asked for the capsules to be tested as a matter of priority. When I got the results, I immediately spoke to him and he was adamant that he had nothing to do with it.' Fanshawe patted her arm again, and this time left his hand resting on it. 'It wasn't only the two capsules Forster gave you that had been doctored, Molly, it was all of them. They've found partial fingerprints on the capsules; I'm guessing we'll find they're a match to your husband. That's why I'm certain it'll be a clear-cut case of self-defence. It looks like he has been trying to kill you since you came back from the hospital, he probably hoped you'd take the painkillers at least once, and once would have been enough.'

She didn't have to ask why. There was only one reason, the same reason Charlie had. Both men had wanted to kill her for the money. She remembered Jack's anger. 'That was why he went ballistic when I told him you'd taken them,' she said, shutting her eyes. 'And of course, it was why he had to get away.'

'He'd have known the game was up,' Fanshawe said. 'I had already issued a warrant for his arrest and sent officers around to warn you. They arrived seconds after your call. I'm afraid, you're going to need to replace the second lock now too. For the moment, it's a crime scene.' He sat back. 'You've a whopping great bruise on the side of your face, bruises to your neck and the paramedics say your arm is broken. At the hospital, they'll take photographs of all your injuries, okay?' Carstairs appeared at the open door of the ambulance and stared inside. 'I need to go,' Fanshawe said with a look in his direction. 'There'll be statements to be made,' he said. 'I'll call in to see you tomorrow.'

Shock had covered everything that had happened in a dense fog. Everything felt distant, numb. She guessed when it wore off, the pain would be unbearable, almost as unbearable as telling Freya and Remi that their father had tried to kill her, and that she *had* killed him.

'We'll be heading off in a sec,' the paramedic said, scribbling on a clipboard.

'Would it be possible to make a phone call?' she asked, her voice thick.

'Sure, your mobile is here.' He reached behind, took it from a shelf and held it out. 'Hang on,' he said, 'I can take that off your finger, your Sats are okay.' He unclipped an oxygen saturation monitor from her finger and handed her the phone.

She could ring one of her friends. Amelia or Petra, she knew, would rush over, they'd be horrified, shocked and saddened and would be there for her. There were tough times ahead, she'd need their support.

A wave of sadness and despair swept over her. She needed more than friends, she needed family or the next best thing. Someone who had been with her through the good times, a woman she had laughed and cried with and who loved Freya and Remi almost as much as she did.

Someone she should never have let go.

With one hand it was awkward, but she managed to scroll through to the number she wanted and tap it before holding the phone to her ear. It was a few seconds before it was answered, but as soon as she heard the woman's voice, she took a deep breath.

'Rebecca, how would you like your old job back?'

ACKNOWLEDGMENTS

A huge thanks, as ever, to Bloodhound Books, especially Betsy Reavley, Tara Lyons, Heather Fitt, Morgen Bailey and Ian Skewis.

A special thank you to Freya and Remi Guezo for lending me their names – and an extra thank you to Freya for coming up with the name Lucien Pleasant.

There would be no point at all in writing if I didn't have such wonderful readers – thank you to those who read and to those who review and blog – all much appreciated.

Writing would be a lonely business without writing buddies – as always, grateful thanks to the author Jenny O'Brien who rushes to rescue me from technological disasters and reads an early version of my books to give me honest feedback. My US author friend, Leslie Bratspis, for her ongoing support and editing assistance, and to many others including the authors: Vikki Patis, Rona Halsall, Jim Ody, Pam Lecky, Catherine Kullmann, Kerena Swan, Pot Gitt and Mary Karpin. These and many others make being an author much more fun.

Those readers who read the Dublin Murder Mysteries will notice I've used the name Edel in this book too – in every book, if it's possible, there will be one kind lovely woman called Edel in fond memory of my friend Edel Cunningham who left us in 2019.

And last, but never least, a huge thank you to my amazing family and friends.

If you'd like to contact me – and I love to hear from readers – you can contact me here:

Facebook: www.facebook.com/valeriekeoghnovels
Twitter: @valeriekeogh1
Instagram: valeriekeogh2

CPSIA information can be obtained
at www.ICGtesting.com
Printed in the USA
LVHW112146290720
661911LV00003B/937

9 781913 419615